D1245250

ARCHANGEL
OF SEDONA

Tony Peluso

WPG

WARRIORS PUBLISHING GROUP
NORTH HILLS, CALIFORNIA

ARCHANGEL OF SEDONA

A Warriors Publishing Group book/published by arrangement with the author

This is a work of fiction. Names, characters, military units, places, events, and incidents are either the products of the author's imagination or used in a fictitious manner. Any resemblance to actual persons, living or dead, or actual events is purely coincidental.

PRINTING HISTORY
Warriors Publishing Group edition/December 2014

ISBN 978-0-9897983-5-8

Library of Congress Control Number 2014948075

The name "Warriors Publishing Group" and the logo
are trademarks belonging to Warriors Publishing Group

PRINTED IN THE UNITED STATES OF AMERICA

10 9 8 7 6 5 4 3 2 1

PROLOGUE

Fall Solstice, 1086 A.D.
Upper Verde River Valley
Two miles southeast of Oak Creek Canyon
Sinagua Sacred Ritual Site

ADORNED IN THE ceremonial robe of the Antelope Clan, the old shaman struggled to lead his kinsmen along the rocky footpath to the forbidden site. The Toltec artisans who had fashioned the robe had woven multi-colored parrot feathers and bright cotton threads into the doeskin poncho, creating a mystical effect. While the priest often negotiated the long hike from the river with ease, the beautiful robe—so useful for the secret rites in the kivas along Beaver Creek—proved heavy and unwieldy on the trail.

The priest ignored his growing fatigue. In light of his important task, he bore the weight of the robe as a sign of respect, obedience, and devotion to the blessed Spirit.

Trips to the Sinagua ritual place were rare, and always marked an important celebration: an intertribal wedding, a noble birth, or a sacrifice for divine assistance in hunting, gathering, or harvesting. Time at the holy site was a sacred privilege.

The ritual place lay nestled in a spectacular basin surrounded by a high escarpment to the north and east covered in stunted green pines, needle-leaf junipers, and red-barked manzanitas. To the south and west, water and wind erosion had formed towering buttes of ancient sandstone—stained crimson by the mineral rust of 20,000 millennia. These magnificent pinnacles captured the scarlet, lavender, jade, and gold of the setting sun, focusing the celestial prism on the Sinaqua pilgrims.

Tonight the ceremony would vary from normal practice, as evidenced by the shaman's robe and the presence of the unconscious northern Sinaqua maiden, carried on a litter by four of the stoutest Antelope clansmen. The shaman had a grim duty. As a result of recent celestial reprisals, many Sinaqua tribesmen had perished. The Spirit demanded a reckoning from the sinners before the Verde Valley could regain its fragile balance.

For ten summers, members of the tribe had ignored the taboos imposed by the servants. They'd left the safety of the upper valley and the pine forest's camouflage to dwell in the canyon's cool shadows near the creek that flowed from the escarpment. The servants, who had travelled to the Verde Valley in fiery canoes, had warned against this sacrilege. They'd prophesized that the Spirit would unleash a dreadful devastation, if the Sinaqua failed to heed their omens.

Six moons earlier, a force of unimaginable power had erupted from the earth a day's run from the great rim. The Spirit created a new mountain that belched fire, molten rock, hot ash, noxious gases, and untold numbers of tiny glass stones that rained down on the Sinaqua settlements all the way to where the Verde and Salt Rivers joined.

The eruption devastated the northern Sinaqua. The villages, cornfields, and every member of the once-mighty Bear Clan vanished without a trace. The land's elk, deer, antelope, bear, wolves, cougars, and javelina disappeared. Trout and bass died in the streams and lakes. The people north of the rim could find no edible plants to gather. In desperation, surviving members of the other northern clans descended into the upper Verde Valley to seek sanctuary with their cousins.

No rain had fallen on any Sinagua land since the eruption. All of the creeks, except the sacred stream in the narrow oak valley, had dried up. The Verde River generated a trickle. If they didn't make amends with the Spirit, the surviving tribesmen would leave the safety of their lands and take their chances in the east, where their fierce enemies could destroy them. They could not go west, where an uninhabitable desert stretched to the shores of a limitless, salty, and undrinkable ocean.

The Sinagua had distilled their religious beliefs from the traditions, rituals, and practices of their trading partners: the Mogollon, Anasazi, Hohokam, and Mesoamerican tribes. They did not practice human sacrifice, like the Toltecs from Mesoamerica. Yet they knew that they had to do something radical to perform penance for their sins and to win back the Spirit's favor.

As restitution, the elders selected the most beautiful maiden in all of their polity, a northern refugee of 15 summers. They would offer her to assuage the Spirit's anger.

Unable to engage in the bloodletting of the Mesoamericans, the tribal elders drugged the maiden with mushrooms after numbing her with beer, brewed from the harvested corn. The shaman planned to lower the drugged girl to the bottom of the sacred sinkhole, adjacent to the ceremonial site, leaving her fate to the servants.

Fearing retribution, once they arrived at the site the clansmen hurried to lower the girl into the sinkhole, using a rope that their women had woven from strands of wild cotton plants. They tied the rope to a tall pine and allowed her to remain suspended ten feet above the floor of the sinkhole.

They begged the Spirit to accept the maiden as reparation. After the ceremony, they left, promising to honor the taboos and return to the holy site to preform those customs required by the servants of the Spirit.

All would have been well, but the maiden's clan was northern Sinagua. After sunset, her father and two brothers, who had shadowed the procession, stole into the narrow draw that surrounded the sinkhole.

The father and brothers located the cotton rope tied to the pine tree. When they touched the rope, they knew something dreadful had occurred. The cotton line felt slack and weightless. No body hung from it. Pulling it up, they inspected the end by the light of a small torch that the brother held.

Something sharp had severed the line. The father had never seen a cleaner cut. No edged stone weapon could have made it. The cut end looked blackened and charred. It bore the odor of burned cloth.

The maiden's father cursed the Spirit. Before the men could search the sinkhole, a shooting star shot across the sky from the north to the south—an evil omen. A moment later, the star stopped cold and turned from the south, sped north, then west, and then east at unimaginable speeds.

Nothing in the hunter-gatherer's experience had prepared him. He and his sons froze in place like stalked deer. They watched in horror as the star turned toward them. It slowed down and stopped over the sinkhole. The star grew as it descended, casting a pale, white light on the three northern clansmen.

The father regretted his foolishness. To avoid the wrath of the servants, he and his sons ran from the ceremonial site. They fled southeast on a long slog toward the village.

The next day, the Spirit signaled His satisfaction. The rains began.

The shaman declared that the offering had brought the life-giving moisture to the valley once again. Over the next several years, steady rains and fertile ash from the new volcano turned the upper Verde Valley into a garden. The rains persisted for two generations.

CHAPTER ONE

God created the Grand Canyon, but He lives in Sedona.
—NY Times.

September 2, 1966, 7:15 p.m.
Northern Courtyard, Chapel of the Holy Cross
South of Uptown Sedona, Arizona

DAN OSTERGAARD AND I teetered on the stone bench facing west. We perched high on the retaining wall that formed the northernmost edge of the courtyard surrounding the chapel. Dangling our legs 50 feet above the next outcropping, we sipped beer and nibbled fried chicken, as we watched the magnificent light show develop on the other side of Scheurman Mountain.

"Tony, you were right. This place is gorgeous. I thought you were full of shit when you said it was stunning. This is special. I had no idea," Dan said, while focusing on the miracle above the mountains.

"I told you that you'd like it, dickhead."

"Eat me," Dan said, too distracted to engage in serious repartee.

"Blow me," I said, in the adolescent custom that Dan and I had adopted over our years at Arizona State and Brophy Prep in Phoenix.

By the time Dan and I found ourselves drinking beer on the high butte's cutting edge next to one of Sedona's spectacular architectural marvels, I'd lived in Arizona for 13 years. My family had moved west in 1953. I'd grown up in Phoenix, as the town evolved from a desert oasis into a major metropolis.

My parents were working class. Mom labored as a tailor and dad drove trucks. Children of the Great Depression and World War Two, neither finished high school. Neither valued education as a ticket to greater opportunity. Anything beyond 12th grade was frivolous. No one in the Giordano family had ever gone to college—I was the first.

They were also devout Catholics. After they purchased our house near Camelback Road and Central Avenue, they installed my older sister and me in St. Francis Xavier Grammar School, so that the nuns could indoctrinate us. After eight years with the Sisters of Charity of the Blessed Virgin Mary, known as BVMs, I'd found common cause with the victims of the Spanish Inquisition.

In 1960, I contrived to leave all Catholic education in my wake. I'd attend Central High School and join the Army. I can't remember a time when I didn't want to be a soldier. I also thought about becoming a lawyer. In grammar school, I couldn't reconcile the two goals.

I took the entrance exam into Brophy Prep because a priest at St. Francis predicted that I would fail. To show him, I took the test. I did well enough to get accepted. I don't know how I ended up there in 1961. Chalk it up to a divine thread that's woven through the tapestry of my life. I reject the concept of mere chance or serendipity. Everything happens for a reason.

Brophy turned out to be life-changing. Though separated by 100 yards of classrooms and playgrounds, the Jesuits proved to be the antithesis of the BVMs at St. Francis. The priests, scholastics, and brothers who taught at Brophy were smart, cool, motivated, dedicated, effective, and pious. I blossomed there.

The Jesuits took me most of the way from boy to man. Though I now have three degrees, the faculty at Brophy provided the best educational experience of my life.

Dan's family migrated to Phoenix from Madison, Wisconsin in 1963. Dan's dad was an eminent surgeon, who'd taught at the University of Wisconsin. I never learned what caused Dr. Ostergaard to pull up stakes and move to Phoenix to practice medicine.

I met Dan in Latin class junior year. Though he was new, he never sported the profile of a recent transfer. He seemed confident, funny, arrogant, quirky, and intelligent. Despite his modest physical stature and average looks, his main attribute proved to be his magnetism for members of the opposite sex.

At 16, I hung around with Dan because he always led an entourage of pretty girls from Central High School. His followers adopted a more flexible moral standard and were more cooperative than the girls at Xavier High, Brophy's co-educational counterpart. After graduation, Dan and I attended Arizona State University, though we pledged different fraternities.

Dan's parents understood the value of a college education. His dad paid his way and provided him with a liberal allowance. My family and I argued over college. They wanted me to learn a trade. They felt no duty to contribute to my quest for a degree.

Mom gave me the "my way or the highway" speech a week before my 18th birthday in the summer of 1965. I didn't want a trade. I moved out. I found a room with friends, got a job at Fry's Food Stores, and enrolled at Arizona State University. I worked summers, took out college loans, and hashed at the main cafeteria during the school year.

In the summer of 1966, I worked full-time at the Sperry Rand factory in Deer Valley. Sperry built computers the size of a small garage. Today the average cell phone has more computing power than the ponderous main frames that I helped to fabricate that summer.

I made enough at Sperry to pay my tuition, fees, books, room, board, and buy a 1962 Chevrolet Corvair. Since Ralph Nader had trashed the Corvair in his book, *Unsafe at Any Speed*, I bought a neat, white, low-mileage coupe with leather bucket seats for a song. Despite its engineering flaws, I loved that car. I remember how much fun I had driving it.

I bought the Corvair before Labor Day. I arrived at the fraternity the last week of August, as ASU wanted to start the semester so the administration could schedule exams before Christmas. Since few of my fraternity brothers lived in Arizona and most hailed from other states, a couple of the guys showed up the first week. Most of the others chose to stay home through the long weekend.

Bouncing around that empty frat house over Labor Day didn't appeal to me. I called Dan at his fraternity. We had a mutual friend, John, who attended Northern Arizona University in Flagstaff. He moonlighted as a night clerk in small hotel near NAU.

Our friend encouraged us to come up. He'd find a room for us. We could hang out in the cooler clime and chase NAU girls all weekend.

I picked Dan up in the afternoon on Friday, September 2, 1966. To prepare for the trip, we went to a Mexican restaurant on the east side of the University that accepted our fake IDs. We had chips, salsa, and a pitcher of beer while we planned our itinerary.

In the three years that Dan had lived in Arizona, he'd never travelled farther north than Black Canyon. I had an inspiration, lubricated by the cold beer.

"You've never been to Camp Verde?" I asked.

"Nope."

"Heard of Montezuma's Castle, Montezuma's Well, or Tuzigoot?"

"Yep. But I'm not interested in Indian ruins," Dan said.

"How about Sedona?"

"What about it?

"Dan, Sedona is an incredibly gorgeous place. It's mindboggling."

"Come on. That's over the top."

"Seriously. There's something very special about that place."

"Like what?"

"Well, the buttes are a deep red. There's lots of scrub pine, juniper, cedar, and manzanitas. Those are very green. The sky is crystal clear and a dark blue. The red, green, brown, and blue have a hypnotic effect. I can't do it justice. You have to see it."

"You've been smoking a little dope, Tony?"

"No, man. I'm a juicer. You know that."

"You sound like a hippie on drugs," Dan said.

"Don't do drugs," I said, as I drained my beer and poured another full glass. "Dan, there's a spiritual thing you should see in Sedona."

"What now? Are you telling me that I'll have a religious experience?"

"Maybe."

"Tony, how do you know so much about this town?"

"There's a Catholic chapel there. They built it on the side of a mountain, a couple of hundred feet above the valley. It's spectacular. I'll show it to you this evening."

"What's so spectacular?" Dan asked, sarcasm creeping into his voice.

"You'll see."

"How do you know about this chapel?"

"My family attended services there when I was a kid. We'd take Sunday drives up the Black Canyon Highway through Camp Verde to Sedona. We'd go to Mass there once every few months. It's a mystical place."

"Now, I'm sure that I don't want to go. This weekend is for drinking beer and chasing trim at NAU. Don't try to turn this road trip into a pilgrimage."

"Dan, you'll like this place. Parts of the chapel are very controversial."

"What are you talking about?"

"Frank Lloyd Wright influenced the lady who built the chapel. Its architecture is unconventional. The builder had a sculptor do an unusual version of the crucified Christ for the interior. The priests call it the Christus. It's very moving, but most people hate it. A friend of my dad's says that it's so wrong that it denies Christ's divinity."

"Really?" Dan asked, interested in the side trip for the first time.

"Yeah." I said, as I poured another glass of beer for Dan.

"All right. Let's go see the chapel, the Christus, Sedona, and the red rocks. Maybe it'll give me a hard on."

"Dan, if there's a female within a hundred yards, you'll have a hard on."

I drained my beer and picked up the tab.

Other than holiday traffic, the trek through Phoenix went well. We stopped at a convenience store. With the aid of my fake Hawaiian driver's license, we scored a case of Coors. We hit the Colonel Sander's and got a bucket of KFC. We had a full tank of gas, money in our pockets, and an open road.

When we arrived at Camp Verde, it was early evening. The sun lay low in the west above the mountains. I turned onto State Road 179 and headed north toward Sedona.

Dan started teasing me about the superlatives that I'd used to describe Sedona. I had grown up in the provinces and didn't have his opportunities to travel the world. If I'd seen the sights in New York, London, Paris, and Rome, the deep crimson sandstone buttes around Sedona might seem less impressive.

When Dan got his first glimpse of Courthouse Butte, Bell Rock, and Cathedral Rock, he stopped carping. He looked shocked and craned his neck to get better views. I could have stopped, but it was late. I wanted to get up to the Chapel of the Holy Cross by sunset.

A few miles south of town, the chapel loomed above the road to the east. The architects situated it on a promontory, sandwiched in a narrow draw, two or three hundred feet above the road. The chapel is a rectangular arch, encapsulating a vertical cross that's about a hundred feet high. The sandy-colored chapel—set off by the dark red rock and framed against a deep blue sky—creates a stunning affect.

"Holy fuck!" Dan said, when he first saw the chapel.

"Exactly," I agreed.

"Unbelievable," Dan said.

I parked my Corvair in the lot at the bottom of the hill. Dan and I walked up the ramp to the chapel, carrying two six-packs of beer and the bucket of chicken.

After we ascended to the entrance on the chapel's east side, we put the beer and chicken on the stone benches that surrounded the courtyard. We walked to the main door, trying to be respectful. We were Catholic boys. This was a church.

I tried the door. Someone had locked it.

"What the fuck is this?" Dan asked. "Nobody locks a church."

"Yeah, it's locked, all right," I said, as I rattled the big door.

"We're in the middle of nowhere. Pilgrims in need of spiritual succor and they lock us out? My immortal soul is in peril and I can't get no satisfaction," Dan sang off-key, trying to mimic Mick Jagger.

Dan was pissed. He spent five minutes railing against the bishop of Gallup, New Mexico, who had dominion over the chapel in those days. I'd been drinking with Dan on the way north. I had a mild buzz. Dan's tirade cracked me up.

"Dan, I doubt that the bishop in New Mexico locked the chapel to spite you. I'm sure that he doesn't know what the local priest does around here."

"I wanted to see this Christus," Dan said.

"Why?"

"You said it was grotesque and controversial, right?"

"It is."

"Some people think it's an abomination, correct?"

"Yep—my dad's lawyer-buddy, for example."

"I want to experience it," Dan said, with more passion than I expected.

"Dan, look through this window. You can see the whole thing. It's a little hard to focus, 'cause the sun is setting behind it and there's glare through the west-facing windows," I said, pressing my face against the window that bordered the big chapel door.

Dan went over to the window on the door's other side. He got as close to the glass as possible, shading his eyes with his right hand. He stared at the Christus for several minutes without speaking. He pulled back, gathering his thoughts.

"You're right. That's gross. It's not Christ-like at all. It's dark—like it suffered in flames. Is it screaming in agony? It doesn't look human. The arms are way too long. The legs are too long and skinny. The trunk is too narrow. It resembles a praying mantis that fell into a fire. I can see why no one likes it."

"I didn't say no one liked it. I said a lot of people don't. I think it's spiritual and conveys the sculptor's impression of suffering from torture."

"Jeez, Tony, you get that crap in Art Appreciation 101? The only way that thing could depict Christ is if the Romans stretched him on a rack, burned him at the stake, and then crucified him. That doesn't fit with the story in the New Testament or the concept of His resurrection. That thing is horrible."

"Sacrilege is in the mind of the beholder," I said. "I saw a crucifix at the Newman Center at ASU. It had a varnished, mahogany cross. They dressed the Christus in colorful robes. The figure held a scepter in his left hand and gave a blessing with his right. It represented Christ as prophet and king, ignoring the gruesome nature of crucifixion. That sanitized crucifix in Tempe was plain wrong."

"Enough. I don't want to talk about religion. I want to get laid. Let's have a beer, watch the sunset, and head up to Flagstaff," Dan said, as we walked away from the chapel to fetch our beer and chicken.

After Dan and I settled in on the retaining wall, the sun had begun to drop behind the western mountains. Arizona is renowned for its remarkable sunsets. The one I saw that night could have eclipsed any in recorded history.

Fat, bulbous cumulus clouds drifted from the northwest across the upper Verde Valley. As the sun's waning rays ricocheted off the stratosphere and pierced the clouds, brilliant colors burst across the dark blue-black sky in an explosion of scarlet, rose, mauve, emerald, sapphire, and gold. Every tone and shade in the band of light made an appearance in that evening sky. The sunset alone was worth the trip.

While we sipped beer and watched the light show, I noticed that a small family had made their way up from the parking lot—a young man, a pretty woman with a toddler, and a dog of mixed pedigree, showing some German shepherd.

By their conversation, the sunset had impressed them too. The mother, carrying her toddler on her hip, walked over to us. She saw that we had beer. "Are you guys old enough to be drinking that beer?"

Before I could respond with a wise-ass remark, Dan reached over, grabbed a fresh can of Coors, pulled out the church key, made two openings in the top of the can, and—without comment—extended the beer to the woman.

Faced with the moral dilemma of becoming an accessory-after-the-fact to underage drinking or adhering to a higher moral standard, the lady reached for the beer with her free hand, held the opened can to her lips, and took a healthy swig.

I opened a second beer and handed it to the husband. The guy was fortunate. His wife had a sensuality that I could feel from ten feet away.

The couple stood behind us sipping their beers, as the sunset bled from the sky and the dark blue evolved into an inky black. Ten minutes later it was black as pitch.

At that altitude, the crystal clear air and the lack of ambient light meant we could see a gazillion stars—even though the clouds continued to pass overhead. I don't remember a moon.

The husband moved so that he could put his arm around his wife. Dan opened two more beers for them and passed them up. They accepted. They ignored us to engage in a private banter that implied intimacy in their future.

As I opened another beer, a shooting star fired out of the clouds in the north above the Mogollon Rim. It shot at a terrific speed to the south-southwest.

"Bob, isn't that beautiful?" the wife asked. "What a perfect end to a beautiful evening."

It would have been, had the light been a shooting star. Both Dan and I had seen the light. We followed its long diagonal track across the valley.

With no warning, the star stopped on a celestial dime, high above the valley to the southwest. I couldn't believe what I saw. I'd taken physics. It was impossible for a meteorite burning through the stratosphere to stop in midair. The current position of that body violated the law of gravity.

"What the hell!" Dan said as we watched the bright light hover in the distance. "What in the fuck is that?"

"That's no shooting star," the husband said.

I said nothing. I watched, mesmerized.

The light hung in the sky for several seconds. Without warning, the light exploded to the northeast at an unfathomable speed. It disappeared over the buttes behind us.

"Jesus, what was that?" Dan asked, as he dropped his can of beer. Two seconds later, I could hear it careening off the rocks below.

"I have no fucking idea," I said.

"Bob, are we OK here?" The woman asked, her voice quaking.

"Whatever that was, it's gone," Bob said.

The light rematerialized, flashing to the south and seeming to gain altitude until it passed Bell Rock, three or four miles south of the chapel.

"Holy shit!" Dan shouted. "There it goes again."

"There's one thing I'm sure of," I said. "That's no meteor."

"But what is it? No airplane or helicopter could fly so fast, hover, and fly again without making a sound," Dan said.

"Exactly." Bob said. "What machine on earth could do that?"

The light made a right-angle turn and shot west across the valley. Before we lost sight of it, the light flipped in an impossible 180-degree turn. It headed for the chapel.

Everyone, save the toddler, uttered an expletive. The little boy whined and hid his face in his mother's shoulder. The dog bared his teeth and growled after inserting himself between the oncoming light and his family.

As the light neared the chapel, it executed a series of right-angle turns, figure eights, and aerial maneuvers so complex that I can't describe them. The light continued its behavior for several minutes. We watched in awe.

The light stopped, moved over the chapel, and descended until it hovered over us, revealing a blurry round disk. It emitted a pale light twice the intensity of a full harvest moon. The disk illuminated the courtyard, the family, Dan, and me.

"Bob, get Rommel," his wife said, referring to the dog that had been running all over the courtyard, barking at the disk above us.

It took three days of running this incident over in my mind for me to realize that the woman had named her shepherd after the notorious German Field Marshal. Bob picked up the dog and held him tight in his arms. Carrying the child and the dog, the couple disappeared down the ramp, heading toward the parking lot below.

Dan and I remained in the courtyard, though we'd gotten up from our perch on the wall. We looked up, gaping at the spectacle.

I remember being apprehensive, but not frightened. I later became a Paratrooper and served in Vietnam. I know fear. I experienced no fear that night.

After many minutes, the light gained altitude. It blasted across the valley to the northwest. After it cleared the mountains, the disk turned north. I watched it until it faded into the blackness. We waited in silence for another 30 minutes. The disk did not return.

Dan and I cleaned up the garbage around us. We walked down to the parking lot without discussion. After we settled into my Corvair, I pulled out of the lot and headed north toward State Road 89A, which intersects with SR 179 south of Uptown Sedona. SR 89A continues north, up Oak Creek Canyon, and clears the lip of the Mogollon Rim 15 miles outside of town.

During the day, the ride up or down Oak Creek Canyon is a delight. It's a beautiful, tree-lined passage that includes ponderosa pines, oaks, and aspens along with the other species from the valley below. It parallels the creek. There are places where the view is beyond picturesque. The canyon loses much of this ambiance in the dark.

After the unexplained phenomenon, neither Dan nor I appreciated the canyon's beauty. We'd become lost in the metaphysical moment.

"Dan, we've got to tell someone." I said, as we passed Slide Rock.

"Tell who about what?" Dan asked, with an angry tone.

"Come on. You know what I'm talking about. The lights over the chapel."

"I didn't see any lights. I didn't see anything tonight. If you say you did, I'll tell them you were drunk."

"What the fuck is the matter with you, Dan?"

"Nothing. I didn't see a thing."

"Why are you being so obtuse?"

"Tony, what are you going to do? Go to the Sheriff? Stop a Highway Patrolman? Would you tell them that you saw a fucking UFO?"

"Sure, why not?" I asked, though I knew I wouldn't.

"Then you're as stupid as you look. Do you remember what happened to those folks in Michigan, who saw the UFO last March?"

"No, I don't."

"A couple of cops and several citizens claimed that they saw a UFO. It was on the national news. Everybody thinks they're crazy. The Air Force investigated and concluded that it was swamp gas."

"Dan, we're in the high desert on the border of the Mogollon Rim and a huge forest. There's no swamp gas around here."

"Tony, who cares? We've been drinking all afternoon. We're 19 years old. No one will take us seriously. The Sheriff of this hick county will conclude that you're drunk, driving a car, and delusional. That'll look great on your record. Might even get you tossed out of ASU. You'll lose your draft deferment. They'll send your crazy ass to Vietnam. You're an idiot. I didn't see a fucking thing."

Dan's tirade pissed me off. We passed the next 20 miles in silence as we drove to Flagstaff. When we got to town, we found the small hotel where John worked.

As promised, he'd gotten us a room. Despite his efforts, no beautiful coeds materialized. The three of us got trashed in the hotel room. Neither Dan nor I spoke of the incident at the chapel then—or at any other time.

After we returned to ASU, Dan and I saw little of each other over the next two semesters. I kept the event to myself. I didn't speak of it with anyone for over three decades.

CHAPTER TWO

A YEAR AFTER THE chapel incident, I dropped out of ASU. My friends labeled me as self-destructive.

My parents thought that I'd failed to clear the low academic bar that I'd set for myself. My decision reinforced their belief that I should follow a trade.

Though I rejected all criticism, my irresponsible behavior in my sophomore year in college gave weight to their views. During the months that followed the incident at the chapel—while still in school—I'd had two close flirtations with the grim reaper. I felt fortunate to be alive.

In the late fall of 1966, my roommate and I ran off a 40-foot cliff at the edge of a desert mesa near where the Salt and Verde Rivers meet. Eric and I weren't suicidal, but we were drunk and careless.

We were hauling a keg of beer away from a bonfire. We attempted to hide it from the state Alcohol and Beverage Control fascists, who'd raided our Saturday night frat party in the desert.

Imagine our surprise when the ground went out from under us. In the pitch dark, we plunged from the top of the mesa onto the rocks and rubble five stories below. Though I sustained a concussion, broke my right hand, and lost 16 gallons of cold beer, I survived. Eric broke an ankle. It was a bona fide miracle that we lived.

An hour later, my roommate and I managed to limp and crawl back up to the top of the mesa. We looked like hell, broken and bleeding from our near death experience. My fraternity big brother—Randy—walked up to me out of earshot of the ABC cops.

"You gonna be OK?" Randy asked.

"I think so," I said, cradling my fractured right hand with my left.

"You know you're a pussy!"

"What?" I said, not believing what I'd heard.

"Going over that cliff, a real man would've yelled: Banzai!" Randy said, emphasizing the last word with a terrible Japanese accent and a high pitched drunken screech.

If I hadn't broken my hand, I would've busted his silly grin.

In the spring of 1967—my hand and wrist freed from the cast—another frat brother, Jerry, and I travelled to Tucson late on a Friday. We wanted to visit girlfriends at the University of Arizona. Jerry drove. I fell asleep in the front seat of his Plymouth Lark, as he negotiated the interstate south of Chandler.

I slept through a horrific accident. I woke up pinned inside the vehicle. Jerry had lost control of the compact car on the highway north of Picacho Peak. We'd left the interstate at over 80 miles per hour.

After swerving off the right lane and clearing the embankment next to the highway, the Lark sailed over two fences and the access road before we landed in the desert and rolled twice.

Trapped for half an hour and covered in gasoline, I suffered only minor cuts and bruises. Later that day, Jerry, his father, and I viewed what was left of the vehicle at the accident scene.

"You two idiots are lucky to be alive," Jerry's dad said, as we examined the wreck.

"Yes, sir," I responded.

"Look at this mess!" Jerry's Dad said. "The roof's compressed to the window line. The engine broke through the firewall and covers the front seat. The gas tank ruptured. God, Tony, you're damned fortunate that this pile of shit didn't explode. Jerry, if you'd been wearing the seat belt, you'd have been crushed. Your guardian angels were sure working overtime."

Amen. I thought.

In that remote part of the Northern Sonoran Desert, I'd experienced another miracle. In my ignorance, I chalked it up to happenstance.

After the accident, majoring in Sociology at ASU seemed like an absurd waste. When the semester ended, I enlisted in the Army Airborne, knowing it was a ticket to Vietnam. Something in me had changed. Some powerful, irresistible force compelled me to abandon the safety of college and embark on a dangerous adventure.

After Basic, Advanced Infantry Training, and Jump School, the Army gave me leave before deployment to Southeast Asia. During this furlough, my family and I spent a few days in Sedona.

I'd not gone back to the Verde Valley since the incident with the unexplained lights. I felt wary, but our time in Sedona proved to be placid and spiritual. I visited the chapel every day. I prayed that I'd do my duty in Vietnam and return home in one piece.

I took solace from the grim visage of the Christus. I saw compelling qualities in the gruesome portrayal. I gained equilibrium in the shadow of that great crucifix. Praying in the chapel gave me confidence in the future.

After Sedona, I left Phoenix. I traveled to McChord Air Force Base to catch a chartered flight to the war. I landed at Cam Rahn Bay in transit to the 173rd Airborne Brigade on the fifth day of the Tet Offensive of 1968.

I had close calls in Vietnam. I shouldn't have survived. Somebody or something looked out for me.

By May of 1968, I'd transferred from the Fourth Battalion of the 503rd Infantry to a billet in the Support Battalion at our basecamp near the Vietnamese village of An Khe. Though it was safer at An Khe than the area assigned to my old battalion, we often absorbed serious mortar, rocket, and sapper attacks.

The North Vietnamese sappers were a tough, brave, and determined bunch. Their tactics required a squad-sized unit to rush a weak point on our perimeter in the middle of the night and overwhelm it—killing the Americans entrenched in the targeted position. Once inside our defenses, they would scatter through the basecamp causing as much mayhem, destruction, and death as possible.

Each sapper would carry several Chicom grenades and an AK-47 assault rifle. Some would also carry explosive charges in webbed satchels. As they ran through our camp, the sappers would toss grenades, plant the satchel charges on targets of opportunity, and shoot at anything that moved. Most sappers died in these bold, disruptive, and damaging attacks.

Though their casualties were high, a lucky few might make it to the other side of the camp. If they did, they hoped to find our soldiers manning the perimeter to be facing away from them and out into no man's land. The surviving sappers would attack the weakest point they could locate from the inside.

Sometimes they surprised us. The NVA killed and wounded our boys, as they tried to make their escape from the camp over the destroyed emplacements.

In the early morning of May 15, 1968, a reinforced squad of NVA sappers swept into the basecamp over a fortified bunker on the north side of the Green Line. Three soldiers in the 1st Air Cavalry had manned it. After killing all three Americans, the NVA regulars ran through the 1st Cav cantonment area causing significant destruction.

We learned of the attack when we awoke to the firing in the north, followed by the shriek of the camp siren that called my unit into battle. It signaled Condition Red. During any Condition Red deployment, we formed up as part of E Company, Provisional Infantry.

By dawn, almost all of the fighting had ceased. During the night, my platoon had neither seen an enemy soldier nor fired a shot in anger.

We had assembled near the base of Hong Kong Mountain, the highest point in the basecamp. Our new lieutenant gathered us together to brief us.

"Men," the 22-year-old shaved-tail began. "The S-2 has confirmed that at least twelve or thirteen sappers infiltrated the First

Cav's position on the north side of the base camp. They came in around 0230 hours. The best estimate is that the Air Cav legs killed or captured ten of the NVA. Before they died, those slimy bastards killed seven and wounded a dozen Americans. They blew the shit out of two Cobras and damaged three or four slicks. There could be two or three sappers still alive somewhere inside the camp. Colonel Angel thinks they're in our area. He's ordered E Company to form up and sweep east along the south part of the Green Line. Our platoon will be on the right flank of the sweep. Staff Sergeant Walsh."

"Airborne, sir!" Walsh piped up.

"Your squad will be my right flank. Your people will be closest to the wire. Although it's after dawn, all the positions on the Green Line will remain manned and ready. However, one trooper in each position will be facing north, to thwart a surprise attack from inside the camp by the remaining NVA. So be fucking careful. Don't let your guys get trigger happy."

"Yes, sir."

"OK. Let's get moving. Form up on me. Walsh, get your people on the right. Davis, your squad is in the center. Thompson, you're the left. We'll move out when first and third platoons link up with Thompson. Get it done!"

While we waited for the other two platoons, SSG Walsh called for me.

"Specialist Giordano."

"Yes, Sarge," I said, as I trotted over to him.

"Your fire team will be the right flank of our squad and the far right of the whole company. Your people will be closest to the Green Line. Make sure your guys are careful. No fucking mistakes. There are more Americans in the trenches, bunkers, and towers on the right than gooks. No mother fucking accidents. You understand?"

"Of course, Sarge."

"Tony, I'm putting you on the right 'cause I trust your ass."

"Thanks, Sarge. I won't fuck up. I'll watch these guys," I said.

"Watch your own ass, too. Nathaniel Victor has nothing to lose. He'd love to grease a nice Italian boy from New York before he buys the farm."

"Sarge, I'm from Arizona. And we'll be extra careful."

"See that you are. Put Gallagher on the far right. He's the best you got."

"OK, Sarge. Will do."

Once the company sweep began, I went into a super-vigilant mode. My fire team was headed for trouble.

I had to look out for two privates and a private first class. We'd be swinging east along the inside of the perimeter with a bunch of jumpy paratroopers on my right. Somewhere out in front, two or three experienced and committed North Vietnamese soldiers waited. Since it was past dawn, they'd missed their window. They knew that none of them would leave the base camp alive. They had nothing to lose.

We'd dispersed at the proper interval. I sent PFC Gallagher as a scout, a few more yards to the right. I had my head on a swivel, trying to ensure that we didn't get jumped by the sappers or shot by our own guys.

Twenty minutes into the sweep, we entered an area where the engineers had been building an artillery battery emplacement. The construction crews had left two trucks, a bulldozer and Jeep. They'd parked the vehicles in a neat row from east to west, facing south. Something about the vehicles caused the hair on the back of my neck to go up.

I whistled. About 60 yards to the north, SSG Walsh heard me. I signaled that we had vehicles to our front. He alerted the platoon leader. The whole platoon slowed down.

Walsh signaled for me to take the fire team to the south side of the vehicles. The rest of the squad would be on the north.

"Listen up, guys." I stage whispered. "The sappers might be hidden in and around those vehicles. There's a fortified bunker manned by our troopers to the south. The rest of our squad will be on the north side of the trucks. We'll be in the middle. Be fucking careful. There's ten ways to screw this up. Get it right."

As the fire team's two privates swept past the first of the two-and-a-half ton trucks, I looked to the right and spotted an Airborne sergeant about 30 yards to the south. He stood behind a bunker next to the Green Line. He watched our movements with interest. I signaled him. He lowered his M-16 and nodded.

As I looked back out of the corner of my eye, I spotted an NVA sapper 20 yards to my left. He crouched underneath the first deuce-and-a-half. The two double sets of large rear wheels on each side had given him cover from my less-than-vigilant young troopers.

My men had walked right by him. If he'd had his AK 47 ready, he could have killed them both. Although it all took less than five seconds, I still remember what happened next in great detail.

The sapper had unscrewed the end of a Chicom grenade handle. He'd inserted a finger of his right hand into the small metal ring that connected a thin wire to the grenade's fuse through the hollow handle. He prepared to toss the grenade at my men, which would disconnect the wire and arm the fuse. Four seconds later, it would explode. It could kill both of my men.

Though itchy-fingered Paratroopers surrounded me, I had to shoot the son-of-bitch. In less than a second, I brought my M-16 to my shoulder, flipping the selector to full auto. I fired a burst into the enemy soldier, hitting him at least three times.

The force of the impacts caused the sapper to snap backwards and involuntarily fling the grenade forward, arming it. Chicoms resemble the old German potato-masher hand grenade. Once they hit the ground, they bounce erratically. The sapper's armed grenade bounced toward me, landing four yards away.

I yelled, "Grenade!" I dove to a prone position, trying to make myself as thin as possible. When the Chicom exploded, the concussion sucked the air from my lungs. Pieces of shrapnel slammed into my helmet, flak vest, load-carrying equipment, and my rifle.

I looked over at the sapper. He'd slumped to the ground. I could see his body writhing and blood spurting from his shoulder. A wave of fear swept over me, then a strange calm.

I started to check myself out. Gallagher got to me first.

"Tony, don't move. Let me see where you're hit. Stay still."

"Get your ass back on that flank, PFC Gallagher!" I shouted. "They're other sappers around. Watch your ass!"

SSG Walsh and the lieutenant came up after Gallagher got back in line, while I was still on the ground. They examined me, as my two negligent troopers secured the sapper, who was still alive.

"I'll be damned," SSG Walsh said.

"What?" The lieutenant asked.

"Giordano is the luckiest mother fucker in the Herd. He may have to change his underwear and get new LCE, but I don't think he's wounded at all."

"Are you sure?" 2LT Andrews asked.

"Yes, sir. Let's get him on his feet. He's a little dazed by the blast, but he's OK."

"You sure got an angel on your shoulder, bud," SSG Walsh said.

"I'll say," my platoon leader agreed. "No Purple Heart for you."

"No confirmed kill, either," Walsh said, as he looked at the wounded sapper.

"Sir, let's get the medics over here. The sapper could have a ton of information about who else is lurking outside the perimeter."

Less than 20 minutes after I shot the NVA soldier, the first platoon on our left encountered four sappers near a culvert that engineers had built across a small stream. Alerted by our earlier contact, our boys spotted the enemy before they could ambush anyone. After a brisk firefight, four NVA soldiers died. Two Americans received minor wounds.

The next day, at the express direction of my First Sergeant—a man that I still admire above almost all others—I held informal counseling sessions for my negligent subordinates behind the company shit house. Top supervised as I counseled each one in a dismounted Airborne bare-knuckle drill. The first session went well. The second proved far more challenging—but ended on the right note.

When it was all over, both of my men apologized and swore that they would never fuck up again. For the next several weeks, we became so close that one of the guys named his second son after me ten years later. The other, Tim Williams, died in my arms at LZ English. My oldest son bears his name.

I had several other close calls in Vietnam.

Six weeks after shooting the sapper, Tim Williams and I were in a C-123 transport that took ground fire on an approach into the landing strip at LZ English near Bong Son. Tracers from .51 caliber machine guns wounded Paratroopers in the webbed seats on both sides of me. One of the rounds hit Tim in the back and exited his chest. The enemy fire disabled the port engine and destroyed the hydraulic lines that controlled the landing gear.

Somehow, the brave and skilled aircrew managed to land the airframe, but other Paratroopers suffered serious injury in the controlled crash landing. Two of my friends, including Tim, died in that incident. After holding Tim until the life ebbed from his body, I walked away with a heavy heart, a ton of guilt, but without a scratch.

Two weeks later, on my 21st birthday in July, I rode shotgun on a Jeep that had business in Qui Nhon, a small Annamese town on the South China Sea. Due to the irresponsibility and gross misjudgment of a horny lieutenant, we missed our convoy back to An Khe in the Central Highlands. Adding insult to injury, the lieutenant ordered that we travel without an escort at dusk, west on Highway 19.

The driver, the officer, and I negotiated the treacherous switchbacks of the An Khe Pass after dark. For the next hour, I could sense an evil presence along the road.

It wasn't until the next day, when the NVA unleashed a massive ambush against a South Korean infantry battalion in An Khe Pass, that we realized that the NVA had followed our Jeep at every turn. Not wanting to spoil the tactical surprise or risk losing the bigger target, the enemy must have decided that three Americans were small potatoes. They let us through unmolested.

In addition to a dedicated, motivated, and deliberate enemy, threats at An Khe included drunken and deranged comrades.

The night that I made sergeant in November of 1968, an intoxicated, homicidal staff sergeant tried to shoot a close friend of mine over an imagined slur. After he fired his first shot at my buddy's head, I attacked the senior man with my bare hands. I managed to disarm him as he fired all the rounds in his pistol's magazine at the wall and ceiling. As he struggled to regain control of the pistol, two other new sergeants and I beat him savagely. Later, I could never explain how any of us survived.

In March of 1969, at the end of my self-extended tour of duty, I was the non-commissioned officer in charge of a detail in Saigon. It was supposed to be a boondoggle—an R&R disguised as an official mission.

On the last night of our sojourn, the NVA sent a barrage of 122 mm rockets into Saigon. One rocket hit our hotel in Cholon, destroying the fourth floor and setting the building on fire. My men and I remained on the 11th floor for several hours, trapped by the conflagration.

By all rights and every law of physics, the whole place should have burned to the ground. No fire department ever arrived to fight the flames. Miraculously, the fire burned out before it reached our floor. Americans died in the attack. Once again, I made it through unscathed.

I wasn't blind. I could see how lucky I'd been. I wondered why I was the recipient of such good fortune. It wasn't the guilt of the survivor. Something more profound was at work.

Becoming a Paratrooper and serving in Vietnam fulfilled a dream that I had since sixth grade, when I read a book about the Airborne that Sister Mary Assumption had purchased for our class library. The experience proved to be all that I'd hoped and feared it would be—and much, much more. The Army finished the job that the Jesuits started.

CHAPTER THREE

I WOULDN'T TRADE my experiences as an enlisted man and non-commissioned officer for anything. Only my wife, sons, daughters, and grandchildren have more value.

In the three decades after the war, I had many successes and some dismal failures. After Vietnam, I married an Army nurse. We had two daughters. We put each other through college: grad school for her and law school for me.

In 1974, I returned to active duty in the Army as a Captain in the Judge Advocate General's Corps. I'd found a way to reconcile my two treasured goals. My first assignment as an officer was with the 82nd Airborne Division. For the next few years, I jumped out of airplanes and tried criminal cases in courts-martial.

My extraordinary good fortune continued during my first tour at Bragg. In 1976, I survived a helicopter crash in an OH-58 Kiowa that had lost all power during takeoff.

As he was lifting from the Division Headquarters' pad at the edge of the ridgeline overlooking Gruber Avenue, the pilot tried to auto-rotate the 100 feet to the ground. He had limited success. The helicopter crashed into a space between several stout pine trees, destroying the main rotor, fracturing the airframe, and catching on fire. Although the crew and I limped away, the pilot had compressed several vertebrae. He never flew again. Once again, my overworked guardian angel had kept me safe.

My first marriage did not survive Fort Bragg. After we broke up, I remained single for eight years. In the interim, I earned an advanced legal degree at George Washington University, served at the Army War College, did a second tour at Bragg, and taught Constitutional and Criminal Law at the Judge Advocate General's School at the University of Virginia.

In 1984, I married a female officer in the JAG Corps. It took.

The Army assigned us to posts near Washington, D.C. In 1986, during the Iran-Contra Scandal, the Army posted me as the General Counsel of the White House Office of Emergency Operations. Almost everything about that job was classified. I can tell you that I had to travel a lot.

On a very snowy morning in January of 1987, I tried to drive from the District to a site in Western Virginia. I got as far as Gainesville on I-66. Five or six inches of snow and ice accumulated on the road, as the storm turned into a blizzard. The highway clearing crews had not gotten very far west by 0400 hours.

I had no traction in my powerful but very light 280ZX. I'd been stupid to even attempt the trip.

To make any headway at all, I fell in line behind an 18-wheeler traveling around 40 miles per hour. I set my front tires in the truck's tracks, though my wheelbase was much narrower than his.

A half mile east of the exit for Gainesville, the big truck hit an ice patch and spun wildly to the right. As soon as I reached that patch, my little sports car began to do a full 360-degree rotation. No matter what I did, I could not gain purchase on the roadway.

When I got to the 180-degree point and faced east, another large truck bore down on me. Time slowed. The driver was doing everything that he could to avoid hitting me, but he had no control either.

The large truck would slam into me. I would die. I felt no fear. I said a quick prayer to Saint Michael the Archangel to ask God to watch over my wife and new son, Tim.

Though I can't explain why, the truck missed a direct hit at the last instant. It popped my left rear quarter and spun the little Z like a hockey puck on an ice rink. I rotated at least three full revolutions across I-66 and ended up buried to the windshield in a snow bank on the median. When the State Troopers arrived, they couldn't believe that I'd survived at all. One of them mentioned that I must have a four-leaf clover tattooed on my ass.

I didn't argue. I was almost 40. I'd begun to realize that someone very powerful had been watching out for me.

After my near catastrophe in 1987, Gretchen criticized my cavalier attitude for my own safety. She insisted that I take more precautions. Our family was growing. She didn't want to be a widow and raise two orphans.

In the late spring, Gretchen, Tim, and I moved into a house in Springfield, a mile south of the Washington Beltway. We'd been renting in Alexandria for two years. Gretchen was now pregnant with John. We needed more space and had to move to a bigger house. I took leave from the White House and managed the job myself with the help of several Army buddies.

By the end of a sunny Saturday in May, we had boxes lying all over the new townhouse. To show our appreciation, we served beer and hamburgers to our helpful friends. While we were drinking and chatting, my toddler had found a box sitting next to the family room's fireplace. Clever like his mom, he'd discovered a way to open it. He'd begun to remove the contents: a number of ancient looking stuffed animals.

Then I noticed the logo and writing on the box. I couldn't believe my eyes.

The box had been unpacked from a larger container that Gretchen's mom had sent her from Texas a month earlier. Gretchen was an Army brat. The box had been in storage for 12 years, since she'd packed it up after graduating from Ball High School in Galveston. I'd never laid eyes on it before.

The box contained her childhood collection of stuffed animals. She'd packed them for storage since she wouldn't take them with her to Texas A&M University.

"Holy shit." I said, as I walked over to the box and examined it. "This is not fucking possible. The odds are incalculable."

"What are you babbling about?" my friend Bill asked, sipping his beer.

"Look at this shit, Bill." I picked up the box and turned it so he could see the logo on the front.

"Shut the front door," Bill said.

In 1975, Gretchen's dad had obtained the box from a liquor store on Galveston Island. He needed several boxes to prepare for his retirement from the Army, which coincided with Gretchen's decision to attend TAMU in College Station.

This box had once transported liquor from Italy. The winery shipped it to America sometime in 1975.

The logo read: Giordano. Under the logo, the Giordano Company listed their products. They sold acqueviti, liquori, spumanti, and vini. However, it wasn't the logo with my family name that caused the stir. To the left of the Giordano logo, the high school girl had written her first name to identify the contents as her property. She put her name on that box at least ten years before we ever met.

The words Gretchen Giordano appeared on the front of the box containing her stuffed animals in that sequence and proximity.

Be honest. How many women named Gretchen have you ever met? I'll bet you've never even heard of a Giordano. In the entire Milky Way galaxy, there is precisely one Gretchen Giordano.

Calculate the odds for yourselves. They are beyond miniscule that a high school girl in Texas would write her own first name on a box next to a logo that was also a rare Italian surname—and that logo would turn out to be the last name of the man that she would meet and marry in Virginia ten years later.

No one who's ever seen the box can explain it. An atheist friend suggested that it was mere serendipity. Sure it is.

Encountering that box was another epiphany. Of all my life and near-death experiences, the Giordano box—and its cryptic message predicting my marriage to Gretchen—convinced me that everything happens for a reason.

In 1990, as a Lieutenant Colonel, I received an assignment to the U.S. Attorney's Office in Tampa to help the feds prosecute a munitions fraud case. After the first Gulf War, the U.S. Attorney asked me to stay. I'd served 20 years on active duty and was almost retirement eligible. He sweetened the deal by hiring Gretchen, too.

By the 1990s, I had a new dream—to litigate long, complex, criminal cases in Federal Court. The U.S. Attorney gave me a chance to show my stuff. Over the next 16 years, I had the time of my professional life.

At home, I mentored my sons, Tim and John, as I watched them grow. Raising two boys proved to be fulfilling and rewarding. Though I missed the Army, someone very wise wanted me to leave my military life with the endless trips, deployments, commitments, and challenges. My job was to focus on my boys, be a good example, and teach my sons how to be better men than I could ever be.

I'm a lapsed Catholic. I never obtained an annulment from my first marriage since I have two precious daughters. The Church would not sanction my marriage to Gretchen. Despite this serious difficulty, I chose to raise my sons as Catholics. They attended Incarnation Elementary School and, much later, Jesuit High School in Tampa. They were top students in both places and established themselves as first-class leaders. Both of my sons turned out to be excellent football players.

I wanted Tim and John to have the same educational advantage that the Jesuits gave me. My sons are now practicing attorneys. They agree that their time with the Jesuits was the best education they could have gotten anywhere.

In 1998, the new U.S. Attorney directed me to help prosecute the biggest health care fraud in American history. By May of 1999, I prepared for a ten-week contested trial.

In the spring, I had been finishing up the motions practice and organizing my portion of the trial-on-the-merits, which was really basic, like identifying and marking exhibits. Since our case involved thousands of documents, it was tedious. The Secretary of Health and Human Services assigned clerical personnel to help out.

One of the very best clerks was a female HHS college intern—a strikingly attractive black woman named Yvette. Like many hip college girls, she wore a small nose ring. I always thought that it detracted from her otherwise stunning appearance.

Yvette was wicked smart and analytical. In short order, she grasped my situation and helped to modify a Microsoft database into a unique resource for tracking, sorting, and illuminating the thousands of exhibits. During the trial, this database proved invaluable.

I tried to convince Yvette to go to law school. She declined. She wanted to be a criminal investigator. She thought the FBI would be a good fit, but she was willing to work for any of the other federal agencies that employed special agents.

Once, as we catalogued evidence, she mentioned that she was an Army brat and that her dad was near retirement. After learning that, I made a point of asking after her father on those occasions when we worked together.

In May 1999, after her graduation from UT, she stopped by my office to tell me that HHS had hired her as a special agent and criminal investigator. They'd agreed to assign her to Los Angeles so that she could be closer to her mom and dad. I wished her well and asked where her father had decided to live after retirement.

"Oh, they're already there. They took terminal leave. They moved to Arizona."

"Really? I grew up there. Where in Arizona?"

"They moved to Sedona."

"Have you been there yet? It's so beautiful."

"No. I've flown over Arizona on the way to California. I'm looking forward to seeing this place. Mom and Poppa think it's awesome."

"It is. I spent a lot of time there before Vietnam. I went there once after the war. I'd finished up at ASU on my way to law school in Texas. When you go out there, you have to see the Chapel of the Holy Cross."

"Is that the one that's built into the mountain? Mom sent me a postcard with a picture of the chapel. Very impressive."

For reasons that I can't explain, I launched into the first description of my close encounter in 1966. I'd seen Spielberg's movie decades earlier. The term close encounter conveyed the substance of my experience.

Yvette listened. Halfway through my story, she sported a look of complete incredulity. Dan Ostergaard's common sense warning for me to keep my mouth shut had come to fruition.

"You look like you think I'm crazy," I said. "I know it seems hard to believe. I sometimes wonder myself. Nothing like that has happened in the last thirty years."

"I don't think you're crazy."

"Why the look then?"

"Tony, I spoke with Poppa last Sunday. He's a squared-away guy. Like you, he was both enlisted and an officer. He also retired as a light colonel. He's down to earth, all business, no nonsense. He told me about an experience that he had hiking between Bell Rock and a place called Courthouse Butte."

"So what's the connection?"

"Other than the different site, his story is identical to yours," she said.

"No shit?"

"None."

"Well, I'll be damned."

"Maybe," she said.

"Bell Rock and Court House Butte are four miles south of the chapel," I said.

"In galactic terms, that's a bull's eye," she said.

"Who says that this is other worldly?" I asked.

"You think it's something secret? Where's Area 51?" she asked.

"What do you know about Area 51?"

"Just stuff on TV."

"Area 51 is northwest of Sedona. Must be a couple of hundred miles. Maybe they've got something now that could do the things that I saw, but in the mid-sixties? I don't think so."

"OK. We don't know what the phenomenon is. We know you aren't crazy, unless Poppa is too. Could be something they fed you guys in the Army."

"Nice theory, but my close encounter predates my Army service."

We left the issue at that. We exchanged pleasantries and promised to keep up. We never did. I didn't have contact with her until 14 years later.

CHAPTER FOUR

June 4, 2013, 11:30 PM
1908 Port Colony Way
Tampa, Florida

I'D RETIRED FROM the Department of Justice in 2006. I went to work for the local Sheriff. Since my youngest son, John, had recently graduated from a top tier law school and because I maintained an expensive mistress—Gretchen—I had no plans to retire and live out my golden years in peace and comfort.

It had been a miserable day. I'd been wrestling with the unresponsive bureaucracy of the Social Security Administration. To calm myself before I went to bed, I sought out a soothing video on YouTube.

It had become my habit late in the evening to watch something placid and soothing. While I watched, I would pray on a special rosary. A friend had purchased it for me from the gift shop at the Chapel of the Holy Cross on a trip she'd made to Sedona. Since I'd encouraged her to go see the red rocks, she bought the rosary as an unexpected present.

Praying on this rosary in the quiet of my empty nest comforted me. I don't go to Mass anymore. The Sedona rosary has been my connection to the Divine Spark.

I carry the Sedona rosary with me everywhere. I also have a gold St. Michael the Archangel medal. St. Michael is the patron saint of Paratroopers and police officers. Twenty years earlier, I had a jeweler engrave the designations of the three Airborne units in which I'd served on the back of my medal.

I'm a klutz beyond the imagination of Inspector Clouseau. I'm hard on the things that I carry around. Sometime in late 2010, I lost the Christ figure from the little wooden cross on my rosary. I felt horrible.

I chose to keep the Sedona rosary, rather than replace it with a newer one. At the time, I didn't realize that the loss of the Christ figure wasn't an accident, but a foretelling of my future.

Despite its importance to this story, there's nothing miraculous about my rosary. I view it as a cell phone for talking to God. Atheists will claim that my use of the rosary is an act of desperation by a man beyond middle age. I don't care.

You've heard my story so far. I've been fortunate. I've seen too many things that convince me that there is far more than we mere mortals can fathom. I don't pretend to know what lies beyond—but there is something.

I opened YouTube that night and searched for a soothing video. I found one that used photographs of special sites around Sedona as the backdrop to new-age music. I noticed an interesting video on the list to right of the one I'd played.

That video led me to a link to an extraordinary article written by an Anglican Bishop from St. Luke's Episcopal Church in Sedona. The author, the Right-Reverend David McMannes, had written a bizarre tale about the history of the Christus and the Chapel of the Holy Cross, which is now part of St. John Vianney's Roman-Catholic Parish.

This should be good. The Anglicans are writing an expose about the Roman Catholics, I thought. While the Anglicans and Catholics have similar beliefs and rituals, they can be very competitive.

The article, dated in 1997, began as a recapitulation of the genesis of the chapel and the phases that followed. It described the motivation of its benefactor, Marguerite Staude. It cataloged the work of the architects and the sculptor of the Christus, including the original controversy surrounding the grotesque appearance of the Christus.

I would have dismissed it as another interesting piece on the Internet had it not dropped a nuclear revelation: the compelling and grotesque Christus figure had disappeared without a trace. It no longer hung on the mammoth stone cross inside the Chapel.

According to Bishop McMannes, sometime in the late '70s, the Christus vanished. No one knows how or why. There are theories and speculation that range from the mundane to the macabre, but no facts. More intriguing, the Anglican Bishop revealed that the Roman Catholics stopped having religious services at the chapel at the time it disappeared.

The local Catholic parish built a gift shop in the old priest's quarters in the chapel's basement. The gift shop did brisk business selling Catholic artifacts, like my rosary, to the hundreds of thousands of tourists who now flock to see the chapel every year.

I couldn't believe that anyone would turn this mystical place into a cash cow. I wondered what they were thinking in the Diocese of Phoenix, the Catholic principality that has assumed control over the chapel from the Diocese of Gallup.

It struck me as more than a coincidence that the Christus had disappeared around the time the Catholics stopped having religious services at the chapel. Being an attorney over four decades has made me morbidly suspicious.

It was inexplicable that the Anglicans would address this mystery—and not the Catholics who suffered the loss and stopped the services. Why would that be?

Over the next few weeks, I searched the Internet. I gathered all the data that I could about the chapel, the Christus, the benefactor, the architects, and the rumors of the disappearance. I found no article, paper, report, explanation, equivocation, clarification, rationalization, denial, or justification from any Catholic source that would illuminate any part of this mystery. Utter silence.

"Dad, you're obsessed," my son, Tim, said as we chatted on FaceTime a month later. I'd finished my latest report to him about my research. Tim and his wife, Heather, live in Washington, D.C., where he practices law in a K Street bluestocking firm.

"Tim, that's harsh. I'm on a quest, an investigation into a great mystery."

"Dad, you remind me of that guy in *Close Encounters of the Third Kind*. You know. He saw a UFO, got sunburned, became obsessed, and built a replica of a Wyoming mountain in his basement."

"I'm better looking than Richard Dreyfuss," I said. "I'm not obsessed. It's a coincidence that I constructed a scale model of the chapel on the lanai and sculpted a replica of the Christus from five hundred pounds of stainless steel," I joked.

While we talked, Tim's comment about the aliens jogged a memory. As soon as we ended the call, I went on the Internet and found a clip of Spielberg's movie. I also watched independent videos that embellish the story that Spielberg told in his film.

Some of the other videos focused on the physical appearance of the aliens in Close Encounters. Several of these depictions seemed eerily similar to the Christus, though the Christus appears quite a bit taller and a little thinner. You can see these aliens for yourself on the Internet and compare them to the picture of the Christus in the McMannes article.

This new discovery caused me to double my efforts. Over the next week, my wife became concerned about my behavior. She'd begun to worry about my obsession, which she attributed to the not-so-early onset of dementia.

"Tony, we need a vacation," Gretchen said. "You're consumed with this Christus. We need to get you away from computers. We haven't had a bona fide holiday in years. All of our trips involve moving furniture to college dorms or attending law school graduations."

"Yeah, I'd like to get away," I said. "I've got plenty of leave."

"We could go to one of those all-inclusive places in the Caribbean or in the Bahamas. I've never been to Bermuda."

"How about a cruise?" I asked. "Alaska, the Rhine River?"

"A cruise doesn't blow my skirt up. Not enough to do."

"You're afraid that I'll get you alone on a boat," I said with a sly smile.

"Maybe, but I'd like to do something different."

"Let's go to Sedona," I said. "You've never been there. You've been promising that you'd go for twenty years. I'm calling you on it."

"Tony, I'd love to go to Arizona. Mom adored her trip there with Dad—but I don't want to enable your addiction. If we go, it's to have fun, enjoy the experience, and have some time together. It's not a search for evidence of alien invaders. OK?"

"Sure, I promise. You do understand that we have to go to the chapel, right?"

"Fine," she said in the superior way women use to dismiss their men.

"Will you make the airline reservations?" I asked.

"Yeah, I will—as always. I'll tell you what; I'll get a round trip ticket for me and a one way ticket for you, just in case."

"In case, what?"

"In case you get abducted, silly."

CHAPTER FIVE

11:15 PM, August 21, 2013
Room 549, L'Auberge Resort & Spa
301 Little Lane, Sedona, Arizona

YOU'VE ALREADY GUESSED that my primary motivation for this Sedona trip was to gather information about the missing Christus. I admit that I promised Gretchen that I'd put my obsession on hold, but she knew that I was lying. I wasn't being honest when I said it. You knew that I was insincere when you read it.

I'm not a dishonest man. I'm a realist.

No marriage survives 30 years without liberal fabrications by both spouses on a full spectrum of topics. Wives lie about the finances that they control.

"This little old thing? Honey, I've had it for years," they'll deceitfully claim when you spot a suspicious new dress or pair of expensive Italian high heels.

Women mislead their men about their sexual interests. And they exaggerate their satisfaction with performance when they do interact intimately. I didn't say that wives were cruel, though they can...well, I'd better stop there.

Husbands exaggerate and lie when the topic is their prior achievements in sports, military service, hunting, fishing, and romance. Wives know this. They tolerate the aberrant behavior because it's expedient.

Wives don't care how many touchdowns or tackles you made, fish you caught, deer you slayed, enemy soldiers you vanquished, or prior girlfriends you seduced. They're too busy hiding the receipts from the mall and cooking the family books.

I did want to go to Sedona to have fun. It's a great venue for all kinds of recreation, hiking, climbing, biking, jogging, sightseeing, eating, appreciating art, and shopping.

You know how beautiful I think the place is. Look at the pictures. Judge for yourself. Be aware. None of the magnificent photographs on the internet do Sedona the least bit of justice. You have to experience this place for yourself.

I'm not a member of the Sedona Chamber of Commerce. I don't own property there or have financial skin in the game, other than hoping that you'll read this story.

I'm a man who has come to the fall of his life. I've taken on a quest. I want to know what happened to an important spiritual icon of my youth. I have a personal connection with the Christus…and it's missing.

I thought that I could use my investigative skills to examine the mystery of the missing Christ figure. I hoped that I might learn something more than the Anglicans knew 16 years ago. I guess there's no fool like an old fool.

Though we accept that I was lying about my motives, I had to be subtle or risk pissing Gretchen off. I didn't want to lose all hope for romance on this trip. I had to ensure that we'd have fun, too.

After we landed at Sky Harbor Airport in Phoenix on August 21st, we rented a car. We drove to Sedona along the Interstate 17, passing through the Phoenix metropolitan area and then climbing with the highway into the high desert plains to the north.

Gretchen was in a sour mood. She felt disappointed because she'd much rather have gone to the Caribbean than visit any place in my home state.

Gretchen has never liked Arizona. She'd never been to Sedona. She had been to Phoenix once in our entire 30-year marriage. That sad trip had to do with my dad's last illness and death. Not a time for sightseeing or recreation.

My bride has not been shy about criticizing Phoenix, which she describes as a "hell-hole." When we were there in August of 2005, the temperature in the afternoons did exceed 120 degrees every afternoon. Even so, anyone who's spent time in my hometown knows it's a wonderful place to live or to visit—especially if it's not summer.

All along the trip, Gretchen kept up a critical dialogue about the barren terrain in Phoenix and in the mountains north of the city. As we descended into the Verde Valley, Gretchen reminded me that this trip was my idea, that I owed her for her unbridled altruism, and that I would have to make it up to her.

Though I'd gone on plenty of trips with her that I didn't like, I didn't argue with her. I knew that as soon as she saw the place, Sedona would seduce her.

When we turned north on State Road 179, I had a flashback to my trip with Dan Ostergaard. Though a lot has changed in five decades, the impact of the red rocks when they first heave into view remains undiluted.

As soon as Gretchen saw Court House Butte, she stopped carping. Though my wife can be very persistent in cataloguing my shortcomings and explaining her position on any topic, she ceased all complaints and criticisms.

As we drove deeper into the red rock country, she had no reluctance to describe each new geologic delight with unbridled enthusiasm. It was the most rapid, complete, and comprehensive attitude transformation that I'd seen in our long marriage.

While we drove north toward Uptown Sedona, Gretchen pulled out her cell phone, called her mom, and informed her that she was selling our house and we were moving to Sedona. No kidding. Talk about seduction.

We checked into L'Auberge, a fancy hotel east of Uptown Sedona that's situated along a breathtaking stretch of Oak Creek. L'Auberge offers separate cabins with every possible amenity, but we chose to stay in the lodge.

The ambiance of our room exceeded our highest expectations. I can summarize our entire morning by saying that I'd never heard Gretchen use the word "wow" so often or with so much enthusiasm. In a weak moment, she admitted that she was glad that I'd insisted on this trip.

After we unpacked, I took my bride to lunch at Tlaquepaque, a swank shopping mall built to look like a simple Sonoran village near Oak Creek, south of Uptown Sedona. Did I mention that they served a killer Margarita in the Mexican restaurant there?

I drink because I do my best investigative work if I'm relaxed. I use alcoholic beverages for professional or medicinal purposes. Seriously. To acclimate to the altitude in Sedona from our sea level life in Tampa, Gretchen and I spent that afternoon at Tlaquepaque.

The faux Mexican mall did not exist in my day. Sedona has changed. It's no longer the art-influenced, laid-back, southwestern cowboy village of my youth. In the 60s, artists lived in Sedona and Oak Creek Canyon. The place is too gorgeous not to attract talented people.

Back then we called these artists *hippies*. While I risked my life in Vietnam, the hippies wore flowers in their hair and cavorted naked in Oak Creek. They smoked Bob Marley-sized joints of marijuana to mellow them out for their marathon sexual activities.

Do I sound envious? Perhaps I am, a little.

I've struggled to survive in 100-degree heat with 100 percent humidity while motivated North Vietnamese sappers did their best to blow me to smithereens. I could have stayed home, dodged the draft, and experimented with drugs. Thus fortified, could I have instead chased some sexy, nubile, blonde hippie nymphomaniac around Cathedral Rock? Hmmm, it's a tough choice.

The New Age movement hit Sedona several years after I left Arizona State to attend law school. This trip was my first experience with the phenomenon. Even after watching videos on the internet and talking to experts at the Center for New Age and Crystal Vortex emporiums in Sedona, I'm still not sure what it is.

I like the music. There's a tune called "Adiemus" that a website plays as it scrolls through pictures of Bell Rock and other Sedona sites. "Adiemus" is a soothing New-Age chant of unintelligible gibberish. I play it before I sit down to take my blood pressure. It's good for a five-point drop after a rough day. Maybe that's the miracle of New Age philosophy.

After additional Margaritas, I called the hotel shuttle for the short ride back to L'Auberge. In Tampa, I work with a lady who's a major player in Mothers Against Drunk Driving. It took me far too long, but—because of her example—I recognize what an irresponsible shit I had been during a couple of decades in my life. Though I've never had a DUI, I no longer drink and drive.

The next morning, August 22nd, I got up early and asked the hotel shuttle to take me to the mall to pick up my car. I returned to L'Auberge and gathered up my wife. We drove north up Oak Creek Canyon to the West Fork Trail Head to get a jump on the crowd.

I'm not articulate enough to describe the beauty that hikers encounter on the West Fork Trail. It's friggin' unbelievable. The trail is so magnificent that it's worth the substantial price of parking, the tariff levied by the Forest Service for each hiker, and the hassle one encounters with large numbers of other day-trippers.

Since it's four miles in and four miles out, it takes six to eight hours to hike the trail. Although West Fork in no way resembles the triple canopy jungle in the Central Highlands of Vietnam, I still had a flashback to less enjoyable times.

I remembered the awful heat, the stifling humidity, the difficult terrain, and the mal-designed, load-carrying equipment that the Herd issued to grunts in 1968. My time in the Infantry preceded the implementation of the Army's so-called ALICE—All Purpose Individual Carrying Equipment—Packs.

On an operation in the field, we carried tons of shit stuffed into the diabolically designed and super uncomfortable LCE.

The gear that I humped included an M-16, water in at least six plastic canteens, C-rations, socks, underwear, hundreds of 5.56 mm rounds for the basic weapon, two hand grenades, a belt of 100 7.62 mm rounds for the M60 machine gunner, a mortar round for the 11 charlies or claymore mines, a large hunting knife, entrenching tool, first-aid packet, insect repellant, a flashlight, compass, map, personal items, poncho liner, and towels to pad the straps and to soak up the torrents of sweat that humping the boonies generated. I'm sure that I've forgotten some of the other stuff that we humped.

In contrast to Vietnam, the hike through West Fork Trail was a joy. The trail sits at 5,400 feet above sea level. Even in August, it remained shady and temperate all along the beautiful trek.

My modern camelback pack allowed for a three-liter water bladder in an insulated pocket. I kept the water cool with a small frozen bottle of water stuffed into the pocket alongside the bladder. I had room to carry all the navigation, safety, medical, and comfort equipment that I could heft. Of course, my bride thought I'd over-planned the whole episode. Once we hit the trail, she began to complain.

"Anything that can be done, can be overdone, huh sweetie?" she asked.

"If we get lost, hurt, injured, or snake-bit, you'll be glad that I prepared."

"Sure, babe," she said. "But how will you get lost? You have an expensive compass, good maps, and three different GPS apps on your phone. The trail is well-marked and it follows the freaking west fork of Oak Creek."

"Expect the worst. Hope for the best. That's my philosophy," I said.

"You're certifiable!"

"That's why you love me."

"No, it's not. I love you because I'm certifiable."

Despite Gretchen's unfair and unfounded criticism, the hike was a glorious adventure through one of the most scenic trails anywhere on the planet. The modern equipment made carrying the load a breeze. I hardly noticed it.

That exertion through the canyons and over 13 separate fords across the serpentine creek satisfied my hyperactive wife for the day.

When we got back to our car, she told me that she wanted to go to Tlaquepaque to shop for presents for her girlfriends. She assured me that these gifts would not include jewelry, clothes, or shoes.

I wondered what she would buy for her posse. Resisting the impulse to engage Gretchen with questions, I agreed to drop her off so that I could go to the Chapel of the Holy Cross and begin my quest.

As she got out of the car, Gretchen gave me a knowing smile, but refrained from sarcasm or criticism about my obsession. My acquiescence to her shopping trip proved to be an unearned benefit that she chose not to squander.

Less than 10 minutes later, I arrived at the chapel. I couldn't believe the crowd. Cars filled the parking lot and buses lined the road. Over a hundred tourists milled about on the ramp, in the courtyard, in the chapel, and in the gift shop. I'd never seen so many people at the chapel.

The exterior of the Chapel of the Holy Cross hadn't changed over the last 40 years. The structure had weathered the elements and the altitude. The spiritual nature of the site, on the other hand, had changed dramatically.

Inside the chapel, I was shocked by the absence of the Christus. It felt empty and cold. I knew the figure wouldn't be there. I thought I'd prepared myself.

Seeing the bare, sterile cross, framed against the stunning backdrop of the red sandstone buttes, made me angry. As beautiful as the architecture of the chapel is and as breathtaking as the view from the site, I no longer felt the transcendent experience that I'd felt every other time I'd been inside the sanctuary. The Church had lost, mislaid, or forgotten a treasure of incalculable value.

I felt uncomfortable in a place that had once provided a peace that carried me through a year's worth of fear and fatigue in a deadly combat zone. I couldn't disguise my torment.

"You look upset, fella," a tourist from Massachusetts said, as I stood and stared at the barren cross. I could tell he was from New England by his accent.

"I am."

"Why? This place is serene and beautiful. I've never seen anything quite like it and I've been all over the world."

"I grew up around here. There used to be a figure of Christ on that cross. It's different in here now."

"How's it different?" The man asked, as he took a picture of the inside with his iPhone.

"It used to be a real church. My parents and I went to mass here. Now, it's a barren tourist attraction. They took the Sistine Chapel and made it into a bingo hall."

"Forgive me, fella. I'm not Catholic. Tell the truth, I'm an agnostic. I think there's intelligence out there, but I have a hard time believing in an anthropomorphic divinity that lives in the clouds and interacts with humanity. I'm glad the Catholics decided to be reasonable about this place. It's too valuable to be a church."

"What?" I said, not believing what I'd heard.

"You been downstairs to the gift shop?" The man asked, as he put his phone away.

"Not yet."

"Well, my Catholic friend, take your credit card. It's pricey down there. I'm sure the Pope makes a ton from the proceeds for those trinkets."

"The new Pope is a Jesuit, my agnostic friend. He's the first in the five-hundred-year history of the Order. He took a vow of poverty. He won't see a penny."

"Sure, he won't," the man said, as his wife pulled him away to catch the tour bus at the bottom of the ramp.

"Harry, we'll be late. We're going to the Asylum for dinna," she said in her own Bostonian manner.

The Asylum is a restaurant in Jerome, an old mining town southwest of Sedona on State Road 89A. The restaurant used to be a loony bin. Or if that's too insensitive: a sanctuary for the mentally ill. Seemed like a good place for the New Englanders.

I did go down to the gift shop. The man was right. The Church had attached a healthy bump to the cost of their products. After ten minutes in the shop, I noticed a youthful, quite striking, Hispanic woman behind the counter.

She had long, black, silky hair, deep-brown eyes, a prominent nose—reminiscent of the Aztecs—and a lovely olive-brown complexion. As I watched her, she waited on the customers with an enthusiasm bordering on flirtation.

I smiled, walked over to the counter, waited for her to free up, and then asked her if the gift shop carried any items related to the Christus.

"I'm sorry, sir. I don't know what you mean."

I told her of the story of the Christus that used to reside in the chapel upstairs.

"Really?" She asked. "There was a figure on the Cross upstairs?"

"Yep. It was very dramatic."

"How so?"

"Let me show you," I said, as I pulled out my iPhone, tapped on the Safari icon, and entered *Christus of Sedona*. The software pulled up the McMannes' article. It has a graphic picture of the Christus at the top. I displayed it to the pretty clerk.

"I've never seen this," she said, though her manner changed and she seemed off-kilter. "I've been working here for two years. This wasn't here when I started."

"That's right. According to this article, the Christus hung from the Cross in the chapel from 1956 until sometime in the late seventies," I said.

"That's long before my time."

"Is this the first that you've ever heard of the Christus?"

"I'm pretty sure. Maybe Jim knows something about it," she said.

"Who's Jim?"

"The sales manager. I'll call him over," the girl said, as she signaled to a thirty-something, tall, thin, balding man who was attending to a customer. While we waited for the manager, I introduced myself.

"I'm Tony Giordano."

"I'm Linda Alvarez," the girl said, offering me her well-manicured hand.

"*Con mucho gusto, Senorita,*" I said, trying to be gallant.

"*Senora, Caballero,*" the woman corrected me, beaming while showing me a respectable diamond ring set on her left hand.

"*Lo siento, Senora,*" I apologized. "*¿Puedo practicar mi espanol contigo?*" asking if I could practice my Spanish.

"*Como no.*" Linda said, agreeing.

Linda and I spent a pleasant ten minutes conversing in Spanish. Linda's Spanish was flawless and—oddly—more Castilian in style than Mexican or Sonoran. She had to correct my grammar a couple of times. For such a vivacious personality, she seemed worldly-wise, experienced, and mature.

"Hello, Sir. I'm Jim Wilson," the manager said, extending his hand in greeting as he walked up.

"Tony Giordano." I shook his limp hand and got a very bad vibe.

"Jim, Tony showed me a picture of a figure that hung on the Cross in the chapel upstairs. He calls it the *Christus*. He wants to know if we sell anything like it."

I held the phone up and let Jim examine the photo. He looked at it for quite a while.

"I never saw the Christus in the chapel. We used to sell a postcard that depicts it. May still have a few in the back," Jim admitted. "Mr. Giordano…"

"Call me Tony," I interrupted.

"Tony, where did you find this article?" he asked in a strange tone.

"On the internet."

"Yeah, it looks like the postcard," Jim said, gesturing at the photo.

Our conversation had drawn a small crowd. Other tourists wanted to see the picture. Rather than pass my phone around, I announced the internet link.

"I don't know what happened to that figure," Jim said.

"The article says it went missing sometime in the late seventies. No one knows for sure how it disappeared," I said, generating an audible snort from a lady about my age.

"It got spun up in one of the vortexes," a guy with plaid Bermuda shorts offered.

At this juncture, I must point out that folks in Sedona insist that the plural of vortex is vortexes, not vortices. I can't explain why. Nor can I clarify what a vortex is.

They didn't exist—or no one had discovered them—until the 1980s. I'm not sure that the phenomena of vortexes coincide with New Age beliefs, but they seem to coexist.

I'm not making light of either concept. I've maintained that Sedona is a hauntingly spiritual place. There's a positive, but indefinable, quality to the area. Sedona is the classic example of the totality of something exceeding the sum of its parts.

It's not the beauty or the grandeur of the Upper Verde Valley. The first time that you see the Grand Canyon, it'll rock your world. As spectacular as the Grand Canyon is, it does not have the same mystical quality as Sedona. As the New York Times said in the late '70s, "God created the Grand Canyon, but He lives in Sedona."

I hung around the gift shop for a half hour chatting with the other customers. Since I wasn't advancing the investigatory ball, I decided to leave. Before I did, I said goodbye to Linda while she rang up the postcards of the Christus that Jim found.

"Thanks for your help," I said.

"Didn't help much. Good luck on your quest. *Tenga cuidado y vaya con Dios.*"

"*Gracias, Senora,*" I responded, hoping that I would indeed go on this quest with God. As for careful, that's my middle name.

Linda's use of the word *quest* pulled me up short. I remembered those Grade-B science-fiction movies where there is something menacing afoot. The people in the story seem normal, right up until the time they make a slip and reveal a perverse, evil side. I half expected that as I walked out, I could spin around. Linda, Jim, and all of the customers would be glaring at me with blood red eyes.

OK, I did spin around. They were too fast for me. When I looked, Linda and Jim had gone back to work selling their merchandise. Maybe Gretchen's right about the dementia.

When I got to the rental car, I still had an hour to kill before I had to be back at Tlaquepaque. I decided to visit the local parish rectory.

The Church of St. John Vianney in Sedona is on the west side of town. It's an attractive church that's set apart from other buildings. It's constructed in a southwestern pueblo style, surrounded by a circle of gardens and statues.

I went there to find the Catholic pastor. He was in California attending a month-long retreat. A priest from Ireland was filling in. I asked the receptionist if I could speak with him.

After waiting for 20 minutes, a freckled man with short red hair, about 32 years old, came out into the reception area. He was very fit, about my height, but weighed 20 pounds less. His pleasant face had a hint of mischief in his smile and a glint in his eye. He looked like a tall, thin leprechaun. He introduced himself: "Good afternoon, Sir. I'm Father Patrick O'Malley. Peggy tells me that you'd like to speak to a priest," he said with a charming brogue.

"I'm Tony Giordano, Father. I'd like to speak to someone who knows the history of the Chapel of the Holy Cross."

"I'm sorry. That's not me. This is my first trip west. I've been in Arizona two weeks. That includes about a week here. I've spent some time in the chapel, though. Very impressive, isn't it?"

"It is impressive, Father. I grew up in Phoenix. I used to go to Mass here. I understand that no one says Mass at the chapel anymore. Do you know why?"

"Is that right, Peggy?" Father asked, as he looked over his shoulder at the middle-aged woman who sat behind the counter.

"Is what right, Father Pat?"

"Mr. Gordini…"

"Giordano," I corrected.

"Oh, sorry. Peggy, Mr. Giordano says that he used to come to mass at the chapel."

"Father, we haven't had a mass, benediction, marriage, baptism, reconciliation, confession, or sacrament adoration at the chapel in over thirty years."

"Really? Mr. Giordano is right? We stopped having religious services there?"

"That's correct, Father. When I was girl, they used to say Mass there on Sunday. They stopped a long time ago."

"Why?" Father asked in a way that made it seem that he, too, was curious.

"Haven't a clue. Father Ted might know."

"Sorry, Mr. Giordano," Father Pat said, turning toward me. "It does seem a waste. The chapel is so beautiful. It would be such a joy to say Mass there."

"Father, thanks for your time. Here's my card. The second e-mail address is my personal one. If you talk to Father Ted and he has any additional information, would you please ask him to e-mail me?"

"Of course. Tell me. Why is this issue so important?"

"You're new here, Father. Have you ever heard of the Christus?"

"Not in the context of Sedona or the Chapel. In Ireland, a Christus is a statue of Jesus or the figure of Jesus that hangs on the cross and forms a crucifix."

"Father, since you've been to the chapel, you noticed that the Cross over the altar does not have a Christus, right?"

"Now that you mention it, yes," Father Pat admitted.

"Father, check this out," I said, as I pulled the postcard with the photo of the Christus from my hiking vest pocket. Father Pat looked at the card and registered a mild shock.

"Is that photo accurate?" he asked. "That's a unique rendition of a Christ figure. I've never seen anything quite like it."

"Father, I witnessed this figure hanging on the cross in the chapel from the late fifties until the seventies."

"Show it to Peggy," Father directed, as I stepped over to the counter and held the postcard so that the receptionist could view the photo. "Peggy, do you recognize that figure from the old days?" Father asked.

Peggy put on her reading glasses, stood up, leaned over the counter, and examined the photo. Her pleasant countenance changed.

"Yes, Father Pat," she said with a sigh. "It's been so long. I'd forgotten about that figure. It used to scare me. My father, may he rest in peace, hated it. Lots of people around here were not fond of it."

"What happened to it?" Father Pat asked.

"I don't know. I went off to the University of Arizona in the mid-seventies. I spent all my time in Tucson. Except for breaks, I didn't come back to Cottonwood until 1981. By that time the figure had disappeared."

"Ever hear any rumors about the disappearance of the Christus?" I asked.

"The favored theory is that Ms. Staude snuck in and took it down."

"It's strange that the Church would stop using the chapel for services. Both of these unusual things happen in an architectural work of art—and no one asks why," I said, looking at Father Pat. He watched me, sizing me up.

"You think that there's a connection between the two events, Mr. Giordano?"

"Maybe."

"Any proof?"

"No, Father."

"Best be careful," Father Pat said, the slightest edge in his voice. "I'm sure that there are good, cogent reasons for the two events. I find it hard to believe that they're related."

"Time will tell, Father," I responded to his subtle warning.

"Time always does, Mr. Giordano. Is there anything else?"

"Your blessing, Father."

"Certainly," Father Pat said, as he made an outward Sign of the Cross, "*in nomine Patris, et Filius, et Spiritus Sanctus*. May the Good Lord watch between me and thee, Mr. Giordano, while we are apart one from the other."

"Mizpah!" I responded, surprised that the Irish priest would include that last phrase from Genesis 31:49.

"Thank you, Mr. Giordano. Go in peace."

Driving from West Sedona to Tlaquepaque, my cell phone rang. It was Gretchen.

"Where are you taking me to dinner? I'm famished."

"Depends on how depleted our funds are after your blitzkrieg through the mall."

"Did less than modest damage to our finances," Gretchen said.

"How modest?"

"Very, very modest."

"Can you quantify very, very?"

"Yes," Gretchen said without elaboration.

"Will you give me the gruesome details?"

"Sure, but you should know that the most expensive stuff was the lingerie."

"You bought lingerie for Ellen and Pat?"

"No, silly. I bought the lingerie for me; actually, for you."

"Oh!" I said, surprised at this turn of events.

"I thought we could go back to L'Auberge. I could show you the lingerie. After, we could get a late dinner. If you want, we can order room service," Gretchen offered.

"That sounds like a plan," I said.

My bride must have pulled out the stops on expensive gifts for her friends. I could see that the lingerie was a cynical ploy designed to distract a pathetic older man who—Gretchen assumed—could not reason beyond his own petty lust. Her plan worked perfectly.

Gretchen had fabulous taste in lingerie. She's ten years younger than me. She's five feet five inches tall and weighs 115 pounds. I always thought that she was very pretty and—in many ways—is more attractive at 56 than she was at 26. She has medium-length blonde hair that ends at her shoulders, framing a light complexion and deep blue eyes. When I first saw her at the Officer's Club at the JAG School in Charlottesville, I thought that she was the best-looking woman I'd ever seen in an Army uniform. Her fabulous legs added to the allure.

Gretchen has kept in shape by jogging. I'd been a runner for 45 years. I don't run on the street anymore. These days, I terrorize everyone at the gym by attacking the elliptical StairMaster.

We've had tension, as we've gone our separate ways in pursuit of fitness. I can still hike with the best of them, as I demonstrated on the West Fork Trail. To mollify and distract my hyperactive bride on this trip and to assuage her sense of adventure, I'd agreed to try the Predator Zip Lines in Camp Verde.

Here's the concept. At the Out of Africa Wildlife Sanctuary on State Road 260, clever entrepreneurs have constructed high towers and steel cables over several acres of a nature park that houses lions, tigers, and bears—oh my! You pay them $100 per person. You take 15 minutes indoctrination on the equipment. You sign a waiver written by callous Arizona lawyers. Since I'm an attorney, I embrace the hypocrisy of that last statement.

Thereafter, despite the clear language of the waiver, you allow the polite, energetic, and enthusiastic zip-line guides to convince you that it's safe to ride thin steel cables for hundreds of yards, 100 feet above ravenous carnivores. I'm serious. Of course, Gretchen thought zip-lining would be the best thing ever.

After my private modeling session, we had a terrific meal. Room service delivered a four-star filet, accompanied by an inspiring, lively Shiraz that pleased the palate and left the right hint of an oaky vanilla aftertaste. I felt so grateful that I agreed to the zip-line. The second private modeling session sealed the deal.

Bright and early the next morning, Gretchen and I set out for Camp Verde.

I know that you've been paying attention. You realize that I served in the Army Airborne for over two decades, and had at least three tours on jump status. You must think that to an experienced Paratrooper, a simple zip-line would be a piece of cake.

You'd be wrong. I do have 80 jumps logged on my various manifests, including five with the Canadian Airborne Regiment, when it was stationed in Edmonton. Though I wear my American and Canadian wings on my 5-11 hiking vest, I've never lost my deep respect for high places.

I didn't want to do the zip-line, but Gretchen had been so supportive the night before that I couldn't say no. Despite my angst, the staff proved to be professional and competent. I didn't become fodder for predators and the lines turned out to be a lot of fun.

We have photos—taken by the park's photographer—that show Gretchen skimming high over the carnivores, arms thrown wide, head back, laughing delightfully, without a care in the world or hint of fear. You will never see my photos because they show an old man gripping the belt connecting me to the trolley in abject desperation.

It took two-and-a-half hours to complete the training and negotiate the separate lines. When we finished, it was afternoon. Since it was August, the day became hot, even at over 4,000 feet above sea level.

I grew up in Arizona. While it is dry, when the temperature hits 100 degrees, it's too hot for strenuous outdoor activity. Don't buy into the bullshit about dry heat. You can follow the bleached bones of silly tourists—who flaunted this advice—across the desert and mountains from Nogales to Page, Yuma to Winslow.

When it's 95 degrees in Tampa with 90% humidity, you can still do things outside, though you may not want to. When it's 110 degrees in the high desert, you better watch your ass, wear a hat, hydrate, or—better yet—stay inside and drink Margaritas, but don't drive.

After the zip-lines, I took Gretchen to the Page Springs Cellars near Cornville, a small community south of Sedona, along the lower Oak Creek. The winery sits in a beautiful narrow valley, surrounded by acres of cultivated vines along the hillsides, old cottonwoods, elms, maples, and willows. It's a gorgeous venue that's competing in national markets with fine wine made of Arizona grapes.

Famished, we inhaled a pleasant lunch. Gretchen had a robust cabernet. The ambience and fare at the winery were superb. It was the perfect cap to a great mini-adventure. At lunch, I told Gretchen that I had a surprise for her.

"What might that be?" Gretchen wondered.

"I booked you the whole afternoon and evening at the spa at L'Auberge," I said.

"That's mighty generous. Why didn't you ask me first?"

"Don't you want to be pampered like a goddess by the spa staff?"

"Sure. But what are you up to? Where will you be? I don't see Mister Macho Paratrooper getting a pedicure."

"True. But you deserve a little pampering. I thought you would like this surprise."

"Oh, I do. But I don't trust you. I think this is a cynical ploy to distract me, while you go searching for the Christus."

"Is it working?" I asked.

Gretchen looked at me for a long moment, her face a stern masque. After a moment, she allowed her lips to form a slight smile.

"Yes, it is. When does the pampering begin?"

"In about twenty minutes. We have time to pay the check and get back to L'Auberge."

"OK, Tony. Let's go. If the aliens don't get you and you meet me after the spa, I might show you the other lingerie."

"Other?"

"Yep."

"Like what?"

"Don't be late and you'll see."

"Powerful incentive to be punctual."

While Gretchen experienced the best the L'Auberge spa could offer, I continued my quest by visiting the Center for New Age in Sedona. It's an interesting place where one can get exposure to the full spectrum of New Age philosophy.

New Age thinking is a big tent. It accommodates a variety of intellectual disciplines and religious beliefs. Whether you're a Wiccan, Muslim, Christian, LDS, Jew, Jain, Hindu, Buddhist, Shinto, Druid, Pagan, or whatever, there is something for you at the Center,

After an hour at the store, I passed on a psychic reading by a Reiki master. Reiki involves maximizing spiritual life forces to attain contentment and good health. I'm not sure what a Reiki master does, but I didn't want to know the gritty details of my future. Ignorance of one's fate is bliss.

I had the opportunity to book a UFO and vortex tour, but decided against a field trip. Thanks to Gretchen's offer, I had something much better planned for later that evening. Besides, I'd had my own intense encounter with a UFO decades earlier. It occurred without the benefit of the New Age guidance. I figured that if the intelligence that operated the lights in 1966 wanted to contact me—and it had the technology to overcome Einstein's theory regarding light speed—it would know how to find my e-mail address. If people who want to help me grow a larger penis can find that address so often, advanced beings could Google it. Maybe they'd use Bing or Yahoo.

I spent time at the Sedona Crystal Vortex and Ye Olde UFO stores. Same result.

I noticed one interesting thing. All of the stores that I visited that catered to New Age thinking included medals, statutes, paintings, illustrations, or literature about angels.

I'm not an expert on angels, but I am Jesuit trained. I've always considered the concept of angels to be fascinating. I bought into the notion, as evidenced by the large gold St. Michael's medal that I wear 24/7. With apologies to American Express, I never leave home without it. I never do anything without that medal around my neck.

You may have a different spin on the concept of angels, but within the confines of my obsession to find the Christus, here's how I saw it. An angel is a celestial being, imbued with preternatural knowledge. In other words, they're actual beings of unknown composition and morphology that are far smarter and far more advanced than humans.

Angels are not divine. They are not gods or demi-gods. Bible references claim that God created angels. He uses them as messengers and servants. In certain cases, they act as protectors and guardians. Angels come in several different classes or ranks, like Seraphim and Cherubim. There are at least eight other groupings that I can't pronounce.

In the past, these superior beings had a civil war. The vanquished, fallen angels found themselves disenfranchised and tossed out of Paradise by the likes of my personal hero, Michael the Archangel. The leader of the bad angels is Satan, a/k/a Lucifer, a/k/a the Devil. His followers are demons.

Fallen angels have a perpetual case of the ass. They lost the war.

Demons try to undermine God's plan. They're doomed to failure, but they are all about the journey. Besides, they have nothing else to do. They're condemned to suffer for eternity. If they can take some humans with them into the abyss, they get bonus points. These points have no value.

It's like playing games at Chucky Cheese until the end of time, except for the pain and torment. On further thought, Hell must be a lot like an afternoon with 60 cranky five-year-olds at Chucky Cheese.

While driving from the Center for New Age, it struck me that the Chapel of the Holy Cross gift shop had some of the same statutes and paraphernalia depicting St. Michael that were available at the Center. I found comfort, knowing that my belief system had widespread acceptance by so broad a constituency, at least for retail purposes.

I got back to L'Auberge in time to meet Gretchen. The spa experience had been so soothing and fulfilling that after being massaged, washed, wrapped, and waxed into submission, she fell asleep while I showered. She slept like baby through the night.

The next morning, August 23rd, as part of our Sedona Adventure, we got up early to hike the Broken Arrow Trail. This trail begins about a mile south of Uptown Sedona.

Sedona is too small, even today, to have a downtown. They have to call the main tourist area something, ergo: Uptown Sedona.

From the east end of Morgan Road, the trail winds south through a narrow valley between the Mogollon Rim and a couple of high, magnificent, crimson sandstone structures known as the Twin Buttes. About a half-mile from the trailhead, you encounter an ancient sinkhole called the Devil's Dining Room.

I don't know why the locals named this place the Devil's Dining Room. I asked a few experts and got different answers. It's like asking 12 Brits what Boxing Day is. Other than the 26th of December, you'll get a dozen different reasons why the Commonwealth celebrates the day after Christmas as a holiday. Same for the Devil's Dining Room.

I'll note that the Devil had a dining room in Sedona, a kitchen across the valley near Soldier's Pass, and a bridge on the other side of Capitol Butte. This part of the Verde Valley was sacred to the Native American inhabitants. To compete with the Holy Spirit, the Devil must have been very active here.

When Gretchen and I got to the Devil's Dining Room, my smug demeanor evaporated. I had a powerful feeling of déjà vu, though I'm certain that I'd never been to this geological feature. My arms broke out in goose bumps and a cold chill made me shiver in the 80-degree morning air.

"Tony, what's the matter?" Gretchen asked.

"I don't know," I said as I wiped my forehead. I was sweating and shivering at the same time. This was a first for me.

Wise environmental managers have placed a barbed wire fence around the sinkhole on the Broken Arrow Trail. You have to be stupid, inconsiderate, and a scofflaw to go inside the wire.

The ground around the edge of the sinkhole is unstable. In time, it will fracture and fall into the hole. Standing on the edge is a slow-motion death wish.

Bats hibernate in this dining room. Bats perform a critical service for the ecosystem because they eat tons of insects every night. They hang upside down from the ceiling of the sinkhole during the day while they sleep.

Signs inform the hikers that stupid and inconsiderate humans can disturb the baby bats, causing them to lose their grip and fall to floor of the sinkhole. The sign warns that the baby bats, known as pups, can be injured or killed as a result.

Falling head first to the bottom of the sinkhole causes the babies to flounder around in the accumulated guano deposited over decades. Plummeting headfirst into 30 years of shit makes the pups question the whole bat lifestyle. Entire species of bats are thus endangered by the mental trauma that bats endure, not as a result of insensitive humans, but because of their own gastrointestinal extravagance.

Believe me, I respect the environment. I didn't want to contribute to mass bat extinction. But something other than disdain for the law and the ecosystem compelled me to squeeze under that fence. I stood at the edge of the sinkhole for five minutes. The whole time, I shivered as sweat poured from my head and chest.

The sinkhole is 90 feet deep. Broken limestone rocks covered the bottom. I noticed trash, but not in a large volume. I had a flashback to the Chapel Incident in 1966, when our beer cans and chicken bones ended up on the rocks below the retaining wall.

I didn't see anything extraordinary. I didn't observe a single bat or other flying mammal. No bats were injured or traumatized during the research, writing, editing, or publishing of this story.

Gretchen and I spent 20 minutes at the Devil's Dining Room. During my déjà vu experience, Gretchen had become bored. She tried to use her cell phone, but the reception sucks south of Marg's Draw, east of the Twin Buttes. My bride's patience, short during the best of times, evaporated.

Gretchen settled down as we headed south along the Broken Arrow Trail. This hike is different from the West Fork Trail. West Fork tracks a small tributary of Oak Creek through narrow canyons south and east of the Mogollon Rim. Broken Arrow is a path to the east of Twin Buttes. It's open, airy, dry, sunny, and breathtaking. Be careful. Carry lots of water on Broken Arrow.

When we got to the cutoff for Submarine Rock, Gretchen loosened up. I suggested that we head east to explore the rock, but my wife declined. She wanted to press on to Chicken Point. Since I'd exhausted my exemptions at the Devil's Dining Room, I didn't disagree. Her behavior surprised me because she's always pushing me to do more.

We stayed on the trail and trekked up to Chicken Point. When we arrived, a platoon of mountain bikers, hikers, and pink Jeep tourists had beaten us to the goal.

Gretchen and I spent ten minutes resting, hydrating, and watching deranged mountain bikers do wheelies along the rocky cliff around Chicken Point. Their suicidal behavior made my episode on the lip of the Devil's Dining Room seem tame.

When my wife was ready to resume our hike, I convinced her that we should head west on the Little Horse Trail. I wanted to see the Chapel of the Holy Cross again.

Little Horse Trail intersects with the Chapel Trail on the west side of the Twin Buttes. Once on the Chapel Trail, you pass megaliths named the Two Sisters, as in Nuns. They are large, ponderous, menacing, and unmoving, like the BVMs who taught at St. Francis.

Once beyond the sisters, it's an easy trek north along a narrow ridgeline to the Chapel of the Holy Cross in the shadow of Elephant Rock.

Gretchen and I had been walking for two miles from Chicken Point when we made the parking lot of the chapel. The lot was not as crowded as two days earlier, but scores of tourists meandered all over the property. In the old days, the chapel was renowned, but not so popular. You could find peace and solitude there.

Gretchen loved the chapel. She thought it struck the right balance of architectural beauty, compatibility with the stunning environment, and responsible use of fragile resources.

"The view is spectacular," she said as we stood in the northern courtyard and sipped on our water. "This is where you saw the aliens, right?"

"Gretch, I never said the lights were aliens. I don't know what they were."

"Right, Tony. Nothing in this world operates like that."

"Then you believe that I saw something."

"Sweetie, I've lived with you for thirty years. You're a handful, but you've never been delusional. You believe that you saw something. If it wasn't aliens, what could it be?"

"Gretch, I don't know what those lights were. You could get similar performance from modern jet-propelled drones. The humans operating them wouldn't experience the crushing G forces that those right-angle turns generate. The pilots would be safe in some Air Force computer center playing with their joysticks while hammering back shots of Jeremiah Weed. Honey, I'm not here about lights," I said. "I'm here about the Christus."

"I think the two are connected somehow," Gretchen said.

"Until the McMannes' article, I never saw a correlation. After the original incident, I experienced the Christus here twice, once in 1968 and once in 1971, with no unexplained phenomena during either of those trips."

"You don't like this place anymore, do you?" My wife asked.

"I still think it's impressive. It's not as spiritual."

"You're upset because it's different. They want to attract a broader base of people who can appreciate this beauty."

"You said, 'they want to attract.' Who is the they?"

"The Catholic Church, smart ass," Gretchen shot back.

"The Catholic Church stopped having religious services here. They opened an emporium. They do a brisk business. A unique spiritual symbol is now a sophisticated scenic overlook with a religious theme and a lucrative gift shop."

"Speaking of the gift shop, I told Mom that I'd get her something. Let's go down and look around."

When we went down to the shop in the old priest's quarters, Gretchen set out to examine the various religious items that could pass for jewelry. Linda, the pretty sales clerk, spotted me right away and came over to talk.

"Tony, we hoped that you'd come back. Jim told me that if you wandered back in the shop that I should ask you wait. He has something to tell you about the Christus."

"Super. Where is he?

"Jim's in the back," Linda said, looking over her shoulder toward the rear of the shop. "There he is now." She waved until he noticed, then motioned him over.

"Hey Tony," Jim said, as he gave me a cheerful greeting.

"Hey, you know something about the Christus?"

"Yeah. I hoped you'd come back. Your inquiry a couple of days ago caused a little stir. You went over to the parish and spoke with Father O'Malley, right?"

"Yes, I did. I didn't offend anyone, did I?"

"No. Father O'Malley is an inquisitive Irishman. You got him excited. He called Father Ted. Father O'Malley told me that, according to the pastor, the Christus was controversial."

"That's right. Saw that myself. That's what the bishop said in the article."

"Tony, I read that article last night. It's wild that the Christus disappeared."

"It's suspicious," I said.

"I agree," Jim said. "Father Ted thinks that Father Hansen knows about the Christus."

"Where can I find this Catholic priest?" I asked.

"Is that Don Hansen?" Linda chimed in. "He's the famous trail guide, New Age counselor, tantric massage therapist, and Reiki master. He's a Catholic priest?"

"That's the guy," Jim said. "But he's not Catholic. He's not a priest anymore. He was an Episcopalian priest until about ten years ago. He quit and became a trail guide. He's a character. He grew up around here. He knows every nook and cranny from Flagstaff to Prescott."

"How do I contact him?" I asked.

"I'll write down his number," Jim said, as he grabbed a pad and pen from the counter. "I talked to him this morning. He's interested in meeting you. He's expecting your call. He told me that if I saw you, I should tell you that he's free late this afternoon."

"Jim, I grateful. I'll call him right away," I said, as Gretchen approached with a full bag and a long receipt from the cashier.

"Save that receipt," I told Gretchen. "I'll attach it to the petition I'll have to file in the Bankruptcy Court in Tampa."

"Very funny, sweetie. I'm doing my part for the Catholic Church."

"But you're not Catholic," I said.

"My sons are Catholic. Remember, you made me go to all those masses? Besides, by not being a Catholic, that makes my generosity all the more admirable."

"OK, but Mother Teresa, you're not. Gretch, Jim is the manager here and Linda works the counter," I said, gesturing to my left. "Jim gave me the number of a man who may know something about the Christus. We have to hustle back to the trailhead to get the car. I want to see the guy this afternoon. Where do you want me to take you?"

"I'm going with you this time."

"Sure that you want to go? You'll be enabling my obsession."

"Wouldn't miss it for the world. I'll have a couple of margaritas first."

"Well, that's a happy coincidence," Jim said.

"What is?" I asked.

"Hansen wants to meet you at the Cowboy Club in Uptown Sedona. It's near where you're staying," Jim said.

The manager's words struck me like a baseball bat to the knee. "How do you know where we're staying? I never told you that."

"That's right. Father O'Malley told me."

"How did he learn about our hotel?"

"That's parish business. Tony, Sedona is a small town. It would take me twenty minutes to track a tourist down here. We get some deadbeats and some bad paper. We've got to protect the financial interest of the Church. We have an excellent working relationship with the Sedona Police and the Coconino and Yavapai Sheriffs' Offices."

"Thanks, Jim," I said. "I don't merit the chapel's bad credit treatment!"

"Oh, I see. Sorry, I didn't mean it that way. No one is impugning your integrity, Tony. In fact, you're a kindred spirit, right? Father Pat said that you're a lawyer who works for a Sheriff in Florida, right?"

That one floored me. I looked over at Gretchen. She shrugged it off.

"Jim, what's going on here? Why is the parish so interested in my background?"

"I told you that you caused a stir. If you're curious, you can ask Father Pat."

"Believe me, I will. Is he at the parish now?"

"No, but you can ask him later. He'll be at the meeting with Don Hansen."

"Really?" Gretchen said. "What's his interest in Tony's quest?"

"That's beyond my pay grade folks. I'm only the messenger."

Gretchen and I took our leave. Linda and Jim smiled. They told us to have a good afternoon and pleasant stay in Sedona.

As we walked out, I didn't spin around. There was no need. I knew they had blood red eyes and an evil intent.

CHAPTER SIX

UPTOWN SEDONA HAS a different character than it did in simpler times. The venue for our meeting, the Cowboy Club, sits on the property that used to be the Oak Creek Tavern.

The Tavern was the classic diamond in the rough. Located north of the fork created by State Roads 89A and 179 at the bottom of Oak Creek Canyon, it served as a watering hole and community forum for locals, ranchers, cowboys, miners, loggers, artists, and tourists who would stumble in from the road. Corporate powerbrokers rubbed elbows with grizzled old ranch hands. Artists discussed their creations with ranchers and loggers. The atmosphere was friendly, boisterous, and equalitarian.

At the Tavern, the food was good, the beer better, and the company best of all. The décor was eclectic cowboy. The owner and operator, Ms. Bird, had diverse tastes, including the stuffed eight-foot-tall polar bear that she set to one side of the tavern.

As a kid, my family and I often ate lunch there after mass at the chapel. Some of my best memories of my family are from the Tavern.

Nothing is ever the way you remember it after the passage of significant time. None of the old timers would concede an improvement. Still, everyone agrees that the Cowboy Club is a great place.

The food at the Club is fantastic. In addition to everything you'd expect in a superb restaurant, you can get buffalo, elk, and rattle snake. Try finding that in your local five-star bistro. The service is good and the prices are reasonable.

The Club was walking distance from L'Auberge. After our hike around the Twin Buttes, I'd worked up a thirst. I looked forward to a couple of beers.

As we walked up the steep grade to the restaurant, I cautioned Gretchen to be careful on this evening. Some of what transpired at the chapel seemed ominous.

"You're paranoid," my wife said. "You've been out playing intergalactic detective. You've implied to the local Catholic priest that the Church has covered something up. That might make them a tad defensive."

"Why did they do a background check?" I asked.

"They didn't do a background check. Anyone with access to the Internet can Google your name and get tons of data about you, including everything that the store manager mentioned."

"I repeat. Why do that?"

"I can think of two reasons," Gretchen said.

"Enlighten me."

"First, it's easy to do. Your daughter-in-law was sweet enough to set up a website for your publisher in California to showcase your great American novel. You know, the one you wrote that has made no one's bestseller's list. Thanks to Heather, half your history is on that site. It would take a total stranger less than thirty seconds to get access to the story of your life. Try it. You'll see."

I probably should have mentioned that after ten years of trying, I convinced a small, boutique military-style publishing house on the West Coast to publish a novel I'd written about the heroic adventures of the father of an Army buddy. The book seemed to be selling, but it hadn't gone viral.

"There's even more stuff about you on the Sheriff's website. Remember?"

"OK. What's the second part?" I asked.

"They want to know what kind of lunatic they're dealing with. The Church gets accused of a lot of things. You've implied that the bishop and priests are hiding something nefarious about the Christus, and that—whatever they're hiding—caused them to stop services at the chapel. That allegation might make them cautious. They want to know if they need security when they meet with you. In their place, I'd have done the same thing."

"I think Henry Kissinger—describing Richard Nixon—said that even paranoids have enemies. So be careful," I said.

"You know me," Gretchen said.

"That's why I'm worried."

"I wouldn't be counting on any lingerie modeling later," Gretchen warned.

"By the way, I cancelled the credit cards while you dried your hair," I said.

"Fuck off!"

"Hit a nerve?"

"All right, we're almost there. Behave and I may change my mind."

"Who says I'm interested?" I asked.

"Pleeeeese!" Gretchen said in an exasperated tone, followed by a world-class sigh and a headshake, signaling that she thought that I was the easiest, most pathetic conquest since the British burned Washington, D.C. in 1814.

"Welcome to the Cowboy Club," a clean-cut adolescent-looking cowboy said as Gretchen and I walked in. "I'm Sean. Table for two? Or do you want drinks at the bar?"

"Definitely drinks. We're meeting a couple of men."

"Are you here to see Don?" the host asked.

"Don Hansen?"

"Yeah. He's there in the back booth with another gentleman. He told me that Tony and his wife would be here to see him. I'm thinking that you're Tony."

"Guilty."

"Go on over and get comfortable. What would you like to drink?"

"Have a good Chardonnay?" Gretchen asked.

"How about the Kendal Jackson Vintner's Reserve. It's layered with rich tropical fruit and has a lingering toasty finish," Sean said.

"It'll have to do," Gretchen, the wine snob, said.

"Rogue Dead Guy on draft or Fat Tire, but no toasty finish," I said.

"We have Oak Creek Amber on draft."

"Better than perfect. We'll be waiting."

Gretchen and I walked over to the booth. Father Pat sat on the side facing us. He was wearing jeans and a light green pullover shirt. He looked normal—not like a priest at all. He conversed with someone on the other side of the booth. Due to the arrangement of the booth, I couldn't see the other person.

When Father Pat spotted us, he said something to his companion. Father slid to his right to get out of the booth and greet us. The other person slipped to the left, exited the booth, and turned around.

"Don Hansen, I presume," I said, as I offered my hand.

"You must be Tony and this lovely lady, Gretchen," Hansen said.

Hansen was two or three inches taller, 20 pounds heavier, but he didn't have one ounce of fat on his entire body. He looked mid-to-late 40s. He had long brown hair with a shock of grey on his left side. He wore it in a ponytail that ended at his shoulders.

Gretchen and I had showered and changed after our hike. Hansen still had on the hiking pants, shirt, and vest that he wore on his guided tours. I noticed a wide-brimmed safari hat stuffed over in the corner of the booth.

We shook hands and made eye contact. I look a man in his eyes when we meet. A man's eyes can tell you a lot. Hansen's were unsettling. They were grey, like a timber wolf's. They bored into you. He evaluated me with the same intensity that I examined him.

For the second time that day, a strong feeling of déjà vu hit me. This time I didn't shake, sweat, gasp, or fart at the strong, negative vibe.

"Mr. Hansen, I feel like we've met before," I said as we shook hands.

"Call me, Don. I get that a lot. I'm an old soul. Maybe we met in a former life."

"I doubt that, Don. Father will tell you that we don't believe in reincarnation," I said to Hansen, as I reached past him and shook hands with the priest.

"I know that. I was an Episcopalian priest. Our religions have many similarities. I'm in tune to Catholic dogma."

Father Pat slid back in the booth. Gretchen slipped next to him. Hansen took his seat opposite the priest and my wife. I grabbed a chair from a nearby table, spun it around, and set it at the head of the booth. I wanted to look at both Hansen and Father Pat as we talked.

"I know less about Episcopalians than I do about the Catholics," Gretchen said. "My husband indoctrinated me so our sons could go to a Jesuit high school."

"That's commendable," Father Pat said. "It's his duty."

"Why?" Gretchen asked. "The Catholics tossed him out. What's the word, honey?"

"Excommunicated, sweetie," I answered. I'd hoped not to reveal that little tidbit.

"Yeah, Father. You guys excommunicated Tony for marrying me."

"First wife wouldn't go for an annulment?" Hansen asked, showing more interest than I would have credited.

"Gentlemen, let's change the subject from my dispute with the Holy See and have something to drink," I said as a cute female waitress arrived with the wine and beer that we'd ordered. "Father, Don, y'all ready for another round?"

"Sure," Father Pat said. "I need to try something else. Your American beer leaves something to be desired."

"Try Rogue Dead Guy," I suggested. "It's a red ale. Very good."

"It's a Maibock, Tony," Hansen corrected, irritating the crap out of me.

"I'd love a Maibock. I'll try this Dead Guy ale," Father Pat said.

"I'll have another double Macallan, eighteen years old, neat," Hansen said.

"Guide work must pay well, if you've acquired a taste for single malts," I said.

"I get by," Hansen said.

"With a little help from your friends?" Father said, trying to be funny.

"I count heavily on support from special friends," Hansen said.

While we waited for their drinks to arrive, Hansen and Father Pat made small talk with Gretchen. She provided more information about our lifestyle, jobs, sons, neighbors, dogs, and her mother than I thought prudent. Hansen appeared to be interested, though he seemed to know the answers before he asked the questions.

The beer and single-malt scotch arrived. Hansen took his glass and clinked each of our glasses in turn.

"Here's to your trip to Sedona! May your quest be a success," Hansen toasted and then sipped his drink.

"Thank you," I said. "I appreciate your willingness to meet with us. I hope it wasn't too inconvenient."

"Not at all," he said. "Once Father Ted called me from California and told me that someone had been asking after the

Christus, I was intrigued. Haven't heard anything about that item in fifteen years."

"What do you think happened to the Christ figure?" Gretchen asked.

"I don't think it's a big mystery. The Christus was so controversial that Ms. Staude came back into town and took it down in a fit of artistic pique. She was a sensitive artist and a sculptor. The criticism rankled her. There weren't as many visitors to the chapel in those days. The priest was always traveling. She had plenty of opportunities to get inside, take it down, cut it up, and hide it," Hansen said.

"You believe that?" I asked.

"It's the most logical and straightforward explanation."

"It's the official position of the Diocese," Father Pat said.

"That's comforting," I said. "The Church has always been so candid."

"That a cheap shot," Father Pat said, the freckles on his face merging into one large, red blotch.

"OK, Pat," I said, ignoring his title. "What's the Church's official explanation for its decision to end regular religious services at the Chapel?"

Father Pat seemed surprised by that question. Though he should have been, he wasn't prepared for it.

"I don't know," the priest said, his burst of anger quelled. "Father Ted doesn't know either."

"It can't be manpower. Even with one priest in the area, you could have the occasional services there. Sedona is so beautiful that you must have lots of priests from tons of places who would do a voluntary tour here. You claimed that it would be a joy to say Mass in the chapel," I said, piling on.

I'm a trial lawyer. This was my first chance in 40 years to cross-examine a priest. It was pure joy. The only thing better would have been a shot at Sister Mary Erintrude, the sadistic scourge of seventh grade at St. Francis.

"You don't know why the Church stopped having services at the chapel?" Gretchen asked.

"I suppose that's correct," Father Pat said.

"Don," I began, turning toward him. "You said that the last time you heard anything about the Christus was fifteen years ago. That's after the article written by Bishop McMannes."

"Tony, David McMannes created that presentation for a Good Friday Meditation."

"You knew McMannes?" I asked.

"Who doesn't? He's been the Bishop of the Anglican Diocese of Arizona for twenty years."

"Did you ever work with him?" Father Pat asked.

"No. Bishop McMannes is Anglican. I'm Episcopalian. He's the pastor at St. Luke's. It's on SR 179 down the hill from the Chapel of the Holy Cross. When I worked out of Sedona, I helped to tend the flock at St. Marks in West Sedona. They are two entirely different churches in two different Christian sects. Since David named his church St. Luke's Episcopal, some people get confused."

"I'm sorry, Don," Gretchen said. "Are you saying that the Episcopal churches in Sedona are different sects?"

"Yes, that's right. I never ministered with David. After I was ordained, I served mostly in Episcopalian parishes in California and performed ministries north of here. I did come down and fill in at St. Marks from time to time."

"This is a small town," Father Pat said. "You must know about this man. His article is fascinating and unsettling. I'd appreciate your evaluation of him."

"I'd rather not. David has had his challenges," Hansen said.

"What do you mean?" Father Pat asked.

"Let's say that he had issues. Throughout his personal tests, he seemed to have the passionate support of most of his congregation. I'm far more controversial in my own way than he's ever been," Hansen said. "Have you spoken with McMannes, Tony?"

"I tried to call, but for some reason St. Luke's has no voice mail. I tried to use the e-mail on their website, but all my attempts came back as undeliverable."

"Interesting." Gretchen said.

"Yes, I suppose it is. But we all do God's work in our own way. Right, Padre?" Hansen said, looking for support from the Irish priest.

"What happened the last time someone inquired about the Christus?" I asked.

"Don't know. After he made his inquiries, the man disappeared," Hansen said.

"You mean that you never saw him again," Gretchen said.

"No, I mean that he disappeared. I don't know what happened to him."

"Don, that's vague. Tell us about it, if you don't mind," I said.

"I was filling in at St. Mark's in late summer while the pastor vacationed. An accountant from Scottsdale came to Sedona. He walked in and said that he was looking for someone who knew about the piece McMannes had written. I tried to reach David at St. Luke's, but he wasn't available. So I talked to the man," Hansen said.

"That's pretty much what happened to me," Father Pat said. "That's how I met Tony."

"The accountant asked a lot of questions about the Chapel of the Holy Cross and Ms. Staude. He wanted details about the architects and the sculptor. I did my best, but—even though I grew up around here—I didn't know all of the answers."

"What happened then?" I asked.

"I don't know. He disappeared. He never went back to Scottsdale. I remember that it was in September, sometime during the week before the Labor Day Weekend."

"Why do you remember that?" Gretchen asked.

"Labor Day marks a change in the nature of our tourists. In the summer, it's Phoenicians who own property up here, or tenderfeet who want to escape the heat. When it's one-twenty in Phoenix, it's at least twenty to twenty-five degrees cooler here. The folks from the Valley of the Sun come up in droves. Try getting near Slide Rock. After Labor day, we start seeing tourists from everywhere else in the world."

"Don, something else happened. Tell us," I said.

"The guy's family knew he was coming up here. They thought he was a little crazy. He seemed fixated on something that had happened to him back in the day. When he didn't return, they started an investigation. He was an important guy—a senior partner in a big three accounting firm in Phoenix. I had a visit from detectives from both the Maricopa and Coconino County Sheriff's Offices."

While Hansen was telling the story, the déjà vu overwhelmed me. This time I did sweat and shiver. Everyone at the table noticed my change in demeanor.

"Tony, are you OK?" Gretchen asked.

"Are you sure that this occurred in September?" I asked Hansen.

"Positive."

"What year?"

"It had to be 1998," Hansen said after he thought for a moment.

I took out my cell phone and tapped the Safari app. I went to the Google search window and entered a query for a calendar for 1998. I had a strong premonition.

"Honey, what are you doing?" Gretchen asked, as both men watched me.

"Confirming a suspicion," I said, as I brought the calendar up. "Just as I thought."

"What are you talking about?" My wife said in a worried voice.

"Don, was the name of the missing man, Dan Ostergaard?" I asked.

"Yes, I believe it was," Hansen said, while shaking his head. Those evil gray eyes bored right through me.

"Ostergaard went missing sometime around September 2, 1998?" I asked, as I began to sweat through my knit shirt.

"After all these years, I don't recall the exact day. The second seems right. I presume that would be the week before Labor Day that year."

"Did they ever find the man?" Father Pat asked.

"Not to my knowledge. They kept the case open for a while. In 2003, a Maricopa County detective called and said that unless I had something more, they would close the case. I'm not positive, but I recall that Ostergaard's wife had a court in Phoenix declare him to be deceased a year or two after that."

"Tony, Ostergaard was your high school buddy, wasn't he?" Gretchen asked.

"Yeah," I said, startled by the turn of events.

"What is all of this?" Father Pat asked.

Gretchen looked at me. She knew that I wanted her to keep quiet and not explain. She couldn't resist the impulse to reveal everything to these men.

What would follow would usher in the most momentous time of my life. Part of me wanted to bolt from the Cowboy Club and run all the way back to Tampa. Another part of me wanted Gretchen to explain, so I could watch these two men as she spoke. I'm much more of a fighter than a fleer.

I recognized that I would face my life's biggest test. How I fared would determine my fate, maybe for eternity. I suspected that one of these men would try to destroy me and the other would try to save me. I had to learn which was which.

I smiled at Gretchen. Understanding, she went into her information dump mode.

"Tony and Dan were friends in high school and college," she said.

"Are you saying that you knew this missing man, Tony?" Father Pat asked.

"Yes, Father. I did."

"What's the connection to the Christus?"

"Tony brought him up here in September of 1966 to see the Christus. While they were at the Chapel of the Holy Cross, they had an encounter with a UFO," Gretchen said.

"Is this true?" Father Pat asked.

"Yes, it is."

"Were there any other witnesses?" the priest asked.

"Yes. A husband, wife, their kid, and a dog were there too. After a time, the parents took the kid and the dog and ran for it. I never saw them again."

"Do you remember their names?"

"No," I lied. "Father, that was forty-seven years ago."

I dissembled because I didn't know which of these men I could trust. I knew the husband's name was Bob and the dog's name was Rommel. Those facts were two very slim reeds, but they were all that I had. I didn't want to give that information up yet.

"Honey, don't you remember, the dog's name was Adolf Hitler?" Gretchen offered.

"Thanks, baby," I said, grateful that she got the name wrong, but with enough sarcasm that she'd see that I didn't want any more personal or private data revealed.

Don't get me wrong. Gretchen is a five-star prosecutor. She's very careful and circumspect in her cases. She's a great chess player.

This wasn't her case. It was mine.

"I can see why you'd remember that. I never heard of anyone naming a dog after Adolph Hitler," Father Pat said.

"What kind of dog was it?" Hansen asked. His eyes had narrowed even further. He focused on me like a laser.

"It was a mutt, intelligent, obedient, and playful. German shepherd mix."

"Sounds like a perfect dog for that kid," Hansen said.

"I suppose."

"So you're saying that you encountered aliens at the chapel in '66, and now this friend of yours is missing," Father Pat asked, pulling us back from the tangent.

"No, Father. In 1966, Dan and I saw lights do things that were impossible, but we encountered no live alien life forms. I lost track of Dan decades ago. I didn't try to contact him when I started obsessing over this issue. I first learned that he disappeared five minutes ago—during this conversation."

"That's interesting, Tony. But you shouldn't worry too much. UFO sightings are quite common here. Most people in the Verde Valley have seen unexplained objects in the sky and strange lights," Don said.

"Fine, Don. How many of these observers vanish without a trace?"

"A few. The trails, canyons, and wild country outside the small towns and villages from Prescott to Flagstaff can be unforgiving. We lost twenty brave and dedicated firefighters down in Yarnell. Tourists, those who are unprepared, unfit, and unwise lose their lives in mishaps every year. If you take the wrong step on the wrong trail and don't make it back, we may never find you because the wild country is full of critters that will recycle you back into the environment."

"How serious can it be, if you're a mile from an upscale neighborhood like Little Horse Park and you run out of water?" Gretchen asked.

"That happens all the time around here. Sometimes it doesn't end well. The intelligent hikers prepare," Hansen explained. "Have you ever read Jack London's *To Build a Fire?*"

"I don't think so," Gretchen admitted.

"A miner in the Yukon freezes to death less than a mile from safety because he's unlucky and unprepared."

I looked at Gretchen and adopted my smuggest expression. As you already know, she'd carped about the volume of equipment that I brought along for the day trips. She noticed my facial put down. She rubbed her left eye with the middle finger of her left hand.

"Do you believe in UFOs?" Father Pat asked, readdressing the main issue.

"Good question, Father," Hansen said.

"Father Pat, Hansen is the expert on these matters. You can ask him. For me, your question is wrong. The term UFO means unidentified flying object. UFOs exist. We don't know what they are, where they're from, or who's responsible because we haven't identified the source of the phenomena," I explained.

"I see," Father Pat said. "Let me rephrase. I forgot for a moment that you're a lawyer. Do you believe in aliens visiting the Earth?"

"I don't know."

"Mr. Hansen, what do you think?" Father asked.

"Father, the universe is a big place. Tonight we'll be able to see billions of stars in the Sedona sky. If we had the right equipment, we could see whole galaxies over thirteen billion light years distant. We see the galaxies as they existed thirteen billion years ago. It would take thirteen billion years traveling at the speed of light to get to where they are now. If we got there, they'd be farther out in the expanding reality."

"It is hard to conceive," Gretchen added.

"There are billions of galaxies, with billions of stars in each one. There must be trillions, or even quadrillions, of planets orbiting those stars. It's the height of arrogance to assume that Earth is one planet that has life. It's mathematically impossible for Earth to be the one oasis in the whole universe. Scientists have concluded that in our own galaxy it's probable that there could be eight billion planets like earth orbiting in the sweet spot around their suns. Logic dictates that some fraction of those worlds have developed life."

"Then why is there so little evidence of extraterrestrial life?" Gretchen asked. "If life were so prevalent, we'd have seen plenty of evidence. Right?"

"Not necessarily. Carl Sagan used to lecture on this topic. The laws of physics, vast distances, limitations in technology, and the tendency of a species to foul its own nest are all factors in the answer. And why does the life have to be extraterrestrial? Why not inter-dimensional?" Hansen asked my bride.

"What do you mean by inter-dimensional?" she asked.

"We've discussed how vast the universe is. It's also very small and complex," Hansen said. "Three generations ago, we understood that molecules were made up of atoms. Today, we know that sub-atomic structure is as tiny and minute as the universe is vast. Scientists in France and Switzerland are on the brink of confirming the Higgs Boson, the so-called God-particle. It's orders of magnitude smaller than protons, electrons, and neutrons."

"You're losing me," Gretchen said. "I went to law school because there was no math, physics, or science."

"Sorry," Hansen apologized. "I tend to get carried away. In a way, the universe stretches from the infinitesimally small Higgs Boson, quarks, and dark matter to huge galaxies that are a million light years in diameter and billions of light years away. You get that, right?"

"Sure, I'm not a complete loss but I'm not a geek, like you," Gretchen said.

"I guess, I am a geek at that," Hansen admitted. "Try to follow this. The universe as we know it is vast, but it's also not the only universe. There are other parallel dimensions that exist in the same space. We are a three-dimensional species and because of physical limitations, we can only perceive reality in terms of length, width, and height. We also understand passing time, so that's a temporal dimension. The other dimensions exist. They are as complex as our universe, there are billions, trillions or even quadrillions of them."

"That's hard to believe, Don," Father Pat said.

"Are you saying that an omniscient God cannot create the circumstances that I've described?"

"No. He can do anything, even that. I studied science. It's still hard to wrap my thick Irish head around that concept."

"Different issue, Padre. You're a mortal man with above average intelligence who's biologically confined to three dimensions. Think of it this way. You're in a clothing store. You're being fitted for a new suit. You stand in that space with several angled mirrors. If you look at your image in the right way, the reflection gives you the impression there are multiple images that stretch to infinity."

"That's a false metaphor. It's like a mirage," Father Pat said.

"True, but suppose this universe was a card in a deck of one quadrillion cards."

"Are you saying that if these parallel realities exist and intelligent beings populate them, that they can come here?" Gretchen asked.

"Yes. Several advocates of that concept live in Sedona," Hansen explained. "Some folks think that the energy you feel in Sedona is because the Verde Valley is a portal for inter-dimensional travel."

"Have you seen these inter-dimensional beings, Don?" Gretchen asked.

Hansen hesitated for a long moment. He looked at each one of us. You could hear the wheels turning in his head.

"If I'd seen one, I wouldn't admit it to you guys," Hansen said. "You're neophytes. I do know people in Sedona who swear that they've seen these beings."

"What are the beings like?" Gretchen pressed.

"There are species from different parallel universes. There's no standard type."

"Do any look like the Christus?" Father Pat asked.

Hansen paused again. He nodded his head and said, "Yes."

Father Pat looked distressed.

"How do you know this?" I asked.

"Some of my clients have had the encounter. They described the beings. They're identical to the Christus. Eight or nine feet tall, thin, long arms and legs. These features indicate a being that evolved on a planet with less gravitational force than earth."

At this point, the waitress returned and we ordered another round.

"Hope I'm not breaking the bank with my scotch," Hansen said.

"*In vino est veritas*, Don," I said.

"Yes. I'm giving it to you straight," Hansen said.

"Don, if these Christus beings come here, why don't we know about it? Are you suggesting that there's a big government conspiracy?" Gretchen asked.

"Are you familiar with the conquest of the Aztecs in Mexico, or the Incas in Peru?

"No. I was a business major at A&M."

"You're an Aggie?" Hansen asked.

"Gig 'em!" Gretchen responded, showing her right fist, thumb up.

"A big fan of Johnny Football?"

"Of course."

"I went to Arizona for undergrad." Hansen explained.

"Figures," I said. "Why am I not surprised?"

"Tony went to ASU," Gretchen said, smiling.

"Ah, Tempe Normal, the Farm. Tell me, Tony, have they managed to accredit any of the colleges at your alma mater yet?" Hansen asked.

If you think that there's a more bitter rivalry among American universities than Arizona and Arizona State, you are out of your mind. It's too complex to explain here, but I assure you that it's true. It's immature, embarrassing, and unnecessary, but those bastards from Arizona started it. Yes, I'm sure all colleges at ASU are accredited. Anyway, that's what they claim when they ask for alumni donations.

"What he means, Gretch, is that since he matriculated at U of A, he's intellectually superior to you," I counseled my wife.

"No kidding? Are you an arrogant prick?" Gretchen asked Don, batting her eyes innocently.

"I told you he went to U of A, sweetie. So he must..." I began.

"Did she say that?" Father Pat interrupted, as he drained half his pint of Dead Guy. As a priest, his dinners and social outings with parishioners never included profanity. Then again, he never ministered in College Station.

"Padre, she's an Aggie," I said. Father nodded his head as if he understood.

"I'm not an arrogant prick, but I did study the Spanish conquest of the Americas," Hansen responded. "A small number of men with a huge technological advantage conquered two very powerful empires with strong native forces that vastly outnumbered the conquerors. After the conquest, the unique aboriginal cultures with complex religious beliefs imploded."

"You're saying that could happen here if the inter-dimensional beings made themselves known," Gretchen concluded.

"Yeah. That's one issue. Another is that not all of these inter-dimensional beings are benign. Some are good, very good. Some are the worst you can imagine. Some want to help us. Some would harm us or exploit us, like the Spanish exploited the Native Americans."

"You won't tell us if you've seen these beings yourself. Will you tell us if you believe that they come to Earth through a portal here in Sedona?" I asked.

"Yes, I believe that they come here," Hansen said.

"Why?" Father Pat asked.

"Why do they come here, or why do I believe that they do?" Hansen asked.

"Both."

"I believe that they come here because I trust the people who claim to have seen them. I've seen evidence that they've been coming here for millennia."

"What evidence is that?" I asked.

"Have you ever been to the Native American ruins at Schnebly Tank? There are petroglyphs that go back at least ten thousand years. Though rough, they depict deer, elk, bear, mastodons, big cats, ancient humans, and the like. Two prominent petroglyphs are the spitting images of the Christus," Hansen explained.

"Don, assuming that inter-dimensional aliens visit Sedona, why? It can't be to get one of your tantric massages," Gretchen said.

"Don't be so sure, I'm very skilled," Hansen said, as he leered at my wife.

"I'll bet you are," my bride agreed, as she batted her eyes.

"These beings come here for the same reasons that we want to go to Mars. Some are benign. Some are dangerous and cruel," Hansen said.

"Don, I'd like to see the petroglyphs," I said.

"Happy to guide you there when I have a free day. It's a hike. It's a good twenty-five miles north, northeast of Palatki. From the trailhead, it takes at least five hours in and an equal time out. It's moderate to difficult in spots, but you look like you could make it."

"We can't do that. We have one more day here. We're driving up to Flagstaff tomorrow. Tony wants to show me the Sunset Crater," Gretchen countered.

"What's that?" Father Pat asked.

"The crater is the remnant of an ancient volcano north of Flagstaff," Hansen said. "Erupted a thousand years ago. Tore up the real estate. From what we can tell, it devastated the tribes that lived north of the Mogollon Rim. The local tribe, what the archeologists have named the Sinagua—Spanish for without water—fared well enough to hang around for another three centuries. You'll like the crater. It has awesome hiking trails around the base," Hansen said.

"Do these inter-dimensional beings believe in God?" I asked Hansen, trying to get back to the alien issue and pin him down.

Once again, Hansen took his time, thinking through his answer.

Turning to me, he looked me in the eye and said, "The short answer is yes."

"What's the long answer?" I pressed.

"It's too long for our little happy hour. Sorry folks, but I'm booked for Eight p.m. I need to go. A man has to eat."

"Can you meet with us tomorrow?" I asked.

"No, sorry. I'm full up with tourists from Chile. I know that you're leaving. I realize that you have a thousand questions."

"How about one last question, Don?" I asked.

"Shoot," Don said with a phony smile.

"Why did you leave the priesthood?"

"To answer that would take a couple of hours and several more doubles," Hansen observed. "My religion is very tolerant. We accept lifestyle choices that you Catholics would view as aberrant. As I got more interested in New Age, Reiki, tantric massage, extra-terrestrials, and inter-dimensional contacts, I made no secret of my research. The hierarchy became uncomfortable with me. One bishop told me that he was afraid that my notoriety would put too much *alien* in Episcopalian."

Gretchen and I laughed at the intended joke. Father Pat did not.

"I quarreled with the church leadership for about a year. Eventually, they agreed that I should pursue my personal journey outside of my vocation. They released me from my vows. Simple as that."

"When is your next available date to talk?" I asked.

"Tony, here's my e-mail address. When you get back to Tampa, contact me. I'll try to help. Cheers!" Hansen said, as he finished his scotch and passed his card to me.

With his salute, Hansen grabbed his hat, slid out of the booth, waved, turned around, and strode out of the Cowboy Club.

"That was one very interesting man," Gretchen said. "After that, I need another drink and good meal."

"How about it, Father? Want to eat with a lapsed Catholic and his Aggie wife?"

"I need something to soak up the beer," Father Pat responded. "Tony, you hedged quite a bit earlier. Let me ask you a different way. Do you think that there's any truth to Mr. Hansen's claim? If accurate, it would create some chaos in organized religion," Father noted.

"I may be the worst Catholic since Judas, but I hope that I'm a spiritual man."

"You are, honey," Gretchen confirmed.

"Thanks, babe," I said smiling at my wife. "Father, I understand the arguments that my atheist friends make about organized religion. Some of their thinking makes sense because our religion has taken arbitrary and indefensible positions on science for short-term political gains. Later the official views proved to be invalid. Yet, at the time, the hierarchy enforced its will with the full power of the Catholic bureaucracies."

"Can you give me an example?" Father Pat asked.

"Sure, that's easy. Galileo."

"Why Galileo?" Gretchen asked.

"By the mid sixteen hundreds, Galileo was involved in science and religion. Due to his astronomical observations, and relying on the earlier work of Copernicus, he preached that the sun was the center of the solar system and the planets revolved around it."

"Well, that's how it works, right?" Gretchen said.

"Sure, today everyone knows the solar system is heliocentric. Back in the seventeenth century, the pope and his minions fought the Protestant Reformation. They had invested in the theory that the earth was the center of the universe and all the planets, sun, and stars revolved around us. They claimed that scripture supported their view. Since it's Church doctrine that the Pope is infallible on issues of Faith, they could brook no scientific dispute or they'd risk losing more ground to the Protestants."

"No shit?" Gretchen asked.

"Though he's oversimplifying a complex issue, your husband is correct. Cardinal Bellarmine, a Jesuit, helped the Pope to silence Galileo."

"How'd they do that?" Gretchen asked.

"Bellarmine convinced the Pope to try Galileo in an ecclesiastical court. The tribunal found that he was highly suspect of heresy. They could have tortured or killed him, but they commuted his sentence to house arrest for the balance of his life."

"Tony, your precious Jesuits did that?" Gretchen asked.

"Yep, but the Order is very different four hundred years later," I suggested.

"I'm confused." Gretchen said. "What difference does it make to the issue of the existence of God, if the sun revolves around the earth or the earth revolves around the sun?"

"It doesn't," I said. "An omniscient Creator could organize this universe any way that pleases Him. He makes the rules. The scientists, who advocate the existence of multiverses, claim that some have different laws of physics. So, it's not out of the question to have a universe structured in a way that's very different from ours. An act of Creation that includes a universe that stretches from the Higgs Boson all the way out to thirteen billion light years—and may be one in a quadrillion multiverses occupying the same space and time—is a much grander Divine work, than if earth was the center of the only reality and a million stars revolved around it."

"The Church punished Galileo because he advocated an idea, which could undermine the power that the Church exercised. The existence of inter-dimensional beings doesn't call into question the existence of God. Such a phenomenon would make Creation all that more grand," I pontificated. "The theory of evolution does not preclude the existence of a Divine Spark. The Big Bang and Fiat Lux are not mutually exclusive. In fact, they kind of sound similar, don't they?"

"What does *Fiat Lux* mean?" Gretchen asked.

"Let there be light!" Father said.

"Oh, that comes from the Bible, right?" Gretchen asked.

"It comes from the Book of Genesis 1:3. And God said, let there be light! And there was light," Father Pat said.

"Gretch, the Jesuits explained to me decades ago that belief that our universe, our planet, and our species have all evolved over eons does not call into question belief in God, so long as you concede that God had a role in getting it all started," I said.

"Tony, you're a man of many parts, aren't you?" Father Pat suggested.

"Thank you, Father."

At this point, the waitress returned. We postponed our teleological discussion to wade through the options in the unique menu.

Gretchen ordered a rattlesnake appetizer and a venison steak. I ordered buffalo meatloaf. Father Pat didn't feel adventurous. He asked for a chicken Caesar salad.

I promised Father Pat that if we had one more beer, I'd front the money for a pink Jeep back to the rectory. He accepted.

While we waited for the food, we changed the subject. Father told us a bit about himself. He'd grown up a Catholic in Northern Ireland. Later, he studied at Trinity University in Dublin. After graduation, he felt the tug of the priesthood. Four years later, his parents watched his ordination. In September he'd celebrate his fifth anniversary as a priest.

Father Pat was on assignment in America. The Bishop of Phoenix had met him in Boston and invited him to spend a few months at various parishes in Arizona. He'd heard how beautiful the southwestern United States was. He jumped at the chance.

During our dinner, Father Pat counseled me on the concept of annulment. He felt that I should straighten out my issue with the Church. I listened politely.

When we'd finished and the waitress informed us that a Jeep had arrived to take Father Pat back to the parish. We began our goodbyes.

"Hope you enjoy the rest of your American tour, Father," I offered.

"And I hope that you unravel the mystery," He responded. "Gretchen, you are a delight. You should consider converting."

"Not a chance, Father," Gretchen said. "I like being married to a Catholic wannabe. I'm not interested in becoming one. It's too tough on the knees. Besides, I've got a feeling that I have more pluses than minuses in St. Peter's Great Book. I'll see you in Heaven."

"By the way, Father, what do you make of the inter-dimensional beings? I'll bet they didn't address that little issue in the seminary," I said.

"Tony, I think that they may be real. If they are, they could be angels. Some are good. They serve the Creator and protect us from the bad ones. What else could they be?"

"Father, you surprise me with your candor." I said.

"You're right, Tony. We didn't talk about aliens, extra-terrestrials, or inter-dimensional beings at the seminary. I received two bachelor degrees at Trinity College. I have one in physics and one in mathematics. We did consider these issues at university."

"Father, as a scientist, what do you tell your atheist contemporaries when they challenge the scientific basis for your belief system? You must have encountered that, even in Dublin," Gretchen asked.

"I have indeed. I tell them that when they can demonstrate a valid, scientifically provable explanation for a non-Divine cause for the original Singularity—the minute, infinitely dense element with zero volume—that inflated faster than the speed of light and began the evolution into our vast universe at the Big Bang, I'll consider questioning my Faith," Father Pat explained.

"Stephen Hawking has tried," I pointed out.

"Bless that man and his genius," Father said. "Despite his great intellect, I'm not convinced. I don't find his arguments to be compelling."

"Father, you are a man of many parts, as well," I said, as we shook hands.

"Watch your back, mate! Don't follow in the footsteps of your college friend."

I nodded and smiled, but had no comment to the priest's warning. Gretchen and I slid out of the booth and made our way from the restaurant.

CHAPTER SEVEN

August 25, 2013, 8:30 PM
Monti's La Casa Vieja Restaurant
100 S. Mill Ave, Tempe, Arizona

GRETCHEN AND I WERE finishing up our dinner at La Casa Vieja, a restaurant that I'd frequented in the '60s and '70s while I studied at Arizona State. Parts of the building had been the childhood home of Senator Carl Hayden, a renowned statesman.

In the late 1800s, Hayden's home sat on the banks of the Salt River. It served the tiny frontier community as a ferry crossing, general store, restaurant, and hotel. By the 1950s, a New Jersey businessman turned the old homestead into a fine steak house.

I loved the old restaurant, its history, its location near ASU, and its willingness to accommodate an adolescent suitor like me.

In the 1960s, I used it as an upscale place to take a special date. La Casa Vieja was the nicest place in Tempe or East Phoenix that would honor a Hawaiian driver's license. It was pricey for a student with a part time job and a defective Corvair. If I saved my money, I could splurge there two times a semester.

My luck after a good meal and drinks at the La Casa Vieja was phenomenal. In baseball terms, I'd batted 1000 in this particular venue. This evening, my winning streak had ended. Gretchen was as mad at me as she has ever been. The traveling lingerie fashion show had closed for good.

After our dinner at the Cowboy Club two days earlier, Gretchen and I returned to the room at L'Auberge. She crashed. She slept the sleep of the just for eight hours.

I couldn't relax. I had a flashback to the incident at the chapel in 1966. I pondered every detail. I didn't sleep a wink.

I felt haunted by Dan's original, negative reaction to my suggestion that we report the events of that night. Even though he had warned me, he still made his anxiety-filled excursion to Sedona in 1998, 32 years later.

He must have kept our secret for decades. He initiated his own quest when he learned from the McMannes article that the Christus had disappeared. How or when he read the meditation, I couldn't guess. Learning of the missing icon must have caused him the same discomfort that I'd experienced. It drove him to learn the truth.

There is something about Sedona that does that to people. The Internet is full of videos where folks admit that they felt compelled to go to Sedona. Many abandon comfortable life styles in nice places to move there.

It got me thinking. Until I learned of the missing Christus, I'd thought of Sedona as a special place of spiritual affirmation and renewal. I often reflected about the upper Verde Valley because it is so beautiful. I recommended that friends visit the area. I found satisfaction when all of them seemed pleased and thanked me upon their return. But that was all. I felt no passionate desire to return.

When I learned that the Christus had disappeared, I became more obsessed about this mystery than I had ever been about anything in my life.

As a prosecutor, I am known—perhaps not liked—for my intense focus on preparing to meet the heavy burdens to secure a criminal conviction. There is something in my personality that reinforces this compulsion. Now that I'm a senior, I sensed a limited amount of time to resolve the mysteries in my life.

After Gretchen awoke, we cleaned up for our trip to Flagstaff. We set off in the late morning for an abbreviated tour of central Coconino County. We had to prioritize because the county is huge. It's the second largest county in the U.S. and bigger than the State of Massachusetts.

We brought our gear, but when we got to the Sunset Crater north of Flagstaff, we had no interest in any further trekking. Even from the roadways around the ancient volcano, you can see the extent of the devastation that the thousand-year-old eruption had caused.

Though captivated by the San Francisco Peaks and the mountains around Flagstaff, Gretchen seemed distracted and introspective. The discussion the night before had affected her. In the past, she'd never shown a concern for religion or philosophy. She viewed herself as a protestant, but no particular creed interested her. For 30 years, she'd avoided all discussions on these matters.

The night before our trip to Flagstaff, she'd participated in an intense teleological discussion for the very first time in her life. While we drove around Coconino County, Gretchen debated the issue of whether existence erupted from a Divine Spark or—as Steven Hawking suggests—happened spontaneously.

We interrupted our discussion with lunch at the Beaver Street Brewery in Flagstaff. After our meal, we drove around Flagstaff for another two hours and then headed to Sedona. We went the back way so we could go down Oak Creek Canyon again.

We planned on dining at the Asylum in Jerome. We were tired and agreed to a meal at the hotel. We got back to town and Gretchen said that she wanted to take a nap. While she slept, I walked over to Uptown Sedona and cruised around the shops.

After dinner, we turned in without the distraction of expensive lingerie modeling. Despite her nap, Gretchen fell asleep at once, no doubt aided by her share of the two bottles of excellent red wine that we'd shared. Even though I'd had no sleep the night before, I tossed and turned for two hours before I got up and walked outside. I wandered over to the creek and stood by the rippling water, contemplating my life.

When I was about to go inside, a shooting star blitzed across the sky. Unlike the incident at the chapel, there were no further aerial acrobatics. Seeing that celestial event caused me to make a decision. I felt a profound relief.

I had crossed a line. If I went through with my decision, I'd disrupt my job, my marriage, and my life. I would pay a heavy price. I knew I had no choice.

The next morning, we checked out of the hotel. We had a flight back to Florida the following day, so we thought we'd stay in Tempe on our last night in Arizona.

Since we had so much time, I convinced Gretchen that we should drive south on State Road 89A so she could see the high plains and towns like Cottonwood, Jerome, and Prescott.

We spent so much time at the Burning Tree Winery in Cottonwood ordering cases of wine that we got to Prescott for a late lunch. We dined at the Lone Spur Cafe on Gurley Street on the north side of the famous Courthouse Square.

Gretchen grew up in Texas. She liked the place. She started coming out of her shell, when I dropped the bomb.

"Gretch," I began. "I've been thinking."

"That's always a bad sign," she said, trying too hard to be cute.

"You're not going to like what I'm about to say. I'm staying in Arizona for another few days. I want to see the petroglyphs at Schnebly Tank."

"Are you crazy? We broke the bank on this trip. We can't afford for you to stay at the L'Auberge another week and eat at the five-star restaurants in Sedona."

"Gretch, I can stay at the Super 8 in West Sedona. I can get a room for an entire week for the cost of one day at L'Auberge. The car rental is modest. I'll fly back next Monday."

"What about your job, damn it?"

"The Sheriff won't mind. I have the time saved."

"What if something happens to you?"

"Like what? It's not like Sedona is a high crime area. I'll be fine."

"What happened to Dan?" Gretchen asked, emotion creeping into her voice.

"I don't know."

"Exactly. He disappeared," Gretchen pointed out. "There's more going on over this Christus than meets the eye. I have a bad feeling."

"I'm not Ostergaard. I'm a trained Paratrooper. I've been in combat. I did twenty-three years in the Army with three Airborne tours. I was a deputy U.S. marshal. I can take care of myself."

"Tony, you retired from the Army twenty years ago. They made you a special deputy marshal because we had death threats due to your prosecutions. Despite all the extra training, you never had to fire a shot in anger as a marshal. That was ten years ago. What in the fuck are you thinking?"

"If I stay, I may find out why the Christus is missing."

"Tony, Hansen explained that. The lady who built the chapel snuck in and took the Christus down. Father Pat agreed. Your bishop in Phoenix agrees. I read the McMannes article. It makes the most sense. There is no mystery here, bub."

"Gretch, you're the one who said that there is a connection between the lights that I saw and the missing Christus, right?"

My wife looked at me with fire burning in her eyes. She was mad at me for making a stupid decision that would affect her life. She didn't appreciate me turning her words at the chapel against her.

"Well, if there is a connection, it can get you hurt. Ostergaard put his nose in this business and he's been missing for fifteen years," Gretchen said, as her eyes began to fill.

"I've always been a lot tougher than Dan. I don't know what happened to him, but it'll take a lot to do me in."

"The tragedy is that you believe that. Tony, with your exciting Army career, the long successful stint as a Federal prosecutor, your appointment as a deputy marshal, and your eight years with the Sheriff—where they let you play at being a deputy wan-nabe—getting old had been hard for you. I see the depression creeping into your personality. Despite your denial, you're not prepared to trek across the desert in search of aliens, angels, or demons."

While everything that Gretchen said was probably true, the fact that she said it hurt more than I anticipated. It made me angry.

"Maybe you're right," I lied. "Let's pay the check and get on the road. I'd like to get down to Tempe and look around ASU before dinner."

"OK. Promise that you won't go all Don Quixote on me."

"I give you my word that I won't tilt at a single windmill," I responded, a little surprised that Gretchen would cite Cervantes.

I handed her the keys to the rental car. "Here, you drive. I'm too old."

"Fine." Gretchen said, using that tone of hers.

We barely spoke on the road back through Phoenix to Tempe.

Toward the end of dinner at the La Casa Vieja, Gretchen revealed that she wanted me to seek counseling when we got back to Tampa. I chose not to tell her that while she was showering at the Airport Hilton, I'd contacted the Chief Deputy and secured an extension to my leave. I'd decided to reveal my final decision the next day, when it would be too late for her to have a meltdown or try to have me committed.

The next morning was anti-climactic. I hadn't fooled her. When we got up to go to the airport, she dressed and then confronted me.

"Tony, I know you're not coming with me. I'm worried about you. I love you very much. If you have to do this, I'll have to accept it. But don't stay too long."

"Thanks, Gretch. I'll stay for one more week."

"Honey, why don't you keep my Smith and Wesson .38?" Gretchen asked, as she handed me the small, snub-nosed revolver. Since Gretchen and I are law enforcement, we take weapons with us on our trips. It's a hassle to check them in, but they were a comfort on this sojourn.

"You'll need it in Tampa. Besides, I have my Glock," I reminded her.

"I don't want to go through the nut roll to check it in. I have the Model 27 subcompact at home. I'll carry that while you're out here. I'll feel better if you have a backup. I'm worried about what's in store for you. Whatever's going on in that feeble old mind, you're too old to brawl anymore."

"OK, babe. Thanks, I'll take good care of it."

"I hope it takes care of you. Remember: double tap, center mass."

"Yes, ma'am." I said, as I snapped to attention. "Any other instructions?"

"None that I can think of. Here's your boarding pass. Do you want me to make your reservations, like always?"

"Sure," I said, taking the boarding pass, folding it up, and putting it in the pocket of my sports coat.

Gretchen set down her suitcase and looked at the calendar on her iPhone for a long moment. Her face went white. "Next Monday may be a problem, honey."

"Why?"

"It'll be Labor Day. September 2nd."

CHAPTER EIGHT

I'M NOT AN ELITIST. The Super 8 Motel in West Sedona is a fine place to stay. It's clean, comfortable, inexpensive, and has a cheerful, energetic staff. However, if you learn anything from this tale, take heed.

Do not stay at the Super 8 after a week at L'Auberge. Despite their zeal, the folks at Super 8 will not chill your imported champagne to the proper temperature or find the right crackers to compliment the Russian caviar. They do not have a resident masseuse, fluffy bathrobes, or a five-star restaurant on Oak Creek. On the other hand, they will keep you safe, warm, and dry without breaking the bank.

I settled into my room at the Super 8 by two o'clock in the afternoon after I put Gretchen on a plane for Tampa and drove back up to the Verde Valley. As I looked around my quarters, I felt quite lonely. Yet I knew that I had to be there.

Reclining on the comfortable king-sized bed, I consoled myself by cataloging a plan to proceed. I had one week. I'd try five separate strategies.

First, I'd try to contact Bishop McMannes again.

Second, I would research the background and fate of the sculptor of the Christus, Keith Monroe. I could do that with my laptop from the room.

Third, I'd try to contact the relatives of Dan Ostergaard in Scottsdale. I had no idea if any of his family still lived there. I'd start out by Googling Dan's name and see where it took me.

If I could get a phone number, I'd call. I knew that contacting a widow or orphan carried the risk of opening old wounds. Call me inconsiderate and self-centered, but I was prepared to tear at scabs on this quest.

Fourth, I'd make an effort to learn who in Sedona had owned a mutt named Rommel in the '60s. That seemed like a dim prospect. I thought I could use my law enforcement connections to ingratiate myself with the Yavapai and Coconino Sheriffs' Offices and the City Police in Sedona. Through the cops, I'd try to find some local veterinarians who practiced back then.

If I could locate anyone who cared for small animals, I thought I had three excellent clues: the dog's name, the husband's name, and the fact that the mom had been a bona fide babe with a flirtatious manner. Maybe someone would remember her.

Finally, I would find a way to get Don Hansen to guide me to the Paleo-Indian ruins at Schnebly Tank. That was the one strategy that I knew would pay dividends.

Late in the afternoon, my son John called to check in on me. We had a good conversation, though I didn't do much to make him feel better about my decision to stay in Sedona. A little later, Tim called. He was a bit less patient than John. I had to remind him of his own independent streak before he dialed it down a notch. Like I told you earlier, I knew that my boys wouldn't be too happy about my choice, but I felt in my heart that I'd made the right decision.

To bolster my morale, I decided to lay in basic rations. I'd need water, snacks, sodas, good beer, and a couple bottles of excellent red wine. I might not be staying at L'Auberge, but I didn't have to be in purgatory. I was still in my favorite spot on the planet: Sedona, Arizona.

When I was a senior at Brophy, I worked for the A.J. Bayless grocery chain in Phoenix. I bagged groceries 25 hours a week at their store on Central Avenue and Indian School Road. I did this work for $1.15 per hour. After taxes, I made $22.00 a week. I was damn glad to have that money.

Gas for my dad's 1955 Chevy was $0.19 a gallon. The drive-in on 7th Street cost $2.00 a car. A six-pack of beer was $1.50, if I could get someone over 21 to score one for me. I could have a passionate date with my girlfriend for $8.00. Being rich is having more money than you need. J. Paul Getty had nothing on me.

A.J Bayless went bankrupt in the '80s. Bashas took over the Bayless stores, and their brand is known throughout Arizona. I found their market in West Sedona to be nice. The modest prices for wine surprised me. I expected that a grocery in Sedona would gouge the tourists. Not the case at Bashas.

I splurged. I would spend a week in Sedona at the Super 8, but I'd be sipping some excellent full-bodied Cabs and Syrahs.

After settling with the cashier, I walked out of the store into the overpowering scent of western barbeque. A vendor had set up a sophisticated open-air operation at the store's exit. I had an overpowering desire for a hot dog.

I set my grocery cart to the side, stood in a line, and waited my turn. When I got to the front of the line, a distinguished looking black man waited on me. He had a baseball cap with the combat patch of the 101st Airborne cocked back on his head.

"All the way!" I said in the traditional opening gambit of Paratroopers.

"Airborne!" He responded, sizing me up. "You a Screamin' Eagle?"

"Nope. Served with the Herd in Vietnam, the 82nd at Bragg, and 18th Airborne Corps."

"Vietnam with the 173rd?" He asked.

"Yep."

"Where'd you train?"

"Tigerland at Polk. Jump School at Benning," I said.

"Me, too," he said, smiling. "But along with the 101st in the A Shau, I served with the 82nd in Granada and Panama," he revealed.

By this time, about eight customers had queued up behind me and had become impatient with our reunion. The vendor extended his hand to me and said, "I'm Eddie Grimes. Give me your order. It's on the house. Hang around and we'll chat."

All of a sudden, I felt a lot less alone. I had an Airborne buddy in Sedona. The Army Airborne is a tight fraternity. It's a lot like the Marines, but with only 73 years of gallant history, and without the utter shame of being a subservient branch of the Navy Department.

"I'm Tony Giordano," I said, offering my hand. "I'd like a hot dog."

"Don't do dogs. How about an Italian sausage?"

"Already have one," I responded.

"I'm sure," Grimes said as he laughed. "Would you like it barbequed?"

"That would be a big no," I demurred. "I'll load my car and wander back."

"I'm ready to close this down for the night. I've got a couple of cold ones at my place. You interested?"

"Absolutely."

It took Eddie 20 minutes to serve the remaining customers and close down his operation. After packing up his gear, Eddie walked over to me and handed me a grilled Italian sausage on an excellent wheat roll. He had one for himself. He carried a six-pack of diet coke in the crook of his arm. We got inside his truck and began to eat. I'd forgotten how hungry I was. I inhaled the sausage.

"When did you retire?" Eddie asked me.

"1992," I said. "I had my twenty and I got an offer I couldn't refuse."

"What was that?"

"After Vietnam, I got out, finished college, went to law school, and went back in as a JAG. So, in 1991, I was working at the U.S. Attorney's Office in Tampa. They offered me a job as an assistant U.S. Attorney."

"No shit? Tampa?"

"Yeah. Been in Tampa ever since," I said as I finished my first Diet Coke and accepted a second from Eddie.

"My daughter used to live in Tampa," Eddie said. "That was fourteen years ago. She went to U.T. Interned at HHS. She's a special agent and works out of San Francisco now."

I have to stop here. I told you earlier that I think everything happens for a reason. There is no serendipity. Sure, we have free will, but those choices occur in a context.

There is no chance that I would run into Eddie Grimes by mere happenstance. At that moment, I understood that I was meant to stay in Sedona and hook up with Eddie. I knew that I would get somewhere on my journey toward enlightenment.

"Eddie, you have a daughter in HHS?"

"That's right."

"She's beautiful, intelligent, has a great sense of humor, works hard, and wears a nose ring."

Eddie looked at me as if he'd seen a ghost. "You know Yvette?"

"She was an intern and worked on a fraud case that I prosecuted in 1998 and 1999."

"You were the prosecutor on that case? The medical-fraud-of-the-century case?"

"Yes, I was."

"Geez, Yvette talked about you a lot," Eddie explained. "She said that you could be a real son-of-a-bitch. She told me that she liked you as a person, but was glad that she got to go to L.A. She said with you, it was always your way or the highway."

"Gee, Colonel Grimes," I said, remembering that Yvette's father retired was a light colonel. "I suppose when you were in the Army, you'd gather all your soldiers, have them hold hands, feed them pie and cake, take a poll, and let them run your outfit in a kumbaya manner."

"Fuck no! I told Yvette that I never tolerated anyone who complained about a competent leader and didn't give a hundred and ten percent," Eddie said, as we fist bumped.

"What did you retire at?" Eddie asked, wanting to know my highest rank.

"Light colonel, like you."

"What's your date of rank?"

"1 February 1988."

"Shit." Eddie complained.

"I'm senior, huh?"

"Yeah. But I retired as an Infantry officer. What are you doing in Sedona?"

"Do you have an hour? I'll explain."

"Sure, love to hear this. I've got nowhere I have to be."

I started at the beginning and brought Eddie up to speed.

"Tony, that's one wild story," Eddie said an hour later, as he looked at the post card of the Christus.

"Eddie, one of the reasons that I remember your daughter so well is that she told me that after you moved here, you had a similar experience."

Eddie jerked his head back so fast that I feared that he'd have whip lash. He turned toward me and glared.

"Yvette told you that I'd seen strange lights?" He growled.

"She didn't say that it was a confidence. Your encounter was an affirmation. As the years passed, sometimes I'd wonder whether the whole thing in 1966 was a dream."

"My experience in 1999 was real, all right. It was at dawn. Infantrymen get up at dawn. You JAG wimps sleep in."

"That's right, until 0500. What happened?"

"I was in the slot between Bell Rock and Courthouse Butte. It's a beautiful little trail. Even JAGs could manage it. The sky was full of stars and the moon had set. It was calm and cold, a brisk morning."

"Go on."

"I saw a bright light off to the north, moving at a mind-boggling speed. Seconds later it hovered over my position. It began to descend until I could see a glowing disc about the size of a small pie plate. It emitted a pale, white light. It was eerie and hard to describe. I admit that I was mesmerized. I know I should have been afraid, but I felt calm and focused."

"What happened next?"

"It hung over me for three or four minutes. I don't remember a single sound. After a bit, it juked around a lot, back and forth and all around. Then it shot west out of sight."

"Other than your daughter, did you ever tell anyone else?"

"No, of course not. I don't want to spend my retirement in an asylum."

"You've been here fifteen years now, right?

"Yeah, I guess. Boy, time flies."

"Ever see the lights again?"

"Not like the first time, but there's strange stuff in the Sedona sky, day and night."

"You've never discussed your sightings with anyone?"

"You mean, other than my blabby daughter?"

"That's right."

"My wife."

"Will you discuss them with me?" I asked.

"Maybe, but not now. You said that you're here for another week?"

"Yep."

"You still at that fancy resort?"

"No, I'm at the Super 8 down the street."

"Not anymore. You're staying with me. I've got a nice house with two spare bedrooms. You'll be more comfortable there. It'll give us more time to talk, coordinate, and execute our plan to find the Christus."

"Our plan?" I asked, relieved to have discovered an ally.

"Yeah, it's our plan now. You're not doing this by yourself. I've got your back."

CHAPTER NINE

THE FOLKS AT THE Super 8 charged me for one day when I went in to check out. They were more than reasonable.

Eddie's directions were convoluted, but Siri guided me. I wish that the Apple technicians would do a better job with her voice. I'd prefer something closer to Catherine Deneuve.

Eddie lives in one of the western-most subdivisions of West Sedona. His house proved to be a delightful medium-sized, single-family stucco in the southwestern pueblo style. He'd painted it a mauve-toned brown, which complimented the red rocks, natural terrain, and desert flora surrounding his property. When I pulled into the driveway later that night, I saw his big truck close to the house.

After I knocked on the massive wooden door, Eddie opened it, let me in, and gave me a hearty welcome.

"How do you like Casa Grimes?" he asked as he slapped me on the back and thrust a cold Sierra Nevada into my hand.

"It's very nice," I replied as I looked around the foyer and into the great room, which sported an immense two-story window that faced northwest.

The view must be spectacular in the daylight, I thought. "You furnished the place very tastefully, Colonel," I said.

"Yvette's mom did all of that. I'm a grunt. I don't know anything about designer shit, but Mary sure did."

"Did?" I asked, dreading the answer.

"My wife passed about four years ago. Breast cancer. I'm glad that she had ten years in Sedona before the end. She loved it here."

"Sorry, Eddie," I said in weak consolation.

"Yeah, me too. I miss her. She was a truly beautiful woman in body and spirit. She's the reason that we moved here. But hey, let's get you settled."

"Thanks, Eddie. I appreciate your hospitality."

"I'm looking forward to the company and the mission that we're on. Besides, you need watching out for. You don't understand this place anymore or how it can work."

"What do you mean?" I asked.

"Take your gear to the back bedroom. It's down the hall. It has its own separate bath and a little sitting area. You'll be comfortable there. After you unpack, come back to my study and we'll have a serious chat."

"Yes, Sir," I said. I picked up my carry on and put the strap over my shoulder. I pulled the handle out of the larger suitcase and wheeled it down the hallway.

The bedroom turned out to be large and restful. I spent ten minutes unpacking and freshening up before I walked back to talk to Eddie.

"Find everything to your satisfaction?" Eddie asked as I stood in the doorway to his well-appointed study. "Come on in and sit down," Eddie motioned to a comfortable looking chair across from his big wooden desk, where I had a view of his 'I love me' wall with all of his citations, medals—including a Silver Star and a Purple Heart with an oak leaf cluster—and plaques.

"Eddie, this is a neat house. I appreciate you taking me in. That kind of camaraderie is above and beyond the call of duty."

"It's the least I can do for a Paratrooper who used to work with Yvette. Besides, you need someone to look out for you here."

"You mentioned that earlier. What are you talking about?"

"You've noticed that Sedona is not the simple village that you knew forty years ago?"

"True enough. I like it better. It's more livable, hasn't lost its charm, hasn't compromised the red rocks, and is still spiritual."

"You're right about all of that. Yet Sedona remains a small town. While we get millions of visitors a year, less than twenty thousand people live around here full time. A small group of locals might not appreciate the purpose of our quest."

"Explain that please."

"You understand that different religious and philosophical groups interpret the mystical nature of this place according to their own belief systems, right?"

"Sure, I got that loud and clear from the New Age folks."

"The priest told you that if the inter-dimensional aliens existed that they could be the beings that we call angels, right?"

"Yeah, more or less."

"Don Hansen said that the angels can be good and some can be bad, evil, manipulative, and demonic?"

"Yes, which I saw as consistent with the lessons from the Christian and Jewish dogmas. Catholics believe that Michael and Gabriel work on the good side, Satan and his horde on the bad."

"Tony, do you realize that there could be folks around here who follow and venerate the demons?"

"No, but I get your point. I should have considered that possibility. I don't know why I missed it. On the battlefield, you and I have seen the evil that men do. I encountered that evil when I prosecuted violent crime in Florida. In my current job, I see it when I review the violent crime investigations that our deputies and detectives in Tampa generate. Some humans can be totally depraved."

"Yes, they can. Let me ask, you a question."

"OK."

"What do you think happened to your friend?"

"Don't know, yet."

"Bullshit!" Eddie shot back. "From the way that you told the story two hours ago, you've fantasized that inter-dimensional beings abducted him to keep the secret. Right?"

"Isn't that a possibility?" I asked.

"Maybe, but we're getting ahead of ourselves. Let's start out by agreeing that what was on the Cross in the chapel was an iron sculpture. It was never alive in any way. Think this through, Tony."

"I agree. What's your point?"

"That sculpture hung from that Cross in the chapel for over twenty years. Then, someone took it down. The stories that Ms. Staude came back and removed it make the most sense. That's the real explanation."

"If you're right then there's no mystery."

"Not so fast," Eddie began. I've lived here a long time. Before I became the king of local barbeque, I ran an I/T operation that provided computer related services to local small business, including over thirty artists, sculptors, and writers."

"You were a computer geek? I thought you were Infantry blue through and through. One more river to cross, snake eater, and all that. You've been giving me shit for being a Judge Advocate and you're Information Technology?"

"Yeah, you fucker. As a major, I ran one of the first classified and tempested I/T systems for the Joint Chiefs."

"I'm impressed. Why'd you get out of the business?"

"I got tired of fixing everyone else's glitches, problems, and meltdowns. When Mary got sick and I had to care for her, I didn't want those distractions. I sold my business and set up the barbeque gig so I could spotlight my superior culinary skills and make a buck."

"What's all this got to do with the mystery of the missing Christus?"

"Based on years of working with the artists around here, I'm certain that Ms. Staude didn't give a crap what other folks thought of the Christus. It's possible that she took the statue down and destroyed it. But if she did, it wasn't because of public criticism. She had some other reason."

"So?" I asked.

"We find the real reason why Ms. Staude, or whoever, removed the Christus, and we'll learn the true motive for the Catholics to end religious services at the chapel. When we unravel those two riddles, we'll know what happened to Ostergaard. At least we'll know why he disappeared," Eddie said.

"Any speculation, Colonel Grimes?" I asked.

"No, but your abduction theory has some merit."

"So you do think extraterrestrials or inter-dimensional beings vacation in Sedona?" I asked, trying to be jocular.

"Maybe. Like you, I've seen the lights. It's possible. Folks claim closer contact than you and I have had. They're not all crazy."

"What's next, Eddie?"

"We execute your five-point plan. I'll do the computer work. I've never seen a JAG who could find his ass with either hand where computers are concerned. You do the other stuff. Remember, this is far more complicated and a whole lot more serious— even more dangerous—than you thought. We have to be careful."

"Careful is my middle name," I said.

"If this is your idea of careful, we are in a world of shit."

"Thanks, buddy."

"Don't mention it. Want another beer?"

"Yes, I do."

"Good, they're in the refrigerator, bring me one too." Eddie directed.

Life with Eddie Grimes proved to be a hoot. His hospitality was both generous and genuine. His home became our base of operations. Lt. Col. Grimes had many talents and a dry sense of humor. In less than a day, I knew I'd made a friend for life.

After we did our research, Eddie would make terrific meals. I'd wash dishes and clean up. At Casa Grimes, light colonels were on the K.P. roster.

Eddie did exhaustive research on the Christus sculptor. His name was Keith Monroe. His base of operations had been San

Francisco. Mr. Monroe had a captivating, eclectic style, producing statues, sculptures, and fine art of all types.

In addition to the Christus, he had a signature work. It's a larger than life reproduction featuring Marilyn Monroe—no relation—in that scene from *The Seven Year Itch* where she stands over a sidewalk exhaust and her dress blows up provocatively. Thanks to Keith, the good people of Chicago get to admire a huge version of Marilyn's butt in their public spaces. Otherwise, Eddie could establish no connection between Mr. Monroe and the disappearance of the Christus. It turned out to be a dry hole.

On Tuesday, my first full day at Eddie's house, I found three Ostergaards in the Phoenix area. For a fee, a website provided a number for a Claire Ostergaard in Scottsdale.

I showed my discovery to Eddie. He'd arrived at a stopping point on his project. We discussed my approach. He agreed to listen to the conversation. I made the call in the afternoon. I got voice mail on the fourth ring.

"Hi, Ms. Ostergaard," I began. "I'm Tony Giordano. I used to know Dan Ostergaard. I wonder if you're related to him and if you have time to speak to me."

I left my cell number and hung up. Two hours later my cell rang. I recognized the number. It was Claire Ostergaard. I pushed the button for the speaker function.

"Hello, this is Tony Giordano," I began.

"Hello Tony, this is Claire."

"Thanks for calling back. I hope I haven't troubled you. I was …" I began before Claire interrupted.

"Tony, you don't recognize me. I used to be Claire Weston. We attended Saint Francis together. I went on to Xavier while you were at Brophy."

"Claire! Of course, I remember you. You were the prettiest girl in our class and the smartest."

This development surprised me. I'd known Claire Weston since first grade. She'd been the best student in our class. She blossomed in puberty. All of the Brophy Boys thought that Claire was the hottest girl at Xavier High.

She seemed to be attracted to older guys. By sophomore year, she'd begun dating frat boys from ASU. By the time I met Dan Ostergaard, Claire wouldn't have given either of us the time of day.

"What a surprise. You're part of Dan's family?

"I'm Dan's widow."

"Claire, I'm so sorry. I had no idea that you even knew Dan. In high school, you traveled in better social circles than Dan and I."

"I was Dan's second wife. We were married for fifteen years before he disappeared. We hooked up in the '80s, after our first marriages hit the rocks. Dan worked in Scottsdale, but he had a home near the Biltmore. Saint Francis was close enough for him to participate in our charitable programs. We interacted on projects, started dating, fell in love, got annulments, and got married."

"Again, I'm so sorry for your loss," I said.

"I wondered if you would contact me. I've been expecting a call for a dozen years," Claire said.

"Why would you say that," I asked. I looked at Eddie who had a surprised expression.

"You were with Dan at the chapel in Sedona, right? You were with him when you both had the encounter with the object?"

I paused. I had a hundred questions. I looked at Eddie. He waved his hand in a furious circle, indicating that I should get on with it.

"Yes, I was with Dan at the chapel. When did Dan tell you about that?"

"A week before he disappeared. He read about the chapel and a missing Christ figure. He had an emotional reaction. I tried to comfort him. He was so melancholy."

"Why did you think that I'd contact you after all these years?" I asked.

"The last time Dan and I spoke, he called me from his hotel. He told me that he'd knocked over a hornet's nest. He wouldn't explain what he meant over the phone. He told me that he'd lay the whole thing out when he came home. He said that he'd contact you. What he learned would affect you. He made me swear not to call you, unless he was there. He said that if something happened to him, I was not to contact you at all."

"Holy fucking shit!" Eddie whispered.

"So Dan didn't want you to contact me?" I said.

"The last thing he said was that, if you called me and inquired about him, I was to tell you that if you valued your immortal soul, you should abandon any thought of following him. I've been waiting to see if you would make contact. This is a relief. For the longest time, I thought Dan had a breakdown and wasn't rational."

Eddie and I looked at each other, like two stupid kids caught in an inexcusable act of vandalism. We wondered what world of shit we'd fallen into.

"So how is everything in Tampa?" Claire asked.

"How do you know that I live in Tampa, Claire?"

"The area code on your cell phone number. Besides, after that call from Dan, I found out where you lived, just in case. I've followed your career. You did big cases for the Department of Justice. You work for a Sheriff now. You've written a novel. I have it."

"You read my book?" I asked. "How'd you like it?"

At this point Eddie gave me the finger, then did the circular hand gesture again. He was impatient with my interest in Claire's evaluation of my literary work.

"I liked it a lot. It's a neat story. Dan would have liked it too. He loved historical fiction. But tell me, are you retired?"

"Can't retire. I have an expensive mistress named Gretchen. I'll work until I drop. Then she'll run off with a much younger man."

Eddie gave me the hand job sign. He pretended to wipe away a phony tear to mock the plight of a man with a trophy wife.

"Well, I wish you the best."

"Claire, I'm calling from Sedona."

"Tony, leave there immediately! It's beyond dangerous for you. Nothing good can come from you being there. Dan was right. Your life and your very soul are in jeopardy."

"I'll be all right, Claire. Don't worry."

"Those were the exact words Dan used when he ended our final conversation. I'll go to Saint Francis tonight and light candles. God bless you."

"Thanks, Claire," I said, but she'd already hung up the phone.

"What the fuck is going on?" Eddie asked.

I had a flashback to September 2, 1966. Dan stood at the door of the chapel. I shook the door. He complained that he was a religious supplicant, whose soul was in peril. The priest had locked us out. He couldn't get "no satisfaction." I smiled remembering his bad impression of Mick Jagger.

"What are you smiling about?" Eddie asked. "This is serious shit. We're behind the curve by fifteen years. Ostergaard stumbled over some heavy stuff. We have to avoid falling into the trap that got him. It'll be harder since you've been so careless and broadcasted your intentions all over town," Eddie said.

"OK, Colonel. I'll go make calls to local law enforcement. How about you continue the research on Hansen?"

"How about you make the calls and I fix us some chow? We'll eat, have a beer, and work through the afternoon?"

I agreed. We did have to eat.

I felt shaken by the conversation with Claire Weston-Ostergaard. I worried that a terrible fate awaited Eddie and me. I won't deny that I was scared. I was glad that Eddie was around— I wouldn't succumb to fear in the presence of another soldier.

After lunch, I made calls to the Coconino and Yavapai Sheriff's Offices. I got nowhere. I had the same bad luck with the Sedona Police.

Internet queries provided me with the names of veterinarians practicing in the area. I called three that seemed promising. I got one call back from a female vet. She'd purchased her practice five years earlier from an old timer who'd worked the SR 89A corridor of Jerome, Cottonwood, Clarkdale, Page Springs, Sedona, and Oak Creek in the 1960s.

Though I'd made up a convincing lie about looking for the couple because they were heirs to a modest bequest from an aunt in Florida, she declined to give me more data about the retired veterinarian. She promised to reach out to him. I gave her my cell number and asked her to have him call it.

I got nowhere with Bishop McMannes at St. Luke's. I figured that I'd drive over to the church and see if I could make some headway with a personal visit. I'd try later in the week.

Eddie had more luck looking into Don Hansen. Over the last decade Hansen had earned a reputation as a shady character. He had many fans and several serious detractors. Despite leaving several messages, he didn't return our calls.

Later in the evening, Eddie prepared a gourmet grilled flounder. We polished it off with a superb bottle of Viogner from the Burning Tree Cellars in Cottonwood. After I cleaned up the mess, we held a status conference in his study.

"OK," Eddie began. "The sculptor of the Christus is irrelevant. The veterinarian angle is on indefinite hold, right?"

"That's about the size of it," I said.

"No luck with the bishop?"

"Correct, we'll have to drive over there in a day or so."

"Don Hansen is ducking us," Eddie said. "There's no reason that he couldn't have returned the calls. Nobody is that busy."

"I agree."

"Your buddy's widow threw gasoline on this fire."

"I'll say. She scared the shit out of me."

"You must leave immediately. Your soul is in jeopardy!" Eddie said, using a ghoulish accent and emphasizing the last five words.

"If I hadn't heard the actual fear in her voice, I'd think the whole thing was pathetic and melodramatic," I said. "My immortal soul."

"Tony, her fear is based on the fact that her husband disappeared fifteen years ago. She might not be right about the soul in peril, but she's not paranoid. Something bad is operating around here," Eddie said.

"We should find out where Hansen lives and pay him a little visit," I suggested.

"That's not a bad idea, we ..." Eddie began when my cell phone started to play the first 24 bars of the 82nd Airborne *All American* Anthem.

I pulled the phone out of my pocket and saw the number. It was local.

"It might be Hansen," I said. "Hello, Tony Giordano."

"Tony, it's Don Hansen."

"Hey Don, thanks for calling."

"No problem. Got your messages. Sorry, but I'm all booked up this week. I don't have time to take you up to Schnebly Tank. It's too far."

"Look, Don. I'll make it worth your while. I'll pay you triple your normal fee."

"Sorry, can't. As a consolation, I have a colleague who's a retired Coconino County detective. He's been guiding people for a few years. He agreed to take you up there."

"I'm disappointed. I'd hoped that you would take us."

"Who's the us? Is the beautiful Gretchen still here?"

"No, I have an Army buddy that I ran into. He's up for a long hike."

"Dave will have no problem guiding two old soldiers. He was in the Army too."

"What's his full name and number, I'll reach out to him."

"Dave Fleet. Don't worry. He'll call you tonight and arrange the trek. He's very good. He's lived around here for thirty years. He'll take good care of you. Sorry, got to go. Bye."

"What's the deal?" Eddie asked, as I looked over at him.

"Hansen can't go. We have a replacement. He's a former detective, named Fleet."

"Are you sure that he said Fleet?" Eddie asked.

"Yes. What's wrong with Dave Fleet?"

"The papers say that Fleet was one step ahead of termination from the Coconino County Sheriff's Office. Last few of years he's stood accused of using excessive force on two drug dealers in a bust that he made in Flagstaff. It was a very big deal."

"Eddie, I hear that shit all of the time. I have cases pending in Tampa. The claimant's story often breaks down with experienced cross-examination."

"Might be hard to cross-examine these drug dealers," Eddie said.

"Why?"

"Cause Fleet shot them both in the head. The Coconino Sheriff's Internal Affairs folks exonerated him. The County never filed criminal charges. There's speculation that the families of the dealers might initiate one of those suits that you were talking about."

"Colonel, a man who can shoot that well might come in handy if we have to defend our immortal fucking souls," I joked.

"Unless he venerates evil, inter-dimensional demons," Eddie said.

CHAPTER TEN

THE PALEO-INDIAN RUINS at Schnebly Tank didn't resemble any of the other impressive Native American sites on the Mogollon Rim or in the Verde Valley. They were ancient—ten times as old as Palatki, Tuzigoot, and Montezuma's Castle. The inhabitants of this site hunted and gathered along the rim for more than 3,000 years before the Egyptians designed the Pyramids at Giza.

The Paleo-Indians didn't engage in recognizable agriculture. They didn't leave remnants of their dwellings, other than shallow trenches dug out of the limestone that they used as foundations for tents made from animal skins, tree bark, or brush. They did provide posterity with a rich tapestry of complex and detailed petroglyphs.

As I walked alongside the rock wall that served as their primitive canvas, I marveled at the effort that the Paleo-Indians had invested in the intricate work. The glyphs depicted all manner of predators, game animals, human beings, geometric designs, and strange figures that I couldn't recognize. A huge sandstone overhang, at least 25 feet in depth, had protected the ancient etchings over the last ten millennia.

I tried to imagine what it must have been like to live up here 10,000 years ago in an area swarming with deadly predators, never knowing what threat or bounty the hunt would bring. They must have been a hardy band, surviving on guts, wits, and limited natural resources in this small box canyon. The Paleo-Indians propagated and prospered in a difficult environment, and still had time for artistic expression.

The prehistoric artists found a bountiful source of water at the site. In the desert, high plains, and arid scrub forests of central and northern Arizona, a tank is anything natural or manmade that catches rainwater. In the limestone and sandstone formations that form the Mogollon Rim and its foothills, natural bowls, depressions, and tanks are common. Due to the paucity of rain, they're dry most of the time.

Schnebly Tank is the exception that proves the rule. It's large for a tank, with a water surface area roughly two-thirds of an acre. After a heavy rain it can double in surface size and depth. It's never dry because a small, cold, and reliable spring feeds it year-round. The tank sits in a narrow draw off the main canyon at 6,600 feet above sea level, along one of the tree-lined promontories on the Mogollon Rim.

Other springs feed a little creek that local wags have named the Conaqua—Spanish for "with water." The presence of the tank, the other natural springs, and the small creek made it possible for the ancient rock artists to survive for several generations before they disappeared.

I felt giddy from my major discovery, now an hour old. After arriving at the site, we located the etchings that Hansen claimed resembled the Christus.

These petroglyphs depicted a spot-on reproduction of the Christ figure from the chapel. After close examination, the Christus etchings seemed more detailed, proportional, and lifelike than any of the other glyphs at Schnebly Tank.

The detail of the rock carvings alone might have swayed the most committed skeptic, but the background—or more precisely the context—in which the ancient artist had placed his figures, ended all rational debate. Above and to the left of the largest Christus-like figure, a pre-historic scribe had etched an accurate replication of the Big Dipper and the Little Dipper star systems, complete with the Big Dipper ladle edge and the Little Dipper handle pointing at the North Star. Looking at these petroglyphs made the hair on the back of my neck stand up.

When I embarked on the trip to see the rock art, I had no idea what advantage I would gain. I felt that if the Stone Age Indians had recorded the presence of inter-dimensional beings in rock carvings, I might not be as daft as Gretchen feared. Now I knew that I wasn't crazy. I had made a connection of galactic proportions. As I stared at our find, I thought back to how the trek had started.

True to Hansen's promise, Dave Fleet called later on Tuesday evening to set up our trip. We'd leave Wednesday morning at five. Fleet was brusque and all business.

"So, it's you and your Army buddy?" Fleet asked, after we'd dispensed with 30 seconds of preliminaries.

"Yep. We have our own equipment. Hansen said it was a five hour hike each way, but we could do it in a day if we got motivated."

"He did, did he? I've never heard of anyone getting in and out of Schnebly Tank in ten hours travel time, especially in August. It's closer to sixteen hours, added to the dicking around that most tourists do once they get in there. In the heat, it's a two day hike from the trail head that Hansen uses."

"We didn't count on an overnighter," I said.

"Been awhile since you've been in the field, Colonel?"

"No, I hiked West Fork and Broken Arrow last week. We'll have to pack more gear."

"Nope, 'cause we ain't going the way Hansen would. Look, Colonel…"

"Call me, Tony," I interrupted.

"Tony, I don't want to spend two days guiding you up that trail. I use another approach. I come in from the north and east. I have an ATV to negotiate logging roads and fire breaks along the Rim west from 89A. I can get close to the canyon that Schnebly Tank sits inside. It's a two-and-a-half-hour ride from Sedona. We'll have to climb down a steep escarpment for about two hundred feet. It's a piece of cake, if you've done any rappelling in your Army career. The hike from our descent is half a mile to the Tank. It's easy."

"I assume that you have enough equipment for Eddie and me," I said.

"I do. It's state of the art. Swiss seats, back harnesses, links, carabineers, descenders, ascenders, ropes, lines, gloves, helmets: the works. You've got to bring your own personal equipment and a change of underwear, if you're scared of heights."

"I'm Airborne."

"I know. After Hansen called, I looked you up. You've got all that Airborne shit on the website for your novel."

"Are you Airborne?" I asked.

"No, but I'm Air Assault," he said.

"Great," I lied.

Army Air Assault units are the heirs to the airmobile concept. After Vietnam, some dickhead in Washington decided to turn the fabled 101st Airborne into an Air Assault Division. These guys ride around in helicopters. They're trained to rappel or rope down to the ground from airframes hovering at 200 feet, if the mission requires.

"No airplanes to jump from, Tony," Fleet teased. "It's too mountainous. You'll love the ride. I carry water, food, a medical kit, and SATCOM in the ATV. It's safer than Hansen's route for my senior clients."

"What was the highest rank you held, Dave?" I asked, using his first name and ignoring the age-related insult.

"Captain; artillery. Why?"

"I'm a curious sort. OK, where do we meet you?"

"I'll pick you up. I tow the ATV with my GMC SUV. We'll shoot up 89A, unload on a logging road in the Coconino National Forest on top of Mogollon Rim, and head west. If we do this right, I can get us to the rappel point by mid-morning. You can take an hour or two at the site to get your pictures. The four of us can be home for dinner."

"Four of us? You bringing a friend?"

"No, another customer wants to tag along. Hansen arranged it."

"Who is the other customer?" I asked, feeling a little trepidation.

"He's an Irish kid, visiting priest in the local parish. Hansen says that you know him. Father Patty O'Malley," Fleet said.

"What's the deal?" Eddie asked, when I got off the phone with Fleet.

"He's picking us up at five a.m. We're going to air assault into Schnebly Tank."

"Huh? Are you as crazy as you look?"

"Fleet has an ATV. We'll take logging roads along the rim and then rappel down a cliff near the tank," I explained, deadpan.

"You're way crazier than you look."

"Fleet claims that it'll save us sixteen hours of arduous hiking. He'll bring food, water, medical supplies, SATCOM, the climbing equipment, and a chaplain."

"What the fuck are you talking about? A chaplain?" Eddie asked.

"Remember the Irish priest I told you about?"

"Yeah."

"He's accompanying us on our little adventure."

"Who invited him?"

"Hansen."

"Why?"

"I'm not sure, but this is too coincidental to be coincidental," I said.

"I don't like this at all," Eddie said.

"Me either. Look, Eddie, you've been a real pal the last two days. You don't have to go on this fool's errand."

"Yes, I do. I saw the lights too. I like to fuck with you, Tony, but I need to figure out this contact thing. We're supposed to do this together. I know it. You're not going alone. I told you, I've got your back. You've got mine."

"Eddie, I've seen your shadow box with your medals for valor. I couldn't ask for a more courageous friend. I'll be honest—I'm a little worried about this little jaunt."

"Me, too. But other than the risk to my immortal soul, I've seen lots worse."

"I'll bet you have."

"I was at Hamburger Hill." Eddie said.

"Is that where you got the Silver Star?"

"Yeah, along with a Purple Heart. I still don't know how I survived."

"Want to tell me about it?" I asked.

"No. I don't."

"Who were you with?"

"Delta Company, Third Battalion, 187th Airborne Infantry."

"Jesus, Eddie, I had no idea."

Hamburger Hill was the derisive name that the media gave to the American 11-day effort to assault, capture, and secure Hill 937—also known as Ap Bia Mountain—in the remote A Shau Valley near the Laotian Border in May 1969. Although the order of battle was complex and several units took part, the Third Battalion of the 187th Airborne Infantry served as the spear point in the bloody fight. They took horrendous casualties.

Delta Company lost every one of its commissioned officers and most of its sergeants. Although the battalion experienced over 60 percent casualties, LTC Honeycutt kept them in the battle until the end. Survivors in Eddie's unit would have been among the first to capture the summit. The courage, tenacity, and fighting spirit of those Screaming Eagles are legendary.

I left Vietnam in April of 1969. While Eddie was fighting for his life on that distant hill in the forsaken A Shau Valley, I was drinking beer at the NCO Club at Camp Zama in Tokyo. I realized that I was in the presence of a real hero. I thought of the famous quote from Shakespeare's Henry V:

> And gentlemen in England now-a-bed
> Shall think themselves accurs'd they were not here,
> And hold their manhoods cheap whiles any speaks
> That fought with us upon Saint Crispin's day.

"Eddie, I know that you were prior enlisted. Did you have your commission at Hamburger Hill?"

"No, I was a staff sergeant. I got my buck sergeant stripes in Shake and Bake school at Benning in 1968. I got promoted to staff sergeant in March 1969. I went to OCS in 1972, after I got my degree from UW, while I was stationed at Fort Lewis."

"Eddie, I saw some shit in Vietnam, but I never experienced anything like you have."

"Not too many have, thank God." Eddie said.

"You still think of those events?" I asked.

"Every day."

"Are you OK with it?" I asked.

"Yeah, more or less. I do feel guilty, though. I often ask why I made it through when hundreds of other good men didn't."

"Eddie, for many years I've believed that I've been spared because I'm supposed to do something that advances the Grand Plan. I've had too many close calls in and out of the Army for my good fortune to be mere serendipity. I simply don't know what my role is supposed to be."

"Funny you say that, Tony."

"Why?"

"Though I do feel guilty, I also think that everything happens for a reason, like the Hindu concept of karma. After Mary died, I thought a lot about suicide, but I rejected it because I have a sense that I'm supposed to do something more."

"Though I'm worried, I am excited about our trek tomorrow," I said.

"Me too."

"It wasn't a coincidence that we linked up, Colonel," I said.

"I agree."

"Well, my gear is packed and ready. I don't have much to prepare."

"You're carrying, right?" Eddie asked.

"Yeah, I've got a Glock 23, a couple of extra magazines, and Gretchen's .38. I wouldn't have humped all that hardware on a long slog, but if most of this trip is in an ATV, it'll be a piece of cake."

"We'll need more firepower than a couple of handguns," Eddie said.

"Why?" I asked.

Eddie gave me look that made me feel like the dumbest recruit in basic training. He smiled and shook his head.

"I suppose your momma knows that you're away from home?"

"Don't start that momma shit, Colonel Grimes!"

"Tony, there's lots of reasons to be careful out in the Arizona countryside. In addition to evil beings from other dimensions and their vicious followers, there are rattlesnakes, pumas, bears, javelinas, wolves, coyotes—animal and human—human smugglers, drug smugglers, and the unexpected. It's been a few years, but for a time Phoenix was the kidnapping capital of the USA. Remember, the last time anyone tried to find the answer to this riddle, that guy disappeared. This is Arizona. We have open carry. Strangers will be armed. Do you want to do this with handguns?"

"No, but TSA wouldn't let US Airways transport my howitzer."

"Come with me and we'll work on the firepower issue," Eddie directed.

I followed Eddie into his bedroom. He disappeared into a walk-in closet. While I waited, I noticed a picture on his dresser, depicting a gorgeous woman. I understood where Yvette had gotten her good looks. This was the first picture of Eddie's wife that I'd seen in the house. I could understand his suicidal depression. His loss was so enormous.

While I admired the photo, I could hear the tell-tell sounds of a tumbler spinning and a big iron door opening. Two minutes later, Eddie came back into the room with an armful of long weapons. He set them down on the bed for me to examine. Eddie was a collector. He had a pre-ban Russian AK-47, an M4, a rifle that looked like a sporterized M-14, and a semi-automatic 12-gauge shotgun.

"What's your poison?" Eddie asked.

"What's the threat?" I asked.

"Let's see. None of this will be worth a shit if demonic angels with superior intellect and technology attack. I'm thinking that we need to defend against the humans who venerate the evil beings. These would be the people who want to sabotage our little inquiry."

"I think a platoon from the 503rd Infantry might be adequate," I joked.

"Maybe, but there's just us on this trek. I'll take the M-14. It's a Paratrooper model. It's got excellent ballistics, thirty-round mags, a folding stock, a short match-grade barrel, and a red dot sight. It's fully automatic. It would be good in a short or medium distance fight. If I had to, I could reach out and touch someone at two-fifty to three-hundred yards."

"You got an ATF license for that automatic weapon, Colonel?" I asked, the Federal prosecutor speaking.

"Of course. I paid the tax. It's legal for me to carry. All of these are fully automatic," Eddie said, gesturing to the rifles. "What do you want to carry?"

"Is that an FNH SLP twelve-gauge?" I asked. I had serious gun envy. The Fabrique Nationale Herstal Self-Loading Police shotgun was rumored to be the best in the world.

"Yes, it is. You ever fire one?"

"Yeah, at our range in Hillsborough County. Our deputies use Bennellis. But the FN representative lent our range some pistols and shotguns. The FNH SLP is the most effective semi-automatic shotgun that I've ever fired. Six plus one, right?"

"I modified it. I elongated the tube and use a special two-and-three-quarter-inch shell. So it's seven plus one, if you chamber the triple-ought buck shells that I loaded myself."

Triple-ought buckshot shells contain six to eight pellets in .36 caliber. Firing one shell is like shooting all the rounds in a .38 revolver at the same instant, but more deadly.

"You loaded these yourself?"

"Yes, I did," Eddie said.

"Lead or steel buckshot?"

"Neither."

"C'mon Eddie."

"Each shell has eight thirty-six caliber tungsten pellets."

"No fucking way."

"Way."

"Why'd you get the tungsten molded into buckshot?"

"Cause nobody would sell me depleted uranium."

"You're a mad man," I said.

"Why don't you take the M4? It's like an M16. It's something you're familiar with," Eddie said, taunting me.

"No, you fucker. Normally, I'd pick the AK, but I want the FN."

"Maybe I could find you a twenty-two? If a twenty-two caliber is too much weapon, I have a pellet gun for varmints," Eddie said, as he started to laugh.

"No, I want the FN. Eddie, I haven't gone armed into Harm's Way since I went on a raid in Tampa with our Swat Team in 2007."

"Desert Storm for me," Eddie admitted.

"I'm nervous, but I'm looking forward to this," I confessed, surprising myself.

"Me too," Eddie said. "We'll do something dangerous, exhilarating, and—by the way—we might solve a great mystery. Not bad for a couple of old farts."

"Why, Colonel Grimes, you're a classic romantic."

"That's what Jesuit training will do for you," Eddie said.

"You? Where?" I asked knowing from the diploma in his study that he'd graduated from the University of Washington in Seattle.

"Gonzaga Prep in Spokane."

"You went to G Prep?"

"Yeah, AMDG, brother.

"*Ad Majorem Dei Gloriam,*" I responded.

Like I said, there is no serendipity.

Wednesday morning, Fleet arrived five minutes early. Eddie and I waited in the driveway. I hadn't slept much; neither had Eddie. I felt stimulated and anxious.

Fleet got out to shake our hands and to help stow the gear in the back of the SUV. Fleet was at least six foot one and weighed around 190. He had short black hair. His bearing, attitude, and everything about him screamed ex-police officer.

Eddie got in the front. I sat in the back. Ever since my days as the Chief of the Organized Crime Section, I hate to ride on the passenger side of the front seat. That's a favorite spot for capping your gangster buddy in the back of the head.

Less than five minutes after we left Eddie's, we pulled into the parking lot of St. John Vianney's. Father Pat was waiting. He'd dressed in hiking shorts and a long-sleeved top. He looked every inch the European tourist.

"Father Pat, what brings you out at this hour?" I asked after we got settled and I'd made the introductions.

"I want to see the petroglyphs for myself. This business about the Christus disturbs me."

"What's a Crispus?" Fleet asked.

"Christus…" Father Pat corrected.

Before Fleet could ask more questions, Eddie gave him the abridged version of this story. When Eddie stopped, we were half way up Oak Creek Canyon.

"This whole trip is about gathering evidence to support the presence of inter-dimensional beings?" Fleet asked.

"Yes, in a way," Father Pat said.

"Look, gentlemen. Sedona attracts a lot of sketchy people. No offense to present company. I know there's a ton of unexplained phenomena up here, but inter-dimensional beings? C'mon," Fleet said.

"What about the missing Christus?" Eddie argued.

"Now that I know what you're talking about, it's not much of a mystery. The old broad who built the chapel tore the figure down. Several years ago, I worked on a missing person's case where a guy got all wound up about that."

"You were a detective on the Dan Ostergaard case?" I asked.

"Why, yes. That's the one. How do you know that?"

"Tony went to high school and college with Ostergaard," Father Pat said.

Fleet reacted by slowing the truck down and pulling into an overlook along Oak Creek Canyon. He stopped, set the brake, and turned around to look back at me.

"You knew Ostergaard?"

"Sure did."

"My investigation revealed that he believed that he had an encounter with aliens at the chapel in the sixties. He and a friend were there together. No one could or would tell me who that friend might be," Fleet said, as he looked me up and down. "The wife wasn't too cooperative. We never learned who the other guy was or what happened to Ostergaard. I have my suspicions."

"It was September 2nd, 1966. I was there with him when we saw the lights. What do you think happened to Dan?" I asked, avoiding any reference to my conversation with Claire Ostergaard or her warning.

"I don't think that aliens abducted him, Colonel. He was a well-known accountant who did the auditing for a couple of questionable financial investment schemes in Phoenix. Those fuckers had connections to organized crime. When their Ponzi folded, they cost their investors more than a billion. Hundreds of millions are still missing. I shouldn't be telling you guys this 'cause the case is still open, but I'm convinced that Ostergaard staged his disappearance to avoid the repercussions. His wife knows more than she's telling."

"Ostergaard would leave his wife and disappear?" Father Pat asked.

"Fuckin' A!" Fleet said before he could stop himself. "Sorry, Father. But yeah. We had a joint investigation with Arapaio's detectives down in Phoenix and the FBI. Ostergaard was up to his neck in the fraud. He was a smart cookie. He got out ahead of the collapse. I think that he squirreled away at least twenty-five million. That kind of money can buy you a new identity, anonymity, and a much more compliant wife."

"If that were true, why would she cover for him?" I asked.

"She lives well in a ritzy part of Scottsdale. He paid her off."

"Police work made you cynical, didn't it?" Father Pat said.

Fleet gave Father Pat a condescending look and smiled. He turned around, released the brake, shifted into drive, and drove the truck north on 89A. Less than ten minutes later, he turned off the highway and proceeded up a steep unpaved road. About a mile later, Fleet pulled over and we began to unload the ATV and the equipment.

I hadn't looked at the ATV until Fleet backed it off the trailer. It was impressive. It had a woodland camouflage paint job, four seats—two in the front and two in the back—plus a substantial cargo carrier in the rear. It appeared to be very rugged.

"That's an impressive vehicle," I said.

"Yeah, it's a Polaris Ranger Crew. Not quite top of the line. It's a reasonable compromise for my purposes. It has sixty horses, excellent clearance, fantastic traction, and flexibility. It gets me out of a lot of trouble," Fleet said, as he admired his toy.

"How bad is the track up to Schnebly Tank?" Eddie asked.

"Not bad. This baby can negotiate much worse. Your ride won't be uncomfortable. It's long, though. It'll take a little less than two hours to get to where we rope down," Fleet said, as he loaded a bag filled with climbing equipment and a big five-gallon can of water.

"Where do we stow our stuff?" Eddie asked.

"What do you have?" Fleet asked.

"Packs, poles, and weapons," Eddie said.

"What weapons are you carrying?"

"I have an M14. Tony has a shotgun."

"You expect to run into Attila the Hun?" Fleet asked.

"I was an Eagle Scout," Eddie said. "Always prepared."

Fleet thought about Eddie's answer for a long moment before he responded.

"You lifers love your weapons. Be careful. There's no hunting. I didn't sign up to watch you shoot your guns at rocks or trees. If you carry that stuff down to the tank, you will be responsible. When we rope down, all weapons will be safe. If you agree, let's proceed. Otherwise, I'll refund your money and take you home."

Eddie didn't reveal that we had concealed pistols. I kept the secret.

"That's fine." Eddie agreed. "Safety first."

"Good. If it's any comfort, I always pack a Dan Wesson .357 magnum. If we encounter any hostiles, I'll deal with them. If carrying that heavy hardware floats your boat, have at it. But don't ask me to hump if for you."

The trip from 89A west along the logging road and the power line cuts in the Coconino National Forrest was quite pleasant. Although it was August, we were 7,200 feet above sea level, so it never got above 85 degrees. Most often, we drove along the rim and marveled at the stunning views. Other times, we traversed trails in deep pine forests or tracks over alpine meadows. By 8:30, a weather front from California moved in and the overcast sky cut the temperature another five degrees.

Even though the engine made a lot of noise, we carried on a conversation of sorts. Fleet wasn't shy. He told us a lot about his life as a Coconino detective. About an hour into the trip, Eddie mentioned that I worked for the local Sheriff in Florida.

"I heard," Fleet said. "You're a lawyer not a deputy, right?"

"That's right. I was a Special Deputy U.S. Marshal for five years. Does that count?"

"Maybe. Depends on what you did. What do you do now?"

"I represent the Sheriff in state and federal court. I go to bat for guys like you who get sued for use of excessive force."

Fleet took his eye off the road and looked back at me.

"We need to talk. I need a good lawyer. Greedy assholes want to sue me."

"Why?" Father Pat asked.

"'Cause I shot their boys in the head! They tried to kill me during a drug bust."

"Oh." Father Pat said.

"Don't you have a lawyer?" I asked.

"Nope. Might have waited too long. I don't like lawyers. No offense, Counselor."

"None taken," I said, "especially if you're going to belay me down the canyon."

"If it helps with the rappelling, I hate lawyers too." Eddie said, smiling.

We continued our banter for another hour. As the discussion waned, we traversed a deep and wooded stand of tall ponderosa pines. The path was good, but narrow. We turned a bend and came to a fork in the trail. The route to the right bent north and was a bit wider than the track we had navigated. I noticed deep ruts in the path. They continued north out of sight.

"Must be some big logging trucks come through here," Eddie said.

"There's no logging in this part of the forest. Not for years. It's too dry now anyway," Dave said, as he stopped the ATV.

Without warning, a Jeep with two men came over the rise to the north, heading for our ATV. Seeing us, they sped up. Their demeanor seemed menacing. I had a bad feeling.

You realize that my association with the military and law enforcement has made me suspicious. Knowing that Dan Ostergaard had disappeared generated the tiniest paranoia. Claire claimed my soul could be forfeit, if I continued the quest. I wanted to be careful.

I turned to Eddie, who was in the back with me. I didn't have to say a word. He had the M14 in his lap, the business end pointing out. Fleet dismounted the ATV, walked around the front, and positioned himself between the oncoming Jeep and the ATV. I looked at Eddie. He nodded.

We dismounted the ATV. I walked over to a tree to the northeast, as if I were going to take a leak. Eddie went the other way. He'd slung his rifle, but his hand rested on the semi-concealed butt of his Kimber 1911. I reached into the hidden pouch of my 5-11 hiking vest and felt for my Glock. I switched the laser sight on. I pretended to pee.

"Morning, Gentlemen," Fleet said to the two white men in the Jeep as they drew near our vehicle. I scanned the forest. I could see no discernable movement.

"Morning," said the driver—a well-built man in his 30s. He scanned our party taking account of every one of us. "What's your business here?"

"It's a national forest chum," Fleet said. "It's a free country. Our purpose here is not your concern."

The passenger, a smaller balding man, became anxious. The driver said something that seemed to calm his companion down. I made a point of scanning the forest north, east, and south. I trusted that Eddie had the west. I saw nothing unusual.

"We got a lease to log and mine this section," the driver said. "We're about to post no-trespassing signs. We don't want no trouble. We can't allow you to go north up this road. It's for your own safety. We can't be liable for anything that happens to you."

"Thanks for your concern. It's touching," Fleet said.

"Oh, we don't give a fuck about you," the rider said. "We got these lawyer sons of bitches that insist that we keep you folks out."

"Yeah, lawyers fuck it up for everybody, don't they?" Fleet asked.

"They sure do," the rider said. "I had a lawyer. I'd like to meet him again. He was a real motherfucker."

"Sold you out, did he?" Fleet asked.

"Fuck, yeah."

"So how long did you have to spend in Florence?" Fleet asked.

"I did over four…" the passenger started before the driver of the Jeep cut him off.

"We don't need to go into the sad tale of your life," the driver said.

"Gents," he said, turning to us. "You can't go farther north. If you want to go west, there ain't nothing out there but rim and canyon. You can go back the way you came. It's your choice."

"We'll go west; thanks," Fleet said, as he motioned us back into the ATV.

After I got seated, I kept my hand on my Glock and my eye on the Jeep, as we sped away down the left fork of the trail.

As soon as we got out of sight, Eddie started singing a version of "Dueling Banjos" from *Deliverance*. Fleet and I broke up.

Father Pat looked disturbed. He had no idea why the crazy old Army officer in the back seat sang "da da da da dant," then laughed hysterically.

"What's so damn funny?" Father Pat asked, peeved that he didn't get the joke.

"Ever see *Deliverance*, Father?" Fleet asked.

"It that a movie?"

"It was Burt Reynolds' break out performance," I pointed out.

"Who's Burt Reynolds?" Father asked.

"Father, the movie is about four guys who go on a canoe trip down a river in Georgia that's about to be destroyed by a government dam project. They get crossways with some inbred rednecks. Sodomy and homicide ensue," I explained.

"I presume that Eddie is singing music from the movie," Father said.

"That's right," Eddie said, breaking into another rendition and laughing again.

"If those guys are loggers or miners, I'm the fucking Dali Lama," Fleet said. "The passenger looked familiar. Can't place him, but he did time in the State Prison in Pinal County. Might be he and his pal are cultivating in the National Forest."

"What would they grow?" Father Pat asked.

"Marijuana, Father. It's too high and cool up here to grow the powerful stuff, but it's remote. A drug dealer's life is full of tradeoffs. Don't worry. As long as we stay away from their crop, they'll leave us alone. I'll report it after we get back."

A half hour later, we arrived at the rappel point, where a dramatic vista unfolded for 80 miles to the south and west. We shared a magnificent tableau: rolling mountains, purple in the western distance, merging into blue grey where the storm clouds poured heavy rain; bright red and orange rock formations to the south, covered in speckled sunlight; brown and green timbered canyon lands hidden in deep shadows below us.

We dismounted the ATV. Fleet stood at the lip of the rim. He peered toward the storm through a pair of high-powered binoculars.

"I knew that a front would come through, but the damn weather man said that we wouldn't get much rain here. He expected the precipitation to go to the north into Nevada and Utah. Those mountains are getting soaked. They're west of us, some seventy to eighty miles. If that storm is moving the way I think, it could be here in three or four hours. It'll rain here by this afternoon for sure," Fleet said.

"What's the matter with a good rain storm?" Father Pat asked. "The forest could use a good soaking."

"True, Padre. Dave is concerned that if it rains as hard here as out there, we could get caught in a flash flood," Eddie said, pointing west.

"We have flash floods in Ireland. They can disrupt your life. What's a flash flood like out here?" Father Pat asked.

"This land is rocky and dry," I said. "If it rains a lot, the water will not soak in. It'll run off the rocks into the channels that have carved this land over millions of years. It's rain-driven erosion that created the beautiful scene that you see below. During a flash flood, the narrow canyons fill up quickly. If you get caught in a streambed during a flash flood, it can ruin your whole day."

"It can kill you," Fleet said. "A major cause of death among stupid *turistas* is walking or driving in streambeds during a flash flood. That thunderhead in the west worries me. We could get caught down in the canyon and not be able to climb back out today."

"We've come a long way. Are you willing to risk it?" Eddie asked Fleet.

"I suppose. I'll e-mail Hansen. He'll get someone to cover my tourists tomorrow. I have food for overnight if we get stuck down there. We'll have a little camping trip, sing songs, roast marshmallows, and tell ghost stories by the fire," Fleet said, mocking us.

"You're serious?" Father Pat asked.

"Sure, I am. I always bring extra rations. We can rope it all down. There's plenty of water at the Tank. We can leave most of the other stuff in the ATV. I know a little spot where we can hole up if we need to stay dry. However, if I have to wet-nurse you three pilgrims overnight, the rate will be double."

"How will you e-mail anyone? I don't have cell service. No bars, see," Father Pat said, as he pointed to the data frame on his cell phone.

"I have a Delorme, In Reach device. It gives my Smartphone satellite connectivity for data. I'll send Hansen an e-mail. Then I'll set up the ropes. The armed and dangerous, over-the-hill gang can rappel down the canyon wall to recapture a vestige of their misspent youth," Fleet said, as he gestured to Eddie and me.

"Fair enough." Father Pat said. "Let's get started."

The rappelling seemed less dangerous than the zip lining in Camp Verde. The ledge overlooking Conagua Creek hung 250 feet above the target area for our descent. At the rappel point, the cliff face was not straight down. For the first 180 feet from the ledge, it looked to be about 70 degrees. The last 80 feet appeared to be perpendicular.

As advertised, Fleet's equipment was first-rate. He knew his business. He set up the equipment and fixed the anchors. I grew more confident.

After 30 minutes, we began. I'd go first. Eddie would follow. Father Pat was next, and then our guide would come last. I checked my weapons, backpack, and rappelling equipment for the 20th time.

I hadn't done any rappelling in over 25 years. Fleet had to give me a five-minute tutorial on the use of the figure-eight rescue descender. I was awkward with it, but got the knack without falling to my death on the rocks below. Eddie took pictures with his old Nikon as I rappelled to the canyon floor. You won't get to see those cute photos either.

After I landed on the creek bed, I unhooked my equipment. Eddie followed. Like Gretchen, he was far more graceful than I'd been.

Father Pat came down so fast that I thought he'd lost control. Turns out that little shit was an experienced rock climber. He'd scaled cliffs throughout Europe. When he joined Eddie and me at the bottom of the canyon, he drolly offered to give us tips for future rock climbing and rope work.

Fleet was as good as Father Pat. He made it down in 90 seconds.

Fleet stuffed the climbing gear into a bag, which he set it next to large boulder near the hanging rope. After checking our hiking equipment, we set off.

We did the half-mile to the ruins in ten minutes. The trail along Conaqua Creek was smooth and easy. The petroglyphs lay on the northern tip of Schnebly Tank, east of the creek. Unless you knew that the tank and the ruins were there, you could miss the site.

Until I saw the petroglyphs, the area was unimpressive. The rock faces around the tank didn't have the dramatic red sandstone color or unique weathered features of other places of ancient human habitation.

The petroglyphs were another story. I didn't expect to see the volume, the variety, or the quality. Eddie found the etchings of the Christus first. I'm the one who realized that the dots depicted star systems. Once I pointed them out, everyone agreed that I'd made a connection that no one else had ever recognized.

Like Fleet predicted, we dicked around the petroglyphs for two hours, looking for other evidence of inter-dimensional beings that looked like the Christus. No luck.

When Fleet suggested that we call the ball, head back to the ropes, and get ahead of the rain, it began to pour and thunder.

"Too fucking late," Fleet swore. "Gents, I know a place with another overhang. It's seventy yards farther up the canyon. There are no ruins there. We can set up camp, stay dry, and not offend Native American sensibilities. We'll see how long it rains. There's a chance we could rope up this afternoon, but I think we're here until tomorrow."

We took our last pictures and followed Fleet up the trail. The campsite was well situated near the ruins. Others had camped there in the recent past. Another large sandstone overhang extended over the spot for 25 feet. It was more than enough to keep us dry.

Fleet had humped four rubber mats, which we would use to sit and lay on. We might be stuck, but we'd be comfortable.

The ground beneath the overhang consisted of bare sandstone. We decided to light a fire to heat water for our freeze-dried rations. The rain had lowered the temperature 20 degrees. We all felt a chill.

We gathered wood from outside the overhang. Though it was raining, the wood was dry. We had no trouble getting it to burn.

It rained all afternoon. The level of the creek crested. An hour before sunset, a three-foot wave of water rolled through the narrow flood plain. While we remained high, dry, and warm in our cozy site, anyone downstream would be in jeopardy as the flood gained size, speed, and volume.

We had nothing to do but wait out the storm. We sat near the fire and munched on freeze-dried lasagna and trail mix. We chatted until it got dark, discussing our discovery at length.

"What's your take on the petroglyphs?" Eddie asked Father Pat.

"I don't know what to make of them," Father Pat admitted. "The early inhabitants carved those figures in the context of stars. I thought the beings were inter-dimensional."

"Father, at the Cowboy Club—despite your training—you had difficulty grasping the concept of a multiverse. A Stone Age human would never be able to understand it. The ancient inhabitants could see stars in the heavens. The stars reflect an understandable misinterpretation of the origin of the supernatural aliens," I argued.

"Tony, those rock etchings can't depict the Christus. It was an iron sculpture that didn't exist for another nine or ten thousand years," Father Pat said.

"That's right. Father. The rock drawings and Monroe's Christus represent the same thing or the same race of being. The

Paleo-Indians had a vision of an inter-dimensional being ten mil-lennia ago, and the sculptor—or someone who influenced him—had a similar vision of the being's descendants in our time."

"Why descendants? If these beings are from another dimen-sion, who is to say what their life span is?" Eddie asked. "If they're the beings that we call angels, they could live so long that from our perspective they're immortal."

"If I'd known what lunatics I'd be guiding, I'd have skipped this fucking trip," Fleet said as he plopped down on his mat, reached into his pack, and pulled out a fifth of Gentleman Jack Daniels. He opened the bottle, took a healthy swig, and passed it to Eddie.

"Those glyphs are the work of primitives, who hunted and gathered for a living. When they returned from a hunt, they gorged themselves and rested. When they weren't doing chores, making babies, or telling stories, they passed the time carving on the walls. That's it. You guys are crazy, if you think that inter-di-mensional angels have been traveling here for thousands of years," Fleet said.

"Have you ever seen anything that you can't explain, Dave?" Father Pat asked.

"Sure, after half of bottle of that," Fleet said, as he pointed to the fifth that Eddie had passed to me.

"Dave," Eddie said, "this area is full of unexplained sightings. You never experienced any of them?"

Fleet took a deep breath, raised his head, and shook it. "After I joined the Sheriff's Office, I stayed in the Reserves. I deployed to Iraq in the Second Gulf War. I helped uncover the Iraqi victims of Sadam's chemical attacks on his own countrymen. I don't like to think about what I saw there. I was a drug and homicide detective for twenty-five years. I still have bad dreams about the evil that I observed. Humans are depraved. They will prey on their own in the most ruthless and barbaric ways. We don't need devils, bad angels, or evil inter-dimensional beings to influence us to do bad things."

"Dave, that's not an answer to Eddie's question," I said.

"Fuckin' lawyer!" Fleet said, but he was smiling. "Yes, I have, counselor. I've seen strange lights more than half-a-dozen times. Satisfied?"

"What explanation do you have for them?" Father Pat asked.

"Top secret aircraft, experimental drones, alcohol driven hallucinations, mirages, swamp gas."

"Aw, swamp gas," Eddie said. "What swamp would that be Dave?"

"Fuck you, Colonel," Fleet responded, as he took the bottle from Father Pat. "I'll believe in little green men, or tall, thin, dark men from other realities when they land their craft on that creek, walk on water over to this fire, and take a shot of this Gentleman Jack."

Fleet's hostility dampened further discussion. He suggested that we get some sleep so that we could get started first thing in the morning, assuming that the rain stopped, the creek fell, and the ropes dried.

"We'll do four watches," Fleet said. "It's ten p.m. now. I'll take the first watch. Tony, you have from twelve to two, Eddie two to four, Padre four to six. Father, you wake me up, if I'm not already up. If we can get to the ropes, I may be able to use the ascenders to get up the cliff face, even if the ropes are little wet. I have a spare rope in the ATV. I'll re-rig and pull us out of here, OK?"

"Why do we have to do watches?" Father Pat asked. "You said we wouldn't encounter Attila the Hun."

"We have bears in these canyons. There are packs of coyotes, a few pumas, and maybe a stray wolf from Utah or Colorado. The rain and the flood have disrupted their lairs. If they come foraging, they could roll into camp and all hell would break loose. So be alert. If you see any critters moving in, wake us. We'll scare them off."

"Makes sense, Dave," I said, as I lay down on the mat. I zipped up my Scottevest windbreaker. I fell asleep in minutes, thinking how satisfying it had been to act like a soldier all day—rappelling down a cliff, marching to a site, making an important discovery, camping in the field with comrades, and sharing a slug of Jack Daniels.

CHAPTER ELEVEN

August 29, 2013, 12:05 AM
Campsite, 70 Yards North of Schnebly Tank,
Conagua Creek
Coconino National Forest, Arizona

I WOKE UP WITH a start. I'd forgotten for a moment where I was. I had to blink several times to clear my vision. Unless I've been staring at a computer all day, I still have 20/20 vision for anything beyond arm's reach.

I looked around. Everything seemed fine. The fire needed to be stoked a bit. Fleet sat with his back to the fire facing outward, leaning against a large boulder in almost the same position as when I drifted off to sleep. Eddie and Father Pat curled up on their mats. The priest snored softly.

Men my age wake in the night to urinate. My bladder set my first priority. I stood up, stretched—happy that I wasn't stiff—and walked to the north side of the overhang to take a leak. I tried to be quiet, so I wouldn't disturb Eddie and Father Pat.

After I zipped up, I looked at my watch. It was 12:05 a.m. Fleet should have woken me five minutes earlier. Looking over at him, I noticed that he hadn't stirred while I crept around our little camp.

Fucking leg! Air Assault trooper. He had too much Gentleman Jack and fell asleep on guard. I own you now, brother. I chortled to myself.

I closed the ten yards behind Fleet in five steps. By the third step I knew something was wrong.

Relying on instinct, I reached into my vest and pulled my Glock. I squeezed the button on the grip with my middle finger. I could see the laser's red dot on the ground beneath my shadow. I bent into a crouch and moved to the left, using the boulder next to Fleet as cover. I got down on one knee behind what was left of our guide.

The top of Fleet's head was missing. I saw brain tissue spattered all over the side of the boulder, along with copious amounts of dark, red blood. I resisted the urge to retch.

Fleet hadn't woken me because he was dead. At first, I thought that his death could be suicide. Then I saw his pistol in the holster on his belt. No one could shoot himself in the head without making a sound, then re-holster the weapon. Someone had killed him. I could not reason why.

I attribute my survival that night to the fact that I didn't blunder out in front of Fleet. Had I done that, I'd have my own brains splattered on that sandstone boulder.

I looked back at my sleeping pad. I saw the shotgun next to it. Whatever happened next, I would have to use my Glock. I blessed the Sheriff in Florida for requiring that the legal staff practice at the range and qualify to state standards. I felt confident. If I got the chance, I'd put whoever did this in a world of hurt.

I willed my breathing to stabilize. My next priority was to warn Eddie, and then Father Pat, without compromising my position or alerting the enemy, because whoever had killed Fleet had become my enemy.

I looked down at my feet and located several small rocks. Moving more to the left for better cover, I began chucking the rocks at Eddie's chest. On my sixth attempt, I hit Eddie under his chin. He awoke with a start and looked around. When he saw me, he started to get up. He noticed my hand signals and dropped prone.

Though Eddie and I had never served together, we both had learned to communicate with infantry hand signals. I was rusty and clumsy, but Eddie was smart, experienced, and intuitive.

When I pointed to Fleet, I ran my index finger across my throat. Eddie understood and nodded. From his perspective, he could see that someone had shot Fleet in the head. Eddie shook his head, a sad expression on his face. He looked around the campsite.

Evaluating my position, Eddie recognized that I was in good spot from a tactical perspective, but didn't have the shotgun. He searched with his eyes, located it, and picked it up. From the prone position he tossed it to me. I caught it with one hand. The move looked so good, you would have thought that we'd practiced it.

Eddie secured his M14. He'd loaded it earlier because he slid the bolt back a notch, confirmed a round was in the chamber, reseated it, and pushed the safety on the trigger guard forward.

I had no shell in the chamber of the shotgun. There were seven shells in the tube magazine. The rest of the special 12-gauge shells were in my kit, across the way. I didn't lock and load. I couldn't risk the metallic noise of racking a round.

I wondered if I might be dreaming this whole episode until I detected the awful, bitter scent of drying blood and brain matter. After all these years I was back in the shit.

I experienced a wave of dread so profound that for a moment I thought that I'd puke and defecate simultaneously. I looked over at Eddie. He winked at me. I got ahold of myself, smiled, and winked back.

Letting Father Pat sleep was the best course. He'd be no help in this crisis. Distraction could prove to be our undoing—if we had any chance at all.

It was hard to evaluate our situation. All I knew is that someone with a silenced weapon had killed Dave Fleet without rousing us. I had no idea why he shot Dave or how many enemies surrounded us. Time to play it cool.

Several minutes passed. Nothing happened.

All of sudden, Eddie moved his head and stared to his oblique right. He'd detected something. He signaled me that he could hear two hostiles approaching from the right. Not 20 seconds later, I heard something moving over the loose sandstone in front of Fleet. I couldn't tell if it was one or five.

Four men in ski masks sprung up from the ground 25 yards in front of our position. They wore dark clothing. Each one had a Kalashnikov assault rifle. Though lethal, the Kalashnikovs made me feel better. I didn't know any American law enforcement that used them. We wouldn't be engaging the police.

We could see the enemy, but they hadn't made us. Eddie signaled me. He would take the two on the right. I had the two on the left.

I shoved the Glock in my vest holster and hoisted the 12 gauge. When the firing started, I'd have to seat a triple-ought shell first. Recharging the operating handle would take two seconds. I had to chance it. I'm good with the pistol, but I can't match two men with AKs at point-blank range.

The figure in front of me signaled the other three men. They spread out so that the four of them formed a line. Each stood about five yards from the other. Unlike their earlier movements, they weren't stealthy. They'd become overconfident.

The leader gave another signal. The assailants paused for a second then rushed our camp firing their weapons on full automatic. Their rounds tore up the sandstone all around us. Their homicidal charge settled our response.

I racked a round, engaging the leader at 15 yards. With an FNH SLP, that's a gimme shot. Gretchen had counseled double taps. I followed her advice.

I put two shells in the leader's upper chest. He flew backward.

Less than a second later, I swung to the right to catch the second man. The delay in loading had cost me. The second man had reacted too quickly.

Though I fired twice at my second target, I managed to hit him in his right hip. I couldn't be sure that he got all eight of the tungsten pellets. It should have been enough to bring him down, but it wasn't.

He'd aimed his AK toward me and fired a long burst. I could hear some of the rounds hit Fleet's body. Some hit the boulder over my head and rock particles showered me. I flinched. I wanted to duck, but didn't.

I fired three more times at the assassin. I hit him at least once. He also flew backward but didn't go down. He fired another burst, but the shots went high.

Out of shells, I drew my Glock as he turned, rolled, and crawled into the darkness.

I'd focused on my own targets and didn't see Eddie shoot the other two assailants. I heard him fire four bursts. Eddie later bragged that his trigger control was so good that he could squeeze a three-round burst on full auto. The proof was in the pudding.

Two attackers with Kalashnikovs lay dead ten yards from Eddie's position.

I hadn't fired live rounds at another human being in four decades. My ears rang from the shots. The smell of cordite from the shells and the pungent odor of my own fear and perspiration stung my nostrils.

The firing woke Father Pat. When he got up, Eddie pulled him down and rolled on top of him. Eddie clamped a hand over the priest's mouth. He whispered something that I couldn't hear. Pat stopped struggling. Eddie let him go. The priest remained prone.

I looked over at Eddie. With a wan grimace, he gave me the thumbs-up. I signaled thank you. He mouthed that he had my six. He did indeed.

I looked at my watch. It was 12:20 a.m. Eddie took a bottle of our water and poured it on the flames, extinguishing what was left of the fire. It got dark under the sandstone overhang. It took me a few minutes to adjust to the reduced light.

Eddie crawled to one of the men in front of him. He secured the assailant's weapon and examined it in the reduced light, as I covered him with my Glock.

When Eddie finished, he covered me as I crawled to the body of the leader. The assassin lay sprawled on his back. I appropriated his weapon. I searched his clothing. He had cigarettes, a lock-blade knife, two 30-round magazines, but no wallet or papers of any kind. I didn't look under his mask because it was too dark to recognize any facial detail.

I saw a large pool of blood where the second man had been standing. He'd gotten away. I had no way of knowing how badly I'd wounded him.

It was too dark for hand signals. I had to talk to my partner.

"I told you not to come on this jaunt," I said, as I crawled next to Eddie.

"Should have listened. This is a fine mess that you've gotten me into."

"Eddie, these guys are serious. The leader had on a ballistic vest. I could feel the armor. Some of the triple-ought pellets hit him in the throat."

"Well, the ballistics on my M14 are better than your twelve-gauge. The vests on these animals didn't help them."

"Who are these fuckers?" I asked.

"You think they're connected to those marijuana growers up in the forest?" Eddie asked back. "Kalashnikovs, body armor. What in the fuck is that? Why would those guys be so well armed? By the way, did you notice that these are AK-74s, not 47s? These 74s are a lot harder to come by."

"Hate to break it to you, amigo, but the squad leader over there was carrying an AK-103. See for yourself," I said, as I passed the weapon over to Eddie.

"Holy shit. You're right. Whoever these guys are, they're pros."

"Tony, Eddie, what's this all about?" Father Pat asked from his prone position.

"We don't know, Father. But we're in a bad spot."

"Maybe that's all of them," Father Pat said.

"Don't fucking bet on it, Padre," Eddie said. "Our JAG sharp-shooter wounded one of his two assigned targets. We have at least one wounded mother still out there. I heard more movement along the creek as the four thugs formed up for the assault. Now, with the shooting, my hearing's gone for the next hour. Trust me, there are more assholes out there."

"Why?" Father Pat asked, as he gestured at Fleet's slumped corpse.

"Beats me, Padre. We need to haul ass before first light. In the morning we'll be sitting ducks in here," Eddie said.

"Let's think this through. If we can get away from this overhang, we can't go back east the way we came. Whoever is out there will expect us to go for the ropes and get to the ATV. Even if we could get past them, we can't get up that cliff in the dark. In the daylight, even our climbing expert from Ireland would be an easy target," I said.

"We can't go south down Hansen's favorite trail because it's flooded. If we get away and the flood recedes, we don't know how many will chase us. I've looked at the trail map. It's too narrow. We'd get picked off as we tried to get away. Somebody out there has a silenced sniper rifle," Eddie said, as he looked over at Fleet.

"We can't go very far north. We'd have to climb up the rim without equipment. We'd be in the same spot as our first option," I said.

"Agreed," Eddie said. So we have to go west."

"Maybe we can reason with them," Father Pat said.

"Padre, if I hadn't been awake, we'd all be dead. These guys, and whoever is with them, came to kill us all," I said, as I pointed at the dead men.

"Tony—if Fleet died before he woke you to relieve him—why were you awake?"

"Had to pee."

"Classic!" Eddie said. "We owe the rest of our lives to an old man's bladder."

"I'm in Dublin. I'm asleep. I'm having the worst nightmare of my life. Must be Divine retribution for my addiction to Bushmills. I'll wake soon. I'll get good psychiatric care. I'll never drink Protestant whiskey again. It'll be Jameson from now on," Father Pat swore. "Look," he continued. "Let's give diplomacy a try. What do we have to lose?"

"Our lives, and maybe our immortal souls."

"Your souls? What are you talking about?" Father Pat demanded.

Eddie summarized my conversation with Claire Weston-Ostergaard. Although it was dark, I could see a look of complete disbelief on the priest's face.

"You two are daft. Listen, I volunteer to talk with these people. How can it hurt you? In any event, I'm not going to take up a weapon. I'm expendable."

"Father, you know how many of us there are and what our weapons are. The bad guys don't know our capabilities. They do know that we got the upper hand in the opening gambit in this homicidal melodrama," I said.

"I agree. Father, cool it. You stay with us. Tony, tell me, how do we get away from this site without stumbling across whoever is out there?" Eddie asked.

"When we gathered wood earlier, I noticed that there's a little path along the rocks; it tracks north. Those scrub cedars and manzanitas camouflage it, but we could squeeze by if we're very quiet. We'll have to go slow," I said. "By the way, what's west of here? How far is it? What do we have to climb over to get there?"

Eddie thought about it minute. "Let me have your windbreaker," Eddie directed.

I pulled it off and gave it to him. He found his trail map and then hunkered down behind the boulder. Father Pat and I held the windbreaker over him while Eddie examined his trail map by the light of the flashlight app on his iPhone. The boulder and windbreaker blocked all of the light.

"That was neat," Father Pat whispered when Eddie finished. "Did you learn that in the Airborne?"

"Sort of," Eddie explained. "In the second episode of Band of Brothers, the actor playing Dick Winters used a raincoat for the same purpose. I can't imagine that any Paratroopers jumped raincoats into Normandy. It was a cool scene anyway."

"You got that trick from a movie?" Father Pat asked.

"Mini-series episode, actually," Eddie said.

"I'm doomed," Father Pat said.

"Stick with us, Padre; we'll get out of here," I said.

"Tony, we have no chance. Face it," Eddie said.

"OK, Eddie; maybe you're right. Father, will you give us absolution? I have a ton of mortal sins on my soul. I haven't confessed in thirty years."

"I can give absolution to Eddie, if he needs it. I can't give it to you."

"Are you serious?" I whispered. "We're about to be overrun by madmen, and you're withholding absolution?"

"Tony, you're living in an unsanctioned marriage."

"Fuck!" I said too loud for our tactical situation, as the priest blessed Eddie and whispered something to him.

"Dan was right. My soul's in peril." I sang "Can't Get No Satisfaction" under my breath.

"He's crazy, Eddie," Father Pat said, as he pointed at me.

"Padre? Who's crazier? Is it the guys who search for the Christus or the priest who comes along to observe the crazy guys?"

"I didn't say you were crazy, Eddie."

"I have to be fucking insane. If I get out of this, I'll get my daughter to commit me."

Since we had a plan—I know it wasn't a good plan, but it was a plan—Eddie and I made Father Pat hunker down in a corner. Eddie stood watch, while I crawled around the campsite in the dark gathering the gear that we'd need. I'd searched Fleet and his bag for his satellite device. I couldn't locate it. He must have left it in the ATV.

A lot of good it'll do us up there, Captain Air Assault, I thought, though I regretted my rancor at once. *You were a good man, Fleet. I wish we'd been more careful.*

I reloaded the shotgun, chambered a round, and slipped the eighth shell in the tube. I didn't care if the noise carried. Maybe that sound would give our attackers something to think about. I stuffed the remaining shells in the side pocket of my vest.

I continued to pull together the gear that we needed for our trek. While I worked, Eddie briefed us on our goal. He'd discovered that a place called White Horse Lake lay about 12 miles to the west, northwest, as the buzzard flies. He said it was a small body of water, but looked like it had a campground and maybe a small store.

While there were no trails from Schnebly Tank to the lake, the terrain would not be too difficult once we got over the canyon walls to our west. Eddie said that if we went north up the canyon and away from the ruins, in a mile we'd encounter a saddle. The saddle looked negotiable. It formed a pass of sorts over the canyon to the west.

We'd try to sneak out to the north, then head west. We'd escape and evade our pursuers. We'd go as fast as we could manage, back track, lay false trails, and use every trick we could think of. We'd stand and fight, when we had no other option.

We'd have to travel light. After weapons and ammunition, water was the primary item. I had at least four-and-a-half liters. Eddie had a similar amount. We took another two from Dave's kit. Father Pat had two.

I carried a device for water purification. The recent rain would have filled tanks between our campsite and White Horse Lake. Water would not be our problem. If we didn't reach the lake in two days, we'd be dead anyway.

I told the priest that as a non-combatant, he'd carry as much of the water as he could bear. I thought about it for about 20 minutes. We'd take the AK-103. I'd carry it, an extra magazine, the shotgun, and my handguns. It was a load, but I could manage, if Father Pat helped with the water, medical kit, and food.

In the dark, the shotgun was the better weapon. I locked and loaded the AK-103, engaged the safety, folded the stock, and strapped it to my pack. I removed the magazine from my Glock, checked it, confirmed that it was loaded, and reseated it. I re-holstered the automatic in my vest. I stuffed Gretchen's .38 into my waistband.

We could do nothing for Dave Fleet. I didn't want to leave his body behind, but we had no choice. If we got out of this ambush,

I'd come back for him. I grabbed my rosary and said a decade for his soul.

Eddie secured Fleet's pistol. He disassembled the other weapons and scattered the parts around the campsite. He unloaded the magazines for the other AKs. Right before we left, he tossed all the rounds that we weren't taking into the coals of the fire. They wouldn't cook off, but they'd be too hot to reload.

I had a Trimble Outdoors GPS map application on my iPhone. As I waited for Eddie and Father Pat to adjust their gear, I used the phone's GPS satellite technology. So far, it had operated flawlessly on the earlier hikes. I found a dark corner, knelt down, pulled the windbreaker over my head, and I took a moment to view the map of Northern Arizona. Since it was digital, I could zoom in and out. I checked out the path that Eddie claimed would get us over the canyon walls and onto the terrain to the west.

The Trimble confirmed Eddie's analysis. If we could get away from Schnebly Tank, we had a fighting chance to get to White Horse Lake in two days. Either our cell phones would work there, or other campers with vehicles would be there to assist us. I asked Father Pat to say a prayer.

Eddie and I had iPhones. We appropriated Fleet's smartphone as backup. To preserve the battery, I turned Fleet's off. Father Pat had a Blackberry of all things. I'd brought a small, portable phone recharger. If we kept our phones off most of the time, and used the recharger, we'd be OK.

We could check our position from time to time, and communicate if we ever found phone service. Otherwise, our fate was in the hands of the rusty map reading and patrolling skills of two long-retired grunts.

God save us, I thought.

I'd had plenty of warning that something bad could happen on this quest. I'd allowed my obsession to overcome good judgment. Yet nothing that I'd encountered in the run up to the gunfight with the well-armed assailants would have given warning of this level of violence. I blessed our decision to carry the heavier weapons. If we hadn't, we'd be dog meat. Since there is no serendipity, our preparation for the enemy assault must have been part of the Grand Plan.

I recalled firefights in the Central Highlands. I'd fired shots in anger. I had tried to kill my enemy. My heart had felt the rage driven by fear of death and the will to survive.

Though I'd shot and wounded an NVA sapper, before tonight I couldn't claim an individual confirmed kill. Throughout my life, I'd feigned an air of innocence, as if my participation in the violent events in Vietnam had been something less than homicidal.

Now, for the first time, I knew that without a doubt that I'd killed at least one other man, whose body lay broken on the ground, his blood draining into the sandstone from his neck wound. I felt neither elation nor guilt. I'd do it again in a heartbeat.

"OK, Tony, how do you want to proceed?" Eddie asked me, as he cradled the M14 in the crook of his left arm.

"I'll go first. We must maintain total sound and light discipline," I whispered. "Since it's so dark, we have to stay close. Watch for my signals. Father you're second. Pass my signals back to Eddie, who'll be right behind you. No speaking, OK?"

"I don't understand you're bloody signals, mate."

"Father, mimic what I do, and copy my actions. If I crouch, you crouch. If I crawl, you crawl," I explained.

"And if he runs, you run like hell, Padre," Eddie added.

"Last thing Father, if Eddie and I get it, there's a pass about a mile up this creek. Wade across the creek. Then go up the canyon wall to the west. It's steep but for a climber like you, it'll be piece of cake. Father, do you have a compass?"

"No."

"Take my Casio watch," I said. "If you press the button on the top right it'll go into compass mode and give you an azimuth from the twelve o'clock position of the watch. Eddie, what's the azimuth from the pass to the lake?"

"Two-ninety-two degrees."

"Father, once you get to the top of the pass, shoot an azimuth and follow two-ninety-two degrees as best as you can, but watch your back. God be with you both."

"Tony."

"Yes, Father,"

"*Ego te absolvo*," Father Pat said in Latin, as he blessed me.

"Thank you, Father," I said, tears in my eyes. I could feel the weight of all the sins of 30 years leave me. "I thought you said you couldn't give me absolution."

"I changed my mind. We're not going to make it out of here. You'll never see Gretchen again. In the brief time we all have left, you won't have much occasion to sin."

"Sounds right to me," Eddie said.

"Tony."

"Yes, Father?" I asked, impatient to skulk out of the campsite.

"Your penance will be one sincere Act of Contrition."

"OK, Father," I acknowledged the lenient penance.

"And three hundred rosaries. Ten for each year. You've had a cavalier attitude for over three decades. You can wait until we get to White Horse Lake to say the rosaries."

"Father, if we ever get to White Horse Lake, I'll say four hundred rosaries."

CHAPTER TWELVE

August 30, 2013, 10:15 a.m.
Two and a Half Miles Southeast of White Horse Lake
Coconino National Forest, Arizona

TUCKED BEHIND A tall ponderosa pine, I tried to wipe the sweat from my eyes with the soiled left sleeve of my Blackhawk shirt. I hefted the AK-103 and pressed the short stock into my sore shoulder. I moved my face around the stock until I established a comfortable cheek-weld, where I could focus on the front sight. I looked down the barrel toward the bend in the trail where the assailants would appear in the next few moments.

Though apprehensive, I held the pistol grip of the rifle firmly. The index finger of my right hand longed for the trigger.

Through sheer force of will, I managed to regulate my breathing. I had less success controlling the tremble in my right leg. In the prone position, my leg would not interfere with my accuracy.

While I waited for the unknown villains to advance into our kill zone, I remembered my first months in Vietnam and the ambush patrols that I went on with my platoon. During the first days of the Tet Offensive, my battalion had eviscerated the NVA and the VC in our area of operations. In the immediate aftermath, when I joined the unit, we didn't encounter significant enemy fighters on those patrols.

Still, the exercise of setting up an ambush to kill human beings was nerve-wracking. Now my training and experience would pay off. I knew that in a few moments, I would kill again.

As I checked my weapon for the tenth time, I remembered a passage that Ross Carter had written in his World War II reminiscence, *Those Devils in Baggy Pants.* He'd conquered his fear of the Nazis by focusing on what he would do to his enemy and refusing to contemplate what they might do to him. I followed his example.

Consistent with Carter's philosophy, I rehearsed our plan. If I wanted to survive this next encounter, I had to focus. Despite the looming danger, I could not help but recall the last stanza of the poem of "The Young British Soldier" by Rudyard Kipling.

> When you're wounded and left on Afghanistan's plain,
> And the women come out to cut up what remains,
> Jest roll to your rifle and blow out your brains,
> An' go to your Gawd like a soldier.

These might be my last moments. It gave me an inexplicable comfort to think that I might die in battle. If I met my fate this day, I'd avoid all of the misfortunes of senior citizenship. I'd go to my God like a good soldier in the state of grace. There is no serendipity.

The fact that Eddie, Father Pat, and I had escaped from Schnebly Tank and out of the box canyon confirmed that the age of miracles had not passed. As we had planned, Eddie, Father Pat, and I had skulked along the narrow path that stretched north from the overhang along the rock face.

For the first 100 yards, we had thick cover from the foliage. We neither heard nor detected an enemy presence.

When the little trail opened up, we stayed along the rock face. We kept low, stopped, and listened every 50 paces. We made good time over the next 300 yards.

A quarter mile from our campsite, we stopped and listened for five full minutes. Eddie came close and whispered in my ear.

"I heard some movement a few seconds ago," he said.

"Where?"

"Sounded like a couple of hundred yards south of us. So north of our campsite."

"Was it coming this way?"

"Can't tell, ears are still ringing. But I don't think so. We got the jump on them."

I mulled this over for five seconds. "Let's wade the creek here. Once we're across, we head north again. We have three-quarters of a mile to the saddle," I said.

"Why not?" Eddie said.

We whispered a brief direction to Father Pat and began a stealthy movement across the creek. Once we hit the water, two things surprised me. The water was cold as hell and it was deeper than I'd hoped. The flow from the rainstorm had lessened. While we had to struggle in the waist-high water, we didn't get swept away. We made it to the western bank of the swollen creek in ten minutes.

Soaked and cold, we headed north. We increased our pace along the west bank. We maintained our discipline, but the faster we trekked the more noise we made. I stopped us four times, both to rest and to listen before we reached the one-mile point. No one seemed to be following us.

Even in the dark, with the ambient light from a crescent moon in a sky broken by clouds, we recognized the saddle. I made everyone take a long drink. Hydrated, we started up the mountain.

We had 600 vertical feet to the top. The climb was tricky, arduous, and steep. Negotiable is a subjective term for older men carrying a lot of equipment in the dark. In the daylight without the need for stealth, the climb would have been hard. At night, it was a bitch on fire.

About half way up, Father Pat grabbed my arm and whispered in my ear.

"Tony, let me lead. I can find the way faster than you. I may be able to pick a better path to the top."

"Go ahead. Be careful where you put your hands. Watch out for snakes."

With Pat in the lead, we made better progress. He knew his way around a climb.

As we got to the top of the saddle, the sky in the east had begun to lighten. We had less than an hour before dawn. We rested and had a council of war.

"Gentlemen," I began. "I know we planned to move on now, but I think we should wait for a couple of hours. We're tired. We could use the rest. If we did get away undetected, the remaining thugs might assault the campsite at dawn. When they find us gone, they might track us this way. If they try to come after us, we have a huge defensive advantage up here."

"Tony, that's a lot of ifs. Stick to the plan," Eddie said.

"What do you think, Pat?" I asked.

"There's been more bloodshed than I ever want to see. Let's do what we can to avoid more. Let's get a good foot under us and head for the lake," Father Pat said.

"Tony, if they think we went north, they might fuck around in the canyon for a couple of hours trying to figure out which way we got out," Eddie pressed.

"OK. Majority rules. Kumbaya," I said. "But nobody blame me if we have to fight again and don't have this advantage."

"Well, that's settled. Let's get moving toward the lake. The sooner we get there the better," Eddie said.

"I agree," Father Pat said. "Tony, you have a lot of praying to do once we get there."

"Father Pat?" I asked.

"Yes, Tony."

"Are you related to a nun, a BVM named Sister Mary Erintrude? She'd have been a great aunt, very tall, heavy set, dour, mean-spirited, sadistic. She was Irish too."

"Sorry, I don't think so," the priest said.

"I'd have put money on it. You two have so much in common."

We spent the next day-and-a-half executing our plan. Since we had to make false trails and backtrack—and because the terrain was more difficult than we expected—we'd managed seven miles toward the lake by the end of the first day. My trusty Trimble app calculated our actual course. The circuitous trek had covered over 14 difficult miles.

Exhausted, we stopped for the night on a wooded knoll that had an excellent vista to the east where we perceived the greatest threat. Eddie and the priest gathered brush to help camouflage our position. I stood watch and scanned with Fleet's binoculars for any sign of pursuit. I saw deer, antelope, a pack of coyotes prowling through the trees, but no humans.

Though we were in a fight for our lives and were fleeing a dangerous enemy of undetermined strength, as I stood surveying the countryside I felt exhilarated. I told you that there hasn't been a day in my life that I didn't want to be a soldier. That includes every single day since I retired. In the strangest way, this dangerous episode was a gift.

After we finished preparing our primitive lager, we tried all of our phones, but had no cell tower reception. We used the charger to renew the batteries on the iPhones so we would be ready the next day. We'd leave at dawn. With any luck we would make the lake by noon the next day.

All of us were dog-tired. We'd stand watches using the classic two on, four off regimen. We played rock, paper, and scissors for first watch. I won.

Although I woke up at least once an hour, I did manage to get some rest. The night passed without incident.

In the morning, my right knee had swollen from the difficult trek. I'd had surgery 30 years earlier from a Rugby injury. It had never given me trouble. But this was the first time in decades that I'd humped so much weight, over so far a distance, and up so many hills. I tested my knee. I'd make it to the lake. I wouldn't win any sprints.

Before we set out, we had another council. Eddie would take point. I'd bring up the rear. Eddie pulled out his trail map and spread it on the ground. He pointed out the route that we'd take. Although my Trimble said that it was less than six miles to the lake, Eddie's roundabout path would be closer to ten.

"Listen, mates," Father Pat said. "If the mad men had pursued us, we'd have seen some sign of them by now. You two either killed or wounded the primary attackers. The others, if any, have lost their zeal. Let's head straight for the lake."

"Father, you may be the best Irish priest since Saint Patrick, but you're no soldier," Eddie told him. "There are old soldiers like Tony and me, and there are bold soldiers. There are no old, bold soldiers."

"Father Pat," I said, putting a hand on his shoulder. "Eddie and I will get you home or we'll die trying. I give you my word as an Army officer. We go with Eddie's plan."

"What happened to kumbaya?" Father Pat asked.

"Fuck kumbaya! Our complacency and misjudgment cost the life of one of our party. I don't have any spare friends. You're one of my friends. We'll follow Eddie and have a much better chance to get home, Chaplain," I said.

"Chaplain? Who says I'm your bloody chaplain?" Father Pat asked.

"God."

"Are you crazy?"

"Why else are you here, other than to minister to old soldiers on a divinely inspired quest? Think about it. Your presence in Arizona, Sedona—here, in this forest—none of this is an accident. Pat, there is no serendipity."

"If I live through this, I'll never leave Ireland again," he said, shaking his head.

Eddie set a fast pace. Though my knee throbbed, I kept up and didn't complain. I'd never fallen out of a hump. This would be my last one.

By ten a.m. we'd covered over seven miles and were two-and-a-half miles on a straight shot from White Horse Lake. We stopped for our last rest, water, and comfort break.

Eddie had picked the spot well. We settled halfway up the last rise in the terrain before the lake, inside a tree line covered in ponderosa pines. Though we'd crept through the woods on our devious path, to our east a wide-open alpine meadow about a mile long and half-a-mile wide lay stretched out behind us.

While the others relieved themselves, I scanned the east with Fleet's field glasses. I was about to put the glasses down when I spotted movement at the eastern edge of the meadow, inside the tree line. At first, I thought it might be deer or elk. It was neither.

Eddie had returned and noticed my interest to the east.

"What's up?" he asked as he approached me.

"I see three men, inside the tree line, east of us," I answered as I went prone to support my arms and to reduce my personal signature. Eddie flopped down next to me.

"Can I have a look?" Eddie asked, reaching for the glasses.

"Sure," I said, handing the binoculars over. "What do you make of them?"

"Hunters," Eddie suggested.

"What hunting season is this?"

"Poachers?" Eddie offered in the alternative.

Father Pat had come up, noticed our posture, read the reason, and low crawled over to us. He gazed to the east, trying to see what we were observing.

A moment later, three men walked out of the tree line, about a mile east of our position. They moved abreast with one man in the front. The leader stopped, knelt down and examined the ground. All three had weapons, but even with the aid of the binoculars, Eddie couldn't identify the type.

"They're trying to track something," Eddie said.

"Thanks to you, we didn't come that way," I said. "Maybe they are poachers looking for game."

"What's that?" Father Pat asked, as he pointed to the northeast.

Eddie and I looked to where Pat had pointed. A Jeep sped out of the tree line near where we had trekked past this meadow. The Jeep contained two men. It headed for the three men in the meadow.

A minute later, an all-terrain vehicle roared out of the same tree line. As it got closer, we could see two men in the front, and another in the back. The man in the back held onto a large German Shepherd.

Once they all got together, they held a conference. I had a premonition.

"They can't be poachers. It's broad daylight. They're too close to the lake. Some of the campers might hike out this way. Poaching is night work," I said.

"Maybe they're constables," Father Pat said. "Some hiker found the bodies in the canyon, reported it. Wouldn't it make sense that the local Sheriff would form a posse, like in the westerns? That's why they have a dog."

"I hope you're right Father," I said. "I just don't think so."

"Me, either," Eddie agreed.

"Why?" Father Pat asked.

"Instinct," Eddie said. "Those men don't act like law enforcement or soldiers. None of them is wearing a uniform. All are dressed in dark clothes, which tend to stand out on that meadow. Everyone has a long gun. If they were the deputies, some would have pistols. I can't see for certain, but I'll bet each of the weapons is a Kalashnikov. Local deputies don't use that weapon."

Taking the field glasses back, I observed the group. One of the men was upset. You could see it from his angry gestures and posturing.

"What do you think, Eddie?" I asked.

"We need to pick the best spot to stand and fight. They have vehicles. We're close, but it's too far to make a run for the lake. Besides, if they catch us at the lake, they could still wipe us out," Eddie estimated.

I checked the Trimble app while Father Pat used the field glasses. I found a spot about 300 yards farther west at the apex of the rise. A small trail from the lake ran under and along it from east to west.

"Eddie, let's set up here," I suggested as I pointed to the spot. Eddie noted the position. He looked at his trail map and found the place.

"Then what?" He asked.

"We set a false trail down this path toward the lake. If they're tired and think they have us, they may get complacent again. We set up here and here," I said as I pointed to separate positions on the map. "We catch them in a cross fire, and reduce their advantage. Father Pat leaves all of his equipment. He takes two of the phones and hauls his skinny Irish ass for the lake. At the very least, we'll buy time for Pat to get away."

"You plan to ambush those men? I cannot support that. We don't know who they are. I gave you absolution and you're planning mass homicide," Father said.

"Now listen to me," Eddie snapped. "I don't like this anymore than you do. But you don't understand the situation. If it hadn't been for Tony and me, you'd be dead at the campsite. Now do what Tony says or I'll kick your butt and send you on your way, Father."

"You Yanks are so bloody arrogant. I grew up in Belfast at the worst of the Troubles. Don't ever tell me that I don't understand violence, you old bugger. I understand it all too well. I deplore it and the men who use it without just cause."

"Sorry, Pat," Eddie said. "I didn't know."

"Stupid man. I won't abandon my mates and make a run for it. I'm no coward. What happens to you, old man, happens to me. When this is over, we'll see who kicks whose ass!"

"My money's on the Irish kid," I said to Eddie with a smile. "He's scrappy."

Eddie and I laughed out loud. Father Pat looked at us and shook his head.

"I am doomed. I've enlisted in the lunatic brigade."

Recognizing Pat's fear and depression, I started singing an old IRA rebel song, *Come Out Ye Black and Tans*. It's nearly 100 years old. I learned it playing Rugby with the Carlisle Gaelics.

Father Pat first looked astounded, then smiled and joined in.

"If the fucking glee club is done, we need to get moving. The men on foot are boarding the vehicles. They're heading this way. Let's go." Eddie said, as turned from watching the men in the meadow.

Even with all of my equipment and weapons, I managed the 300 yards in less than three minutes. When we got to the trail, we recognized it at once. On the ground, my selected positions seemed more favorable than on the map. We'd have ten feet in elevation over anyone on the trail. The trick would be to get the bad guys to take the bait and proceed down the path into a kill zone.

Since they had a dog and tracker, we walked along the trail past our planned positions, intending to double back. We didn't want to make it too obvious, but we left sign for them to follow. To ensure that the dog would follow the trail, I rolled up my sleeves and rubbed my bare forearms so that the minute dead skin cells would litter the trail. Since I hadn't urinated at the rest stop, I walked down the trail beyond our positions for 20 meters, exposed and evacuating my bladder along the way.

"Tony, I never saw that trick before. Clever," Eddie complimented me.

"Just thought of it," I answered.

"Now you have five hundred rosaries," Father Pat said.

"For what?" I demanded.

"Indecent exposure in furtherance of homicidal mayhem," Father answered, but he had a brave smile on his face.

"Did you ever play Rugby, Father?"

"No, I'm a cricketer. I have a premonition that you have, Tony. It would explain a lot about what's wrong with you."

"Wing forward." I said, describing my position on the All American Rugby Club at Bragg.

"Number Eight," Eddie said, and we fist bumped, "At Campbell."

"Well, it could be worse. I go to Last Judgment with two insane, Jesuit-trained, Airborne Rugby players. You two will spend one hundred thousand years in purgatory. I'm a cinch to go to Heaven."

After we doubled back, we set up with Eddie and me 20 yards apart on the same side of the trail at place where it curved. I had the position furthest west. We had different perspectives on the trail. We could create an effective crossfire with a shallow angle. We didn't have the time or equipment to dig in. I found the biggest tree that I could, and lay behind its trunk with as little as possible exposed.

We dispersed all of our non-lethal equipment to Pat. We insisted that he hunker down 30 yards beyond our position. If it went as I feared, Pat was to run for it.

I ensured that the shotgun was loaded. I laid it to my right, barrel facing the trail.

I unlimbered the AK-103, unsnapping the folding stock. I checked the chamber and verified that I'd seated a round. I pulled the magazine and confirmed that I'd filled it with every bullet it would take. This AK uses a round in the same caliber—but shorter by 12mm—than the bullets in Eddie's M14. After reseating the mag, I turned the weapon over and put the selector in the three-round-burst mode. I set the spare magazine on the ground to my left. I intended to fight from the prone position as long as I could.

I hadn't fired an AK in 20 years and I had never fired a 103. I felt nervous about using an unfamiliar weapon in so dire a circumstance. On the other hand, I'd employed the shotgun two days earlier. I had great confidence in it. I had two pistols. I'd give a good accounting.

We hunkered down and waited. Ten minutes later, we heard them coming through the woods. Eddie and I kept low. As they approached, I could see the bad guys. I confirmed, yet again, that I'd disengaged the safeties on both my main weapons.

The villains had adopted a strong tactical formation. But they were moving fast—maybe a little too fast.

The dog had taken point. It appeared to be a big Alsatian, at least 100 pounds. The handler was medium height and weight. He controlled the dog on a long line. He was a professional.

For a moment, I wondered if these guys might be law enforcement. I'd never heard of gangs of any kind that used trained tracking dogs.

I rejected the law enforcement possibility, when I saw the three men with AKs, walking abreast behind the tracker. One of them was the passenger in the Jeep from two days earlier. I confirmed my suspicion when I got a better look at the Jeep. The driver was the same man, who'd had warned us off his mining claim.

Fleet had been right, I thought. *My conscience is clear. They murdered Fleet. I will kill as many of them as I can before they get me.*

As the handler and his dog approached the portion of the trail that we'd designated as the kill zone, the ATV came into view behind the Jeep. All told, we had eight hostiles and a big dog. Chances were that even if we prevailed, either Eddie or I would buy the farm.

I said an Act of Contrition for me, and a Hail Mary for Eddie. I'd received absolution.

I said a mental good bye to Gretchen, Tim, and John.

I asked St. Michael to pray that God would give me courage. I knew that everything that I'd ever done in my life had been in preparation for the next few minutes. I remembered the prayer of the Astronauts: "Please God, don't let me fuck this up."

Our plan was for me to take out all of the men on the ground. Eddie would focus on the vehicles.

I'd sweep to the right through the dog handler and the rank behind him with the AK-103. I'd then sweep back to the left—using short bursts to provide the coup de grace. If the dog charged me up the hill while I was reloading the AK, I'd take it out with the shotgun.

At the last second, the caravan of killers stopped short of our kill zone. The tracker sensed something amiss, though his dog had bought our ruse hook, line, and sinker.

"What's the hold up, Larry?" The driver of the Jeep called out.

"Don't like it, Steve. Something's wrong," Larry, the dog handler, answered.

The dog sniffed around and pulled impatiently on his line.

"Hey, man; the dogs got the scent. What's your problem?" Steve asked.

"This could be a setup, Steve," Larry said. "These guys are better in the field than we anticipated. They've shown that they can defend themselves."

"Let's get on with it! If they get to a road, we may have to cap more people. If we keep fucking around, they'll get away."

"Steve, this trail is too fucking good. They've been resourceful the last day and a half. This is too obvious. They want us to go down the path. You saw what they did to Ramon and his boys."

Larry's warning caused the other men to shift around, check their weapons, and become more vigilant.

Larry, you fucker! I thought, as I watched him. *In a couple of minutes, you'll be dead. I promise you. You're first on my list.*

Steve thought the situation over. My angst and fear returned. I could feel my heart beat in my chest. My blood pressure teetered on the stroke point.

When I thought the assassins in the Jeep would dismount and look around, Father Pat appeared on the trail about 70 yards west of our kill zone. He must have snuck over there while Eddie and I focused on the killers. He was within view of the tracker, his dog, the men on the ground, and Steve in the Jeep.

"Hello!" Father Pat yelled at the men in an exaggerated brogue. "Are you lads looking for me?"

"Get that fucker!" Steve ordered. "Shoot the son of a bitch!"

Larry unsnapped the line on his dog and gave an order in German. The dog snarled, bared its teeth, and took out after Father Pat. The men and the vehicles all lurched forward, inside the kill zone.

The passenger in the Jeep stood up and leveled a bolt-action rifle with a scope. It had a sound suppressor on the front of the barrel.

I didn't wait for him to fire. I sent a burst of 7.62 x .39 caliber bullets his way. The Jeep was 40 yards from my position. I didn't have time to aim. I didn't care. Even if my shots didn't kill the sniper, they'd distract him so that he couldn't aim the weapon at the Irish kid.

Less than a second later I raked the four men in front. I focused on fire discipline, absorbing the recoil, and not allowing the barrel of the Kalashnikov to rise. All four went down firing back. Several of their rounds hit the tree that I used for cover. The bullets tore branches and peppered the ground all around me.

As Eddie concentrated his fire on the two vehicles, I worked back to the left hitting each of the men on the ground at least twice. None of them got up.

I emptied the magazine in 30 seconds. The bolt on an AK does not lock back when empty. I racked it to confirm. I released the spent mag. I reached to left. The spare mag was not where I'd set it down. I didn't have time to look for it. I set the AK down and reached for the shotgun, glad that I'd taken the time to lock and load it.

Eddie did his usual fine work with the M14. He cleaned out the two thugs in the ATV. They didn't know what hit them. The last thing I saw before we stopped firing was the sniper in the Jeep absorbing the impact of two bursts of Eddie's M14. I'd not taken him out with my first shots.

I surveyed the scene. I looked around for Father Pat and the dog but couldn't see them. I counted seven assailants down. I couldn't locate the driver of the Jeep.

I called to Eddie. He said he was fine. We'd given up our positions, so I felt that we lost nothing in communicating. There was still a homicidal maniac out there somewhere.

We waited. Nothing. Five long minutes passed. I had to pee. Couldn't risk it.

I heard a slight scraping sound behind me. I knew it was the driver. I couldn't fathom how he got out of the kill zone and behind me.

I turned as fast as I could to bring the shotgun to bear. Steve, the killer, was on me before I could raise the weapon. I'm strong, but Steve was stronger. We rolled around and wrestled with the shotgun before he wrenched it from my hands. I was in too close to shoot. He hit me across the head with the barrel.

It was a glancing blow. He drew blood. I saw stars. He tried to stand up, but I grabbed his shirt and pulled him down. I reached for my Glock. He knocked it from my hand with the butt of the shotgun.

I always carry a K-Bar lock-blade knife. I keep it clipped to the inside of my right pants' pocket. I can open it and bring it to bear in less than a second.

I pulled the knife with my right hand, as I gripped the barrel of the shotgun with my left. I stabbed Steve in the abdomen, causing him to cry out and pull the trigger of the shotgun three times. I twisted the knife, pulled it out, and stabbed him again in his left side. I sank all four inches of blade, leaving the knife in him. He howled and pulled at the gun with all his might.

Though I had a grip on the hot barrel of the shotgun with my left hand, and I had stabbed Steve twice, he pulled the barrel from my grasp, firing another two shells in the process. Still too close to bring the weapon to bear; he rapped me hard across the right side of my face with the barrel. He opened up my cheek. I felt a tooth break.

In desperation, Steve tried to pull back. I felt my waistband and located Gretchen's .38. Before Steve could turn the barrel on me, I pulled the revolver. Firing as fast as possible, I shot Steve five times in the face, throat, and neck.

Blood, bone, brain, sinew, muscle, and tissue burst from every wound spraying everything around us. Steve, withered, dropped the shotgun onto my chest, and slipped into a heap next to me, his dark red blood pumping in streams, soiling my shirt, pants, and the ground.

Eddie ran up. He looked me over as I tried to stand.

"Tony, I'd have shot him, but he was too close. Couldn't risk hitting you."

I had a hard time talking. I couldn't breathe. I worried that my jaw might be broken. Small streams of blood poured from the top of my head, my cheek, and my mouth.

"Geez, Tony. This guy's a mess."

"What do you expect? I shot him five times in the head," I slurred.

"Why?" Eddie asked.

"Those were all the bullets I had in the gun!" I garbled through my bloody mouth.

Eddie made me sit down. He retrieved the medical kit and tended to my wounds. He stopped the bleeding, covering the open cuts on my head and cheek.

"The cut on your head is superficial. It'll be fine. You'll need some sutures on this cheek. It looks like oral surgery on your jaw. He fucked up your tooth."

"I was none too gentle with him," I said.

Eddie found small cotton rolls in the kit. We jammed them into my mouth. I looked like I had the world's largest chaw. The bleeding slowed.

I stood up after taking two of the industrial-strength pain pills from the kit. I recovered the AK, shotgun, the Glock, and my knife from Steve's side. I located the missing magazine. An errant round from one of the killers had sent it flying about ten feet.

Eddie and I reloaded our weapons. We walked over to the ambushed caravan. We examined the other seven men. All were as dead as their leader. I walked over to a tree and peed for a full minute.

When we were about to go looking for Father Pat, he came up with the dog in tow. The dog acted as obedient and meek as could be.

"What happened to you, Tony?"

"You should see the other guy, Padre," I garbled through the cotton.

"What's with the dog?" Eddie asked, noting for the first time that the priest was bleeding from deep scratches on both his forearms. There were no bite marks.

"I choked him out," Father said.

"You did what?"

"In Northern Ireland," Father began, "We learned that the Brits train dogs to go for your arm. If you keep cool, you can lure the dog in and grab it by the throat. This beast weighs at least eight stone. But once I got my hands on his throat and lifted him, all he could do is scratch at me. He passed out from the lack of oxygen. When he woke, he was disoriented. He'll cooperate with us now."

Eddie took care of Father Pat's arms while my painkillers kicked in. The dog curled at the feet of the priest. I checked my phone. We still had no bars.

When Eddie finished, the three of us pulled the dead men from the vehicles and lined them up on the side of the path. Eddie had humped his camera, so he photographed everything. We gathered all their weapons and put them in the back of the Jeep.

Eddie tried to start the Jeep. It was useless. He opened the hood.

"Mother fuck!" Eddie swore. "Some dickhead fired into the engine. It's kaput."

"Looks, like the work of an M14," I said, looking over Eddie's shoulder, not wanting to take the blame.

"More like poorly aimed shots from an AK," Eddie said. "Anyway, in battle, shit happens. Let's see if the ATV works. I don't feel like humping this crap out of here."

The ATV started. Blood and human tissue covered the seats, but we weren't choosy. We transferred the weapons to the carrier on the back of the ATV.

While we loaded the vehicle, I realized that we'd compromised this crime scene. But we needed to appropriate a vehicle and get medical assistance. We couldn't leave the weapons in the forest unsecured. We had no way to call the authorities. We'd cross the crime scene bridge with the deputies who came to our aid.

Father said prayers over the dead men, and asked for forgiveness for what Eddie and I had done. I didn't feel the slightest guilt. I didn't see the need for forgiveness. In the last two days, we'd fought off a dozen homicidal madmen. It might have been the medication or the adrenalin but I felt high, six beers high.

We got into the ATV and Father Pat called the dog in German. The Alsatian jumped into the empty seat.

"I think I'll call him 'Adolf,'" Father Pat said. "Like the dog you saw at the chapel all those years ago."

"That dog's name was Rommel, Father," I said.

"But Gretchen said..."

"Long story, Father. I'll explain another time."

I pulled out my phone and turned it on. After entering my code, I opened the Trimble app. I hit the icon for our position and created a waypoint, so that I could give the local Sheriff the exact coordinates of the battlefield. Eddie started the ATV, put it into gear, and we motored down the track past the bodies of the killers.

"Pat," Eddie began loud enough for the kid to hear in the back of the ATV.

"Yes, Eddie."

"What possessed you to go out in front of those killers like that? You had to know how dangerous that was."

"It's an old trick. Let the enemy see you. They chase. Your mates ambush them."

"I don't want to know where you learned that," Eddie said.

"Gentlemen, do you think that's all of them? By my count, you've killed twelve men over the last few days." Father said.

"I hope so, but I'm not so sure," I said.

"Hope for the best, and expect the worst. That's my motto," Eddie added.

Less than 20 minutes later, we pulled into the campgrounds around White Horse Lake. I had three bars on my phone. We could communicate. We stayed away from the other campers. I called the emergency number.

"Coconino County Sheriff, what's your emergency?"

I removed the cotton from my mouth so I could speak better.

"My name is Tony Giordano. I'm law enforcement from Florida. Two of my friends and I have been on a hike to Schnebly Tank. Some unknown assailants killed our guide there. His body and the bodies of at least three of the assailants are still there. He's retired from your agency, Detective David Fleet. We couldn't communicate with you guys, so we ran from the killers.

"We went west," I continued. "Before we could get to White Horse Lake, the rest of the homicidal crew caught up with us. We shot it out with them. I'm wounded. My other two friends are OK. Eight more of the bad guys are dead. We left their bodies on the trail. I have the coordinates."

"Mr. Gordani," the operator started.

"It's Giordano, miss," I snapped.

"Sir, if this is a joke, you should know that there are severe criminal penalties for false police reports in Arizona."

"Miss, I wish this was a false report."

"You say you're wounded?"

"Yes, Ma'am." We're at White Horse Lake Campground. We need assistance."

"We'll dispatch a unit from Williams immediately. How will we recognize you?"

"One white male, sixties, five-feet-eleven, one-ninety-five, brown / grey and bleeding from three head wounds. One black male early sixties, six-foot-one, one-ninety, brown / black and driving a shot up ATV. One white male, thirty-something, five-feet-eleven, one-seventy, blue / red and Irish as Patty's Pig. We'll be sitting here bleeding on the northwest corner of the grounds."

"Dispatching a unit now," the operator said.

"Thanks," I said, as I rang off. I started keying in Gretchen's cell phone.

CHAPTER THIRTEEN

THE COCONINO COUNTY Sheriff's conference room reminded me of scores of similar meeting places in federal and state venues all over the country. It had a long, maple-stained wooden table, suitable for gathering a dozen attendees. The chairs were utilitarian and uncomfortable. They'd painted the walls a neutral off-white. Staged photos of deputies, employees, little-league teams, and police equipment covered the walls.

The room was too cold for my attire. The hospital had allowed me to keep a set of their dark blue surgical scrubs and slippers. The Sheriff had seized all of my clothes and equipment as evidence. I had nothing to complain about. I was safe, dry, and warm enough. The fact that I was still alive was a miracle of biblical proportions.

Where I come from, the Sheriff has over 1,200 law enforcement officers, 900 detention deputies, and 1,400 civilians to help police the unincorporated portions of our county with a population of over 1,200,000 permanent residents and millions of tourists and travelers passing through each year. He and his people do a superb job in a jurisdiction the size of Rhode Island.

In contrast, the Sheriff of Coconino County has fewer than 70 sworn deputies to patrol the second largest county in the nation with more square miles than Massachusetts. Both Sheriffs have excellent reputations in the communities that they serve because of the courage, dedication, and professionalism of their deputies and support staffs.

It is a daunting challenge to be the first responders with so few resources over so vast an area. In Flagstaff, the local police number around 100. They collocate with the Sheriff at the Saw Mill Road operational center.

I sat in the middle of this law enforcement complex, awaiting my fate and recalling the events of the day before.

Almost 40 minutes after my call from White Horse Lake, a unit from the Williams substation arrived. The deputy conducted a cautious and professional evaluation. He assessed my injuries, but insisted that we surrender all weapons to him. We helped him to secure the cache in the back of his four-wheeler.

Our cooperation and my credentials allowed him a degree of comfort regarding our intentions but—based on the violence that I described in my recorded call—he never relaxed his guard. I told you that he was a pro.

In light of my condition, he transported us to Williams after recommending to his dispatcher that the Sheriff send resources to Schnebly Tank and to the coordinates that I'd furnished for the site of the second firefight.

He apologized, but he handcuffed Eddie and me after reading us the rights outlined on his plastic Miranda card. It was the first time in my life that I'd received that kind of treatment. I understood, but I hated every second of it.

Either the deputy had only two sets of handcuffs, or he gave Father Pat a break because the priest traveled to Williams unbound. Adolf curled at Pat's feet in the foot well of the front seat. At the deputy's insistence, we journeyed in silence.

Williams is a small Arizona town. It's a way station and hub for AMTRAC and trains to the Grand Canyon. It has services for the hordes of tourists who come and go along I 40. It does not have a hospital.

The deputy dropped Eddie and Father Pat at the substation. He took me to an urgent care facility in town, where a doctor cleaned my wounds and sutured my face. He could do nothing for my tooth other than to provide pain medication. The deputy took possession of the pills after I swallowed the initial dose.

Still handcuffed, I fell asleep in the back of his four-wheeler. I didn't wake up until we arrived in Flagstaff. The deputy took me to the Medical center where they called in an oral surgeon. After she pulled what was left of the tooth, I spent the night in the hospital, handcuffed to my bed with a Flagstaff police officer hovering nearby.

The next morning, I asked the police officer what the deal was.

"Are you really the chief legal counsel for a Sheriff in Florida?" asked the officer—an experienced man in his forties—as he looked me over, not quite believing the rumor that he'd heard.

"Yes," I said.

"Look, man," the officer began. "I have strict orders not to question you or talk to you about what you guys did."

"No kidding?"

"Yeah, but I hate treating one of our own like this."

"Where are my friends?"

"At the operations center at Saw Mill."

"Am I under arrest for something?" I asked.

"I don't know. The Chief of Police believes that Dave Fleet's been killed along with several others. This is the biggest thing since we lost those boys in that tragedy down in Yarnell."

As I formulated another question, the officer got a call and shushed me. After he hung up, he looked at me and shook his head. "The doc is supposed to release you to my custody. I'll transport you to the operations center. They'll let you know how it's going to be once you get there."

After a quick shower, the hospital discharge, more medication, and a short drive to the Sheriff's Office, I found myself in the conference room with a deputy posted at the door. They'd removed the handcuffs and gave me coffee. I took these as good signs.

I waited in the conference room for over an hour—working on the rosaries that Father Pat had given me—before five people came in. They walked to the opposite side of the table and took seats facing me. Two acted like lawyers. I assumed the other three were cops. They reminded me of a jury returning a verdict in a difficult case.

"Mr. Giordano, I'm Joe Ledger. I'm the managing assistant U.S. Attorney in the Flagstaff Division. This is Mary Smith. She's the Chief of the Felony Prosecution Team in the Coconino County Attorney's Office. Craig Scott is a senior detective with

CSO; Chuck Hudson is a special agent from the ATF; Wayne Bennett's from the DEA," Ledger said as he gestured at each of his colleagues on the other side of the table.

"Nice to meet you," I said. "What's the deal, here? Am I under arrest?"

"No, Tony, but you're not free to go, either."

"How does that compute, Joe?" I asked. "I have a little experience in criminal law. If you're not charging me, you have to let me go."

"Tony, we know all about you. DOJ sent your e-file. You have quite a record, but you found yourself in a real shit storm in the mountains, didn't you? I know that you're hurt and on pain meds, but be patient for a couple of minutes and we'll discuss your future."

"By all means, but where are Eddie and Pat?

"All in good time, OK?"

"Fine. Since I'm a captive audience, please continue," I said.

"Let me summarize for everyone," Ledger said. "A former CSO detective was brutally murdered at Schnebly Tank. CSO deputies found three bodies near him and another corpse seventy yards south. All four died of multiple gunshots. The crime scene was tainted. We found parts of automatic weapons and ammunition all through it."

"Are you looking for comment?" I asked, when Ledger paused.

"Not yet, Mr. Giordano," Mary Smith said. "Let Joe finish."

"Late yesterday afternoon, deputies found eight more bodies near the coordinates that you gave us. Thanks to you, we already had a trunkful of weapons. So Chuck Hudson confirmed— through fingerprints and touch DNA—that most of the guns came from the dead men. We interviewed Mr. Grimes and Father O'Malley yesterday. Their stories are consistent, if not a little bizarre. What's left of the evidence and the crime scenes corroborates self-defense. Your friends are witnesses under our protection."

"So what's the problem? Why am I in custody?"

"Tony, everybody at DOJ and your people at the SO in Tampa tell us that you're a smart guy with a superb record of prosecution. Your Chief Deputy and your wife worry that you've gone off the reservation over whatever happened to you in Sedona decades ago."

"Bullshit, Joe! There are two thousand people in Sedona that are farther over the edge than I ever could be. Do you take any of them into custody?"

"Of course not," Ledger responded. "Who do you think those guys were? You know, the men that you and your pal, Grimes, whacked."

"Best guess is that they were growing illegal marijuana in the national forest. Wanted to protect their operation. Pot growers on federal land have a reputation for violence. If you've done drug cases as an AUSA, you'd know that. I'm sure Mr. Bennett from the DEA will confirm, right Wayne?" I said, as I looked at the DEA agent.

"Tony, you're right." Special Agent Bennett said. "You killed drug dealers and their muscle. I'll concede that. Turns out they were operating one of the largest illegal drug distribution centers in Arizona history. We found their operation this morning by tracking up the forest road that they tried to keep you off. We arrested another six mopes working at the site."

"No shit?" I said.

"It was a regular cornucopia," Bennett said. "They had twenty bales of high-quality powder cocaine, air-dropped from one of the cartels. Gotta be over five hundred kilos. We found kilos. I mean *kilos* of Cocaine Base. It's one of the largest Crack busts in our history. We don't ever see a commercial operation this large and complex for crack."

"No wonder they were so well armed," I said.

"Yeah, and that's not all," Craig Scott jumped in. "They had a huge hydroponic marijuana operation, too."

"Never heard of a hydroponic operation coincidental with the hard stuff," I said.

"Neither had we," Ledger said. "In fact, we're not sure that we've identified all the illegal drugs that are up there. The field tests on the marijuana are through the roof. It's the highest level of THC that we've ever seen. The lab tests will tell us more."

"So they attacked us and killed Fleet to protect their operation," I said.

"It's way more complicated than that," Mary Smith said, looking at Ledger.

"How so?" I asked.

"Let me answer this way," Ledger said. "These guys set up a large illegal drug distribution point to take advantage of the small population in—and the remoteness of—the Coconino National Forest, as well as its proximity to I-40. The interstate provides a straight shot into L.A. and all of Southern California. Once on I-40, there's not a spot on the entire West Coast they couldn't reach in fifteen hours."

"That's pretty bold of these guys," I said. "I've never encountered anything quite so daring."

"Neither had we," Bennett said. "Nor had we seen the escalation to this level of violence. We haven't identified all of the dead guys yet, but the four we've made were all violent felons."

"That makes their possession of weapons in furtherance of drug operations serious separate felonies," I said.

"We don't dispute that, Tony. We expect that the rest of those guys will have violent criminal records too," Ledger said.

"How does that play out?" I asked.

"We're concerned that this distribution point, the kind of men working it, and other evidence we've uncovered demonstrates an effort to export the drug violence south of our border to the American Southwest by a dangerous cult," Ledger said.

"Does that explain why the killers were so well armed and so violent?" I asked.

"Sort of." Chuck Hudson said. "It explains the Kalashnikovs, body armor, and tracking dog. But there's more here."

"More than violent drug dealers trying to import massive violence into your community?" I asked.

"Maybe," Hudson said. "In parts of South and Central America, where the violence has been the worst, a cult has arisen among the folks who cannot see an end to the danger and fear that their lives will be cut short. They call their cult Santo Diablo. It means Saint Devil."

"What bearing does that have on the men we shot?" I asked.

"Three of the men you killed had tattoos of Santo Diablo," Hudson said. "We found several icons and figurines of the cult figure at the drug emporium in the woods."

"I've heard of these guys. As I recall, the Catholic Church has outlawed this cult. No other Christian sect recognizes it," I said.

"I think that's correct," Mary Smith said. "We don't know exactly how all of this shakes out. We do know that you and your pals knocked over a hornet's nest and now you're in grave danger."

The state prosecutor's use of the term *hornet's nest* startled me. It's the same phrase that Dan Ostergaard used when he warned Claire 15 years earlier.

"How do you figure that this cult impacts on Fleet's murder?" I asked.

"The Cult of Santo Diablo celebrates homicide. Its beliefs are based on ancient myths and legends that claim that their patron suffered a stinging defeat from Michael the Archangel. The Santo Diablo followers call themselves the fallen angels," Smith said.

"Here's a picture of the tattoo on one of the guys you and your pal whacked," Hudson said as he slid a photograph across the table.

I picked up the photo and examined the tattoo. The figure stunned me. It was an exact replica of a petroglyph that I saw at Schnebly Tank. It was not the Christus, but it was definitely identical to a different figure carved on that rock face.

I recalled Don Hansen's explanation that inter-dimensional beings comprise different species and races from different universes. The implications frightened me. Eddie, Father Pat, and I had gotten caught up in the ancient war between angels and the demons. Maybe the entire drug war fiasco was a battlefield of that war.

I kept this revelation to myself. I didn't want to give Ledger and Smith another reason to hold me.

"I'm starting to understand. You're worried that the Santo Diablo cult has infiltrated Coconino County and poses the triple threat of illegal arms, contraband drugs, and wholesale violence," I said. "What do you want with me?"

"Tony, nobody will charge you with a criminal offense. All of the evidence supports self-defense. We'll need you as a material witness as we go after the rest of the Santo Diablo conspirators. The case gets complicated. We believe that the Diablos didn't kill Fleet to protect the drug operation," Ledger said.

"Huh?"

"We found a cell phone on the guy whose head you blew off. It was a throw down, but it had text traffic. He's Stevie Lindstrom. Had a record as long as your arm. He realized that it was Fleet guiding you. He texted someone with an untraceable phone who confirmed that Fleet was in the woods with some clients," Craig Scott explained.

"So the bad guys knew it was Fleet when they shot him?" I asked.

"That's about the size of it," Mary said. "The local dealers have wanted to take him out since he capped two of their buddies, possible Diablos, a couple of years ago."

"It'll take a lot more investigation, but we think the person who provided the information knew Fleet. The texts occurred after you guys ran into Stevie in the woods."

"So where does that leave me?" I asked.

"As I explained, you're a material witness in grave danger. If you cooperate, we'll let you stay with Mr. Grimes at his home. Mr. Grimes suggested it. The DEA, Yavapai Sheriff, and Sedona Police will help with your security. You'll have to stay in Arizona for a while."

"If I don't cooperate because I want to go home to Florida?"

"I have a material witness warrant. The Magistrate Judge has already approved it. We'll apprehend you here and take you to the Magistrate for a hearing. He can release you with the conditions that I suggest, or send you to Phoenix where we'll protect you in the Federal lockup. You know how this shit works, Tony. So why don't you cooperate?"

"What about my credentials, IDs, credit cards, guns, knives, and so forth?"

"We're keeping all the firearms and that fancy K-bar. They're evidence. You can have your other personal stuff," Detective Scott replied.

"What about my wife and sons?"

"The U.S. Marshals will provide security for your wife, since she's an AUSA. They'll assign teams to both of your sons and their families."

"What are the conditions of release? Is this like a house arrest?"

"Not quite. You can move around Sedona, but you can't do it unless two state or federal law enforcement officers accompany you. If you behave yourself and don't cause the deputies any trouble, we'll let you go home as soon as it's safe to do so," Mary Smith said.

"Agreed," I said.

"By behaving, we mean that you engage in no investigation on your own."

"Of course," I said.

"Tony, this includes this Christus thing. Put it on hold," Ledger directed.

"Who told you about that?"

"Father O'Malley. Your pal, Eddie, wouldn't discuss it. He claims that you're his lawyer and he won't discuss that issue without you," Hudson said.

"Why do you care about the Christus mystery?" I asked.

"I don't have much evidence to support this yet, but from the phone texts it appears that whoever told Stevie about Fleet knew about your personal quest. If they're part of the Santo Diablo cult, they wanted to make sure that you failed," Craig Scott said.

"Why do you think that?"

"The content of the texts, which is investigation confidential. Right now our best information is that a handful of people knew that Fleet was headed to Schnebly Tank. Three quarters of those folks were you, Grimes, and the priest. We have one good suspect, who happened to be in Sedona at the time. He claims to have an airtight alibi."

"Don Hansen. Right?"

"Bingo!" Ledger agreed.

The ride from Flagstaff down to West Sedona was surreal. It took 40 minutes. Unlike the trip from Williams, I wasn't handcuffed. I got to sit in the front seat of the four-wheeler. The deputy was a handsome white male, mid-thirties, and a seven-year veteran of CSO. He'd also been a Marine sergeant who did a tour in Afghanistan and one in Iraq. He treated me with respect, as you would expect from a kindred spirit.

"You doing all right, Mr. Giordano?" He asked about five minutes into the trip.

"Yeah, I think so."

"This shit up at Schnebly Tank wasn't your first rodeo, was it? We heard that you were a Paratrooper? Been in law enforcement too, right?"

"Right and right," I said.

"I saw what you and Grimes did near White Horse Lake. Good work, Mr. Giordano."

"Call me Tony, please."

"OK, Tony. I'm Randy Stone."

"Thanks for the ride to Sedona, Randy."

"No problem. It's my zone of patrol anyway. You'll be staying right outside my jurisdiction. If you need anything, I can get over there quick. The Yavapai deputies are first rate. I know them. They're briefed on this dirty business. They'll take good care of you."

"Did you know Fleet?" I asked.

"Yeah. He was a pal. I wish I had been with you and Grimes," Randy said.

As I watched Randy's jaw clenching, I had no doubt that he meant every word.

"I knew him for less than a day, but I liked Dave."

"Tony, I saw a lot of shit at Fallujah, if you need to talk."

"Thanks, bud."

"The PTSD can be a mother fucker. It slips up on you when you least expect it."

"Drink beer?" I asked him, as we started down Oak Creek Canyon.

"Been known to hoist a few."

"When you're off duty, come over to Eddie's. We'll swap tall tales."

"Wouldn't miss it, brother," Randy said, paying me the ultimate compliment.

"Gotta be careful drinking with these meds, though," I said.

"True," Randy said. "You do a lot of drug cases as a fed?"

"A dozen or so. When I was an AUSA, I did organized crime, violent crime, and fraud. My wife is the drug prosecutor."

"We're losing the drug war, Tony."

"We seem to be."

"There's a rumor that you saw aliens at the chapel in Sedona," Randy said.

"Wrong. When I was a kid in college, a buddy of mine and I were drinking at the chapel. We saw lights. It could have been an aircraft of some kind. That's all. I never saw any little green men."

"Detective Scott says you're a good man," Randy continued, as he mulled something over in his mind.

"Glad he thinks so. My fate is in his hands."

"He says the deputies in Florida think you're a stand-up guy. You can be trusted."

"Glad to know that, Randy. Where's this going?"

"If I tell you something, do I have attorney/client?"

"Probably not. I don't have an Arizona law license."

"Can you keep a secret, anyway?"

"Depends. If you tell me that you killed someone or committed a crime, I'd be duty bound to report it. I represent a Sheriff after all."

"Craig Scott said you'd take that position. It proves that you're honest."

"Thanks."

"I didn't kill anyone. At least, no one since Afghanistan."

"Good."

"I have seen an alien, though. But I don't want anyone to know. I love this job. I don't want anyone to question my sanity."

"Randy, I'm the last guy who can criticize you. If you want to talk about it, your secret is safe with me."

"It wasn't a little green man."

"Tell me about it."

"Two years ago, I was coming down Schnebly Road above Marg's Draw late at night. It was overcast, no moon or stars. It was real dark, except for the lights from Sedona. I stopped to take a leak. I turned out the lights on the vehicle and walked over to the edge of the road. When I finished, I turned around and standing next to my four by four was an alien being. It stood at least eight feet tall. It was very thin. It had long arms and legs. I'd never seen anything quite like it."

"How'd you react?"

"I wasn't scared. I didn't even think to draw my weapon. I stared at it for at least a full minute, maybe longer."

"What did you hear, smell, and feel?" I asked.

"I heard nothing. I smelled the juniper and pine, nothing else. I felt calm but a little apprehensive," Randy said.

"What happened?"

"Nothing, other than the alien turned to the right and walked up the road into the dark. I watched as it faded from sight, like ten seconds later."

"Borrow your cell phone?" I asked.

"Sure," he said, handing his Smartphone to me.

I pulled up the Internet, and brought up the McMannes' article with a picture of the Christus.

"Did it look like this?" I asked, showing him the photo from the article.

"Holy shit. Dead fucking ringer," Randy claimed, as he took the phone.

"Have you ever seen strange lights in the sky here?" I asked.

"In the last two years, I've seen unexplained craft in the sky at least five times."

"Ever report it?" I asked.

"Did you?" He asked back.

"No."

"Other than to Detective Scott, same," Randy said.

"Detective Scott knows about your encounter?"

"Yeah. We hunt together. I told him when we were deer hunting near Payson. He's the one who suggested that I tell you."

"When you first told Scott, what did he say?"

"He said that the Sheriff would think I was crazy. He'd claim that I'd run into Bigfoot or something. I'd be the target of derision."

"Was the Schnebly Road incident the only time you saw an alien?"

"Once is enough. Right?"

By this time, we'd reached Eddie's house. A Yavapai County four-wheeler sat on the road. A Sedona Police patrol car blocked the driveway. The police officer waved at Randy, gave a thumbs-up sign, and pulled his car up to allow us to drive to the house.

I noticed a black Ford Edge in the driveway. It had California plates.

Randy helped me with the equipment. I was still wobbly from the meds. I walked up the door and rang the bell. When the door swung open, Eddie's daughter, Yvette, greeted me. If anything, she was more beautiful than I remembered. She no longer had a nose ring.

"Yvette, good to see you."

"Tony, come in. You too, officer," Yvette said, gesturing with her right arm.

"Where's Eddie?"

"I made Poppa go to bed. He's been waiting to talk to you. He's been worried about you. He was exhausted. I told him that I'd wake him once you got here."

"I'm pretty tired too. Let him sleep awhile. Maybe I'll crash for a bit."

"Better call your wife first," Yvette directed. "She's worried."

"OK. They kept my cell as evidence. Does Eddie have a house phone?"

"No. He thinks they're a waste. You can use my cell. I'll find it as soon as I get you settled. Officer, is there anything I can do for you?" Yvette asked, as she turned to Randy.

Randy stared at Yvette. He looked a little like a puppy that'd been called by his mistress. He was captivated by Yvette's striking beauty. She must get that a lot from men.

I had to check. He wore no ring on his left hand.

"Hello, deputy," Yvette repeated, but she had a knowing smile on her pretty face.

"Oh, sorry, Ma'am. No, I'm fine. I'll be going. But here's my card. If you need anything, call. I'll be back after I'm off duty. Tony and I have a beer to drink and a discussion to continue," Randy said, but his primary motive for the visit had changed.

Randy and I shook hands and he took his leave. I went back to my room, grabbed a shower, changed clothes, and walked back into Eddie's great room. Yvette was on the phone. When she saw me, she walked over to me and handed me her cell.

"It's Gretchen," Yvette said.

I took the phone and put it to my ear.

"Hey, Gretch."

"Yvette says that you have two little black eyes and the bandages make you look like a raccoon. Somebody beat the snot out of you."

"The other guy fared worse."

"Apparently, since he's dead. Yvette says you're not so distinguished looking at the moment."

"Damn. That means that I won't be able to put the moves on her until I recover my good looks," I said, as I smiled at Yvette, who shook her head and sighed.

"Tell her she can have you. You never listen. I told you not to brawl."

"I did follow your other advice."

"What advice was that?"

"Quintuple tap."

"I believe I said double-tap," Gretchen corrected.

"Sorry, babe, I misunderstood. Don't fret. I'll buy you new bullets."

"Tony, I was so worried about you," Gretchen began, weeping at the other end of the conversation. "I wanted to leave today, but I'm scheduled to start a trial on Monday. Since you're in no immediate danger, Judge Livingston wouldn't continue it over the fucking defense counsel's objection. I'll be out there later in the week after I kick the defendant's ass."

"It's OK. I'd like a couple of days to convalesce anyway. I'll look a lot better by the end of the week."

"Listen, Tony. The Tampa news is all over this. I've been getting calls. I'm not allowed to discuss the case. Look out. When they find out where you are, they'll swarm over you and your pal, Eddie."

"Hold on, Gretch," I said, turning to Yvette. "What's the local news on this?"

"It's big in Phoenix. CSO and the feds haven't released your names. But it's a matter of time. Some neighbor will put two and two together when they figure out the police cars. After that, the media will be camped outside. Enjoy the calm before the storm."

I comforted Gretchen and we spoke for another few minutes. Then, I begged off, claiming that I needed to get a little sleep.

After I ended the call, I got a beer. I walked back to the bedroom. I lay down on the bed on top of the covers and took a big sip. I closed my eyes and fell into the deepest sleep in 20 years. I woke up 12 hours later on a bright Sunday morning.

CHAPTER FOURTEEN

September 2, 2013, 5:30 p.m.
1651 Rodeo Drive
West Sedona, Arizona

SUNDAY, SEPTEMBER 1, turned out to be a day of rest. Eddie and I sat around his house licking our wounds. I took my meds, sipped on tea, and surfed the net for news of our deadly encounter. By Sunday afternoon, our adventure hit the major networks and blogs.

I tried to put the events of Schnebly Tank and their aftermath into some sort of lucid context. I typed up my best recollections. I added them to the draft of the story of the search for the Christus. After I saved the file, I attached a copy to an e-mail that I sent to Gretchen. As a precaution, I sent a copy to each of my sons.

Then I said ten rosaries and took a nap. I slept most of the day.

Monday morning became another thing entirely. Leaks from the state and federal agencies allowed the media outlets to pinpoint our position. Satellite trucks from Phoenix, Tucson, Las Vegas, and Los Angeles lined the suburban streets around Eddie's home. Reporters clamored for interviews. Cameramen trampled all over Eddie's xeriscaping. Crewmen focused their eavesdropping equipment on LTC Grimes' private domain.

It was bedlam. The Yavapai Sheriff assigned more units to control the crowd of interlopers.

Eddie and I spent Monday morning watching the news and making as many insulting, ribald, disparaging, and offensive comments as we could concerning the parentage and sexual prowess—or lack thereof—of the reporters who had been filing stories about us with their respective stations. While we watched Eddie's big screen TV in his great room, I surfed the news sites on my laptop.

All of the stories were long on gore and short on any facts regarding the cause of the violence. The reports agreed that the deaths were related to a large drug operation. The reporters couldn't decide whether the people hiding inside Eddie's house were potential defendants, accessories, victims, domestic terrorists, or undercover informants.

Gretchen had begun her trial in Tampa. She was unavailable for comment or moral support. Yvette filled in as the den mother, when she wasn't talking on her phone to an unknown caller. I assumed that the caller was Randy Stone, who'd spent the entire day with us on Sunday. He was smitten. So was Yvette.

By mid-afternoon, Fox News had a breaking story. Unidentified, but reliable, sources revealed that a major person of interest in the Coconino National Forest homicides was none other than Don Hansen. Hansen had dropped out of sight.

Right after the news bulletin, Deputy Stone arrived. Yvette met him at the door and they chatted for ten minutes. He remembered why he'd come over. He walked into the great room and handed over my cell phone.

"We got everything off the phone that we needed. The Sheriff thought you might want this back," Stone said, as he looked longingly at Yvette.

"Thanks," I said. I closed my laptop, set it next to me in the chair, and started scrolling through the calls on my cell.

I noticed one local call from two days earlier. I had a hunch. I dialed the number. It rang seven times before a man answered. I identified myself. I asked who the man was.

"I'm Dr. Ben Davis. I'm a retired veterinarian. Julie Adams, the girl who bought my practice, said you wanted to talk to me."

"I do. Thanks for calling. I hope you're well."

"I'm doing all right. Not up to practicing anymore. I still get around fine."

"That's good, doctor. I'm from Florida. I'm looking for information about a family that lived here in the sixties. They would have been a very pretty woman, a nice looking man, a little boy, and a dog that you might have treated. Dad's name was Bob or Robert. The dog's name was Rommel."

"What's your interest in them?"

"I met them in 1966. They made an impression. I've always wondered what happened to them," I explained, since I'd decided not to lie about my motives.

"Listen, whoever you are," Doctor Davis responded. "The couple that you're looking for disappeared in 1978. It was local news thirty-five years ago. They were Bob and Cindy Stedman. No one ever figured out what happened. It was a real tragedy. Their boy was thirteen or fourteen when the Cottonwood police found him and the dog alone in the home. I cared for the dog before and after the disappearance, though the dog was getting very old. I lost track of the boy and the dog after the county put the boy in a foster home. Someone adopted the boy. I don't know what happened to old Rommel. Neat dog, He was smart as a whip. Crazy loyal."

"Thanks doctor. Do you remember the boy's first name?"

"I think it was Ronnie. Yeah, Ronnie Stedman."

"Thanks, Doctor. Appreciate your time."

"Don't mention it," the veterinarian said as he hung up.

I got out of my chair and walked over to the long couch where Eddie sprawled with his iPad on his lap, while he watched CNN.

"I have some news."

"This ought to be good," Eddie said, looking up at me. "We're the focus of international media attention for massacring twelve men, and you have news. Riveting!"

"What massacre?" I asked.

"A British paper calls the events in the forest massacres," Eddie said, reading from an article on his iPad. "We are the unknown killers who wantonly murdered twelve peaceful hikers in the pristine western forests. They say that this serial shooting may be what the government needs to finally confiscate or regulate all civilian owned weapons."

"That's pretty far from the mainstream story on this," I said.

"I know. I thought it might amuse you," Eddie said. "What's your news?"

"I talked to the veterinarian that I tried to reach a few days ago," I said

"You mean a lifetime ago," Eddie said.

"Eddie, he knew the family from the chapel. Their names were Bob and Cindy Stedman. Eddie, they went missing too. Sometime around 1978, the Cottonwood authorities found their little boy, Ronnie, living alone with his dog, Rommel. The authorities put the kid in foster care and someone adopted him. Everyone from that night, but that kid and me, has gone missing."

Eddie stood up like he'd been blasted off the couch. Yvette and Randy, who'd been lost in their own conversation across the room, noticed. They walked over to us.

"Tony, did you say that someone adopted the Stedman kid in 1978. His name was Ronnie?" Eddie asked.

"Yes, yes," I said.

Eddie held up his iPad. He manipulated the internal keyboard. He accessed Facebook and sought out a particular page. He found what he wanted. He looked at me.

"The authorities are looking for a person of interest in this nasty business, right? Your pal, Don Hansen?" Eddie asked.

"They can't find him. We know that he's slippery."

"Tony, I went onto Facebook a couple of hours ago. Hansen has a major presence there. I looked at his profile."

"You should friend him," I said. "You two have much in common."

"I open my home to this vagrant. What do I get? Abuse," Eddie said, looking at Yvette for support. She smiled and shrugged.

"What about Hansen's profile?" I asked.

"Look for yourself," Eddie offered.

"No, Poppa. Read it so we can all hear," Yvette insisted.

"OK. Mr. Hansen's profile includes this statement: I'll be forever grateful to the Hansens. They took me in at a difficult time. I'll never be able to repay them."

"No shit!" I said.

"Check this out," Eddie said as he showed me his iPad, which had a photo displayed from Don Hansen's Facebook profile collection, dated 1974.

I examined the picture. It depicted a handsome family standing on the South Rim of the Grand Canyon. It was the same mom, dad, kid, and dog from that night in 1966, only eight years older. Framed against a wonder of the world, the photo showed a handsome man, a beautiful woman in her 30s, a boy nine or ten years old, and a cute German shepherd mix. The caption said, Bob, Cindy, Donnie, and Rommel, South Rim, 1974.

"I guess the vet meant Donnie when he said Ronnie," I deduced.

"Don Hansen was the little boy with you, the night that you saw the lights at the chapel," Eddie concluded.

Like I've been saying, there's no serendipity. Everything happens for a reason. There was no possibility that I stood in Eddie's house in West Sedona, on the 47th anniversary of my encounter, learning that Don Hansen had been the little toddler who witnessed the 1966 sighting with me; and somehow all this had happened by mere chance.

"Eddie, we've got to get to the chapel at sunset," I urged.

"Hold it." Randy injected. "You guys are released on conditions. You can't violate the Magistrate's order. They'll throw you in jail."

"That's right, Randy," I said. "But we can go anywhere in Sedona, as long as we're accompanied by two law enforcement officers. Which two officers would you choose to accompany us, Eddie?" I asked, as I nodded at his daughter and her new suitor.

"I believe that a state and federal task force would work," Eddie responded.

"What if I don't agree to this ploy?" Randy asked.

"Sweetie, don't you want to come with me?" Yvette asked as she pulled him close. "If it gets dangerous, I might need a brave deputy to help me."

Randy looked at Yvette. He knew he was goner. Eddie recognized Randy's capitulation. He could relate.

"Don't feel bad, Son," Eddie said. "I could never refuse Yvette's mom anything either. Promise me that you'll take good care of her."

"What are you talking about, Poppa?" Yvette asked.

"A lot will happen tonight. I can sense it. Yvette, you've been alone since your divorce. I see the chemistry between you and Randy. He seems like a good man—for a Marine. Randy?"

"You have my word, sir!" Randy said.

"Good," Eddie said. "Let's go to my gun safe, then talk about getting to the chapel."

Eddie planned the extraction from his home in five minutes. He'd have been the best G3 any Army division ever had.

At Eddie's direction, Randy informed the Yavapai County deputies that we'd sneak out the back of Eddie's house, hike to State Road 89A, and get something to eat in Sedona. The Sedona Police offered to distract the media and send a separate unit to pick us up. They'd transport us to Uptown Sedona, where we could blend in with the crowd. Randy agreed, but failed to tell the police officer that one of his CSO buddies would pick us up in town and transport us to the Chapel of the Holy Cross.

It took us longer than I expected to hike to 89A. It was sunset by the time we got to Uptown Sedona, and dusk when we made it to the chapel.

I felt anxious. Something was waiting for us. I knew we couldn't miss it. I tried to call Gretchen. Her phone went to voice mail. I left her a loving message. I sent a text as we drove toward the chapel.

When we arrived at the chapel parking lot, Eddie asked the driver, Randy, and Yvette to drop us off and wait in the lower lot. Eddie and I would proceed alone. All three protested, but Eddie prevailed.

When we tried to walk up to the chapel ramp, a security guard stopped us. The chapel closed at Five p.m. No visitors were allowed. He was adamant.

Eddie and I had anticipated this. Google maps showed an alternative route along the rocks to the west of the chapel. It crossed the property of a home next door. We used that route to get to the courtyard.

The owner had posted a sign telling us to beware of his dog. After our adventure in the forest, we could deal with a guard dog. We were armed. Nothing would stop us from getting up to the courtyard. Eddie was a Screaming Eagle. Like the 101st Airborne, we had a rendezvous with destiny.

Our jaunt up the hill was a piece of cake. We made it without breaking a sweat. Once we got to the retaining wall, we climbed over it. We found ourselves in the courtyard, where I'd seen the lights five decades earlier.

We walked over to where Dan and I had perched in 1966. Eddie and I sat down on the stone bench. Eddie pulled off his backpack and reached inside. He produced two bottles of Rogue Dead Guy and a fancy Italian-made corkscrew and bottle opener.

"Eddie, I told you that I drank Coors on that night," I reminded my pal.

"I'm sure any good beer will be fine. Don't you think that Dead Guy is appropriate this evening?"

"Bring any chicken?" I asked.

"How about my signature barbeque chicken? If your alien angels are attracted to chicken and beer, we'll have a gaggle here in minutes," Eddie promised, as he passed me a breast.

The sky had no clouds that evening. The sun had set without fanfare. Nothing dramatic occurred as the sky turned black. Though it was painful for me, Eddie and I munched on our chicken and sipped our beers as day turned into night.

The security guard found us and tried to throw us out. While we argued with the older man, a tall leprechaun walked up the ramp with Adolf—the erstwhile attack dog. Father Pat observed our dilemma and came to our aid. After two minutes of conference, he convinced the security guard to leave us be.

"I thought you two would find a way to come here tonight," Father Pat advised as he and the dog joined us on the Stone Bench facing west.

"You doing all right, Son?" Eddie asked the priest, as he handed him a Dead Guy.

"I can sure use a good red ale right about now," Father admitted.

"It's a Maibock, Father, remember," I said.

Father Pat looked at me for a moment, then smiled and winked.

"I love a Maibock. And I think I'm OK, Eddie, but I never expected the wild ride."

We sat on the stone bench facing west for at least a half an hour. The nature of our quest and the danger we'd shared caused us to become close friends in a very short time. A violent rite of passage—where character, courage, and commitment count—can do that to the men being initiated.

"What have we learned from all of this?" Eddie asked.

"I'm convinced that aliens from somewhere visit the planet. Sedona is the site of one of the portals," I said.

"I have more questions than answers," Father Pat said.

"Like what, Pat?" Eddie asked.

"I want to know the exact nature of our universe and it's place in God's creation."

"That would be good to know," I admitted. "I'd like to know why God created dogs like Adolf with one-seventh of the life span of humans. Whose fucking idea was that?"

"I'd like to know how to win the Power Ball Lottery. I could get by in Sedona on a quarter billion dollars," Eddie said, smiling as he peeled off chicken and offered it to Adolf.

"I'd like to know what part of the Grand Plan caused us to come together like this. How did our adventure advance the Design?" Father Pat asked.

"Life is full of mysteries," I injected.

"So true!" a voice behind us offered.

Eddie, Father Pat, Adolf, and I spun around. Don Hansen stood in the center of the courtyard. He smiled at us, but his expression seemed menacing. Adolf growled and bared his teeth.

"Look who the devil drug in," I said, my anger rising.

"Tony, is this your good buddy, Donnie Stedman-Hansen?" Eddie asked, as he reached for the .45 Commander that he'd stuffed in his belt.

"Mr. Grimes, no need for that. Besides, a gun won't do you any good here," Don said, surprising us with the fact that he knew Eddie's name.

"We'll see about that," Eddie said, as he drew his weapon.

"Be reasonable. You've come looking for answers. I have them. Put that weapon back in your belt. We'll discuss the mysteries of the universe like civilized men."

"Eddie, he appears to be unarmed. If he betrays us again, we'll beat him to death or sick Adolf on him," I promised.

"That's a much better idea. I wanted to blow his balls off for deceiving Fleet and the rest of us. We'll do it your way—for now."

"With these ground rules, are you ready to proceed?" I asked Hansen.

"Sure, ask me anything. Unburden yourselves."

"What happened to the Christus?" Father Pat asked, as he stood up with the dog.

"My stepfather—Jim Hansen, a workman—and I hauled it down on a rainy day in September, 1979."

"September 2nd?" I asked.

"Correct. The workman dismantled it with a cutting torch and hauled the pieces away in his pickup. He buried everything but the head of the statue in the desert. I have the head in a special place where no one can find it."

"Why did your stepfather and his workman destroy the Christus?" I asked as I got up from the bench.

Reacting to my movement, Hansen put up his hand, palm facing me. "Tony, maintain your distance. Let's keep this chat nice and friendly."

"OK," I said, stopping about 15 feet from Hansen. "Answer my question."

"While it's true that the Christus received a lot of negative comments because it was grotesque, a small cadre of folks around here began to make the same connections that you've made. They realized that the figure in the chapel bore more resemblance to possible alien life forms than the traditional vision of the Savior," Hansen explained.

"Why would that matter to you and your stepdad?" Father Pat asked.

"The inspiration for the Christus came from a local artist who claimed to have had a miraculous, personal encounter with the Holy Spirit. The encounter stimulated several drawings that Keith Monroe used to create the iron sculpture," Hansen continued.

"The encounter wasn't with a deity," Eddie concluded. "This artist saw one of the inter-dimensional beings."

"My stepmom was the local artist. Once she and Jim realized the truth, they became allies of the inter-dimensional beings. When the beings transported my real parents to the next level, the Hansens took me in to watch over me."

"What do you mean by the next level? What's that?" I asked.

"It's hard to describe."

"Is it heaven, hell, purgatory?" Father Pat asked.

"No, nothing like that. It's a different consciousness. It's a separate plane that's part of the evolution of living beings that have advanced beyond the physical limitations of this universe."

"Have you been there?" Eddie asked.

"Not yet."

"Are there dogs there?" I asked, not sure that I should take Hansen's ranting seriously.

"I'm pretty certain that some are. The beings promised that I'd see Rommel again."

"Did the Catholics find out about the true nature of the Christus?" I asked.

"More or less. My stepdad convinced them that the Christus did not represent a replication of their Savior," Hansen acknowledged. "The Catholic hierarchy is not stupid. I'm sure they realized the truth. That's why they stopped having services here."

"I still don't understand," Eddie admitted.

"Look, the chapel had been built and consecrated on a fundamental misunderstanding. These non-divine inter-dimensional beings have been coming to Sedona over many millennia. When the valley was unpopulated by humans, or the humans were in a primitive stage of development, the beings could come and go without concern. As human civilization advanced, the beings used subterfuge and guile to keep humans away from the portals. A thousand years ago, they made this part of the valley taboo. They interacted with the humans and used natural disasters, which they could predict with their advanced technology, to frighten the Sinagua."

"Your special friends haven't been able to keep people away from Sedona these last fifty years," I pointed out.

"Realtors and land developers are a fearless and greedy breed. Other than the Sierra Club, the EPA, or high interest rates, nothing frightens them," Hansen said, smiling at his own joke.

"Are these beings from another universe, angels?" I asked.

"The answer to that question is both yes and no," Hansen responded.

"Explain," I demanded.

"These visitors travel to this dimension, using technology that's twenty-thousand years ahead of ours. They can do things that we dream about. Their life spans are hundreds of times longer than ours. On those occasions that humans have encountered them, the difference in intelligence and technology gets misinterpreted," Hansen said.

"That sounds like *Chariots of the Gods,*" I said.

"Not really. Gentlemen, we're fortunate that this particular race has portals here. They're benign. They mean us no harm. They like us. However, they have enemies who are not so gentle. They've been in conflict with the others longer than humans have been a species."

"Are the enemies venerated by the Santo Diablo sect?" I asked.

"Yes, Tony. I can see that you've been doing your homework."

"Why do these benign life forms come here? What benefit accrues?" Eddie asked.

"They're looking for God." Hansen said.

"You said they were advanced, centuries ahead of us. Why would they seek God here, when they travel the universe and pass through several multiverses? Why our planet?"

"Good old planet Earth has been uniquely blessed. The beings believe that we've had contact with the Great Divinity. On Earth, they see the signs everywhere."

"If they're so advanced, what did they think of Jesus?" Father Pat asked.

"They never met Him," Don Hansen revealed. "These beings are not omniscient. They're not divine, nor always here. They come from a dimension where the laws of physics are different. Time is different there too. For example, our northern hemispheric September second coincides with a major solstice on their planet. They miss things. One of their biggest failures was not being in the right place at the right time when Christ was present on the other side of this planet."

"Was that a misfortune, coincidence, or part of the Divine Plan?" I asked.

"Very perceptive, Tony!" Hansen said. "The beings wonder about that, too."

"Why do they keep coming?" I asked.

"Here's a gross oversimplification. As they advanced in knowledge and technology, they embraced—then rejected—the theory that the multiverse spontaneously came into existence because of a random event. The more they learned, the more complex their reality appeared. For example, they know that in this universe the most distant galaxy from earth is much farther than thirteen billion light years. They realize that the Higgs boson is closer to the beginning than the end of sub-atomic structure. Over eons, they abandoned the atheistic viewpoint. Millions of years ago, they began a search for signs of the omniscient Intelligence that created everything. Over vast distances, time frames, and dimensions, they've examined tens of thousands of cultures. They found indisputable signs of the Creator's divine interaction with life forms on a small fraction of the civilizations that they examined. Since the cultures that have had this blessing are rare, the good beings cultivate and protect the precious few that they've found.

There is a human prophecy that the Redeemer will come again. They're here to witness that event when it happens."

"What about the bad angels or whatever you call them?" Eddie asked.

"They come here too. They inspire evil. You men have seen it. The Santo Diablo sect is one of many groups that venerate them," Hansen said. "The demons undermine the efforts of the good angels. They sponsor violence, hopelessness, confusion, and doubt."

"How does all of this affect us?" I asked.

"You're here talking to me, Tony, rather than exploring the parameters of your eternal reward, because of these benign visitors."

"How is that?" I asked.

"Do you and Eddie honestly think that two older men, regardless of experience and training, could defend themselves against twelve vicious killers from a violent cult without some special assistance? Come on. Who woke you in time to defend yourselves at the tank? If you think you and Eddie bested those Diablo's without the assistance of the inter-dimensional beings, you're delusional."

"How do you know those details?" I asked.

"Tony, you can be so naïve. Who cushioned your fall from the cliff in college? Who saved you from your own drunken stupidity in the car accident north of Tucson? Who saved your ass countless times in Vietnam and later? You have no fucking idea how close you came on your twenty-first birthday. You survived all of those events and several others because you have a role to play in a Grand Scheme. Who sent Gretchen on her path to intersect with yours? My special friends connected with you in 1966 and they've been looking out for you ever since."

"Are you saying that I was abducted? I don't remember anything like that."

"You weren't abducted. The beings don't have to kidnap, examine, experiment, or abuse our species like in the trashy movies. When they encountered you, because of the different physical laws in their dimension, they could see your whole life unfold. Throughout the years they've been there in subtle ways to help you, Gretchen, Tim, and John."

"Like guardian angels?" I asked.

"On steroids, Tony," Hansen said.

"That explains Tony, what about Eddie? What about me?" Father Pat asked.

"Eddie's life is connected to Tony's. They passed very near to each other a dozen times. They were stationed together at Fort Bragg. They even made a jump together in 1981."

"That must have been the Fort Irwin jump. What a disaster. That was very close," Eddie said. He stopped to consider the implications. "Tony, were you on that disastrous brigade mass tactical jump at Fort Irwin?"

"Yeah, Eddie. I was one of the straphangers for the brigade's headquarters company. Bad jump. What a mess. I broke my tailbone. There were sixteen Paratroopers killed on that one. I didn't know you were there, too."

"We didn't know each other then," Eddie said.

"How about me? Why am I here?" Father Pat asked.

"Tony was right. He and Eddie needed a chaplain. Besides, we couldn't let Tony move on to the next level with thirty years of sin unresolved. You had to give him absolution."

In the weirdest way, Hansen made perfect sense. By all rights, Eddie, Father Pat and I should have never left the overhang near Schnebly Tank alive. I'd known for decades that someone was running interference for me. Now, I wanted to know why.

"Where are Bob and Cindy Stedman? Where's Dan Ostergaard?" I asked, somewhat mollified by the amazing demonstration of Hansen's prescience.

"You'll find that out later," Hansen promised. "I don't want to spoil the surprise."

One major question remained.

"OK, Donnie," I began. "Why you and me in 1966; and why Eddie, Father Pat, and I now? What specific business do these beings have with us? What's the Grand Plan, Scheme, Design or whatever? What's my role in it?"

"I don't know all of the details," Hansen said. "You'll have to take that up with Michael."

"Who's Michael?" Eddie asked as he looked at Father Pat and me.

"Eddie, ask Tony. He knows who Michael is. Don't you Tony?"

"I don't know what you're talking about," I said.

"Sure you do. You're a big fan of Michael's. That medal around your neck."

"Michael the Archangel?" I asked. "Is that who you mean?"

"Who else?" Hansen said, an arrogant smile on his face.

"Be serious, asshole," Eddie said as he stepped closer to Hansen.

"Eddie, relax. Michael would never let any of you harm me."

"Don, good angels would never protect a man who had David Fleet killed. If any of this is true, Michael the Archangel would never shield you."

"Michael knows that I'm not the man who sold David out to the killers."

"Then who?" I demanded.

"Jim Wilson," Hansen answered.

"The skinny little shit who runs the gift shop here?" I asked.

"The very same."

"Why?" I asked.

"You'll have to ask Michael, but I think that Jim's in tight with the Diablo's."

"I was right. That fucker has blood-red eyes and works for demons."

"What are you talking about?" Father Pat asked, but he kept his eyes on Hansen.

"We'll talk later. You guys at the Parish have a spy in your midst," I said.

"What do we do about this man, Wilson?" Father Pat asked Hansen

"We've taken precautions. We have our own agent to watch him."

"Who?"

"Linda Alvarez. The beings saved her a thousand years ago from an attempt by her people to sacrifice her. They took her to their dimension and trained her to help her species here. They returned her a couple of years ago."

"Why?" I asked.

"Ask Michael."

"Cute. OK Don, I'll ask Michael the Archangel," I said. "Maybe we can do lunch. How about drinks at the Cowboy Club?"

"How about now?" Hansen said as he stepped to the side.

Out of the darkness behind Hansen, a large figure emerged from the shadows. It stood at least nine feet tall, impossibly long arms, long skinny legs and feet. His face was humanoid, complete with eyes, a nose, and a mouth. I could detect no expression.

The figure seemed to glide toward us rather than walk. It moved past Hansen and stopped a mere six feet in front of us. I felt no fear, but no joy or rapture either.

"Holy shit!" Eddie said, as he looked up at the expressionless face of the being Hansen claimed was Saint Michael the Archangel. "Still have my six, Tony?"

"Absolutely, brother!" I said. "You OK, Father? By the way, I haven't finished my rosaries yet."

"Better than OK. I'd get moving on the penance, my friend. Something tells me that we're about to have an accounting at the next level," Father Pat said. "Tony, Eddie, look. Adolf is purring like a cat!"

"Michael before you take them to the next level, these men have some questions for you," Hansen said in the distance.

The Angel turned, looked back at Hansen, then turned back to face us. He looked down on us. I saw his head nod ever so slightly. He spread his arms and hands to their full extent and his face formed the smallest of smiles.

I guess I'll finally get some satisfaction, I thought. *There is no serendipity.*

EPILOGUE

September 2, 2014, 2:30 p.m.
1908 Port Colony Way
Tampa, Florida

THE AFTERNOON SKY was clear and bright. A weather front had passed through from the northeast, bringing rare cool temperatures to Tampa Bay. Taking advantage of this extraordinary gift in the late summer, Gretchen, John, Tim, and Heather Giordano decided to have the meeting with Yvette Grimes-Stone and her husband, Randy, at the wooden table, next to the pool on the lanai.

The presence of Margaritas would blur the somber nature of the gathering. The group sat around the big table on the lanai.

"What did your lawyer say about Judge Holiday's ruling?" Tim asked his mom.

"What could he say? We lost," Gretchen answered, as she sipped her drink.

"He didn't rule against you, mom. He said he'd take your motion under advisement. The decision is without prejudice. Raise it again in six months," John Giordano said.

"Johnny, I'll be bankrupt in six months. I need the proceeds of dad's life insurance policies now. Without his salary, I can't pay the mortgage and maintain this house."

"Mom, the judge granted the motion to make you the guardian of Dad's Thrift Savings Account and the funds in his 401K. You can liquidate them, pay off the mortgage, and put the balance in CDs. If you don't have a mortgage, you'll be able to get by on what you're making at the U.S. Attorney's Office."

"Yeah. I suppose you're right. But I counted on that money for retirement. I guess I'll be working longer than I anticipated," Gretchen concluded. "I wish Holiday had been more reasonable."

"There was nothing he could do, Mom. It takes at least five years to get this relief," Tim said.

"Right, Tim, unless you have strong evidence of death, the minimum waiting period for a judicial declaration is pretty clear," John agreed. "Mom, why don't you publish dad's story? Might make some money from that."

"Maybe. I need more details. DOJ and those Sheriff's Offices in Arizona haven't been much help. They claim that they have no evidence," Gretchen said. "Yvette, you and Randy were the last people to see Tony, your dad, and the priest."

"That's right. We sat at the bottom of the hill and never saw or heard a thing after we watched the priest and his dog walk up the ramp."

"Gretchen," Randy began. "Nobody feels more impotent than I do. The whole episode is unsettling. There was no way that those three men and that dog met with foul play. There's not one shred of physical evidence that suggests violence, mayhem, or kidnapping."

"Gretchen, my dad and Tony were both armed. We know that they wouldn't go without a big fight." Yvette said.

"So are we supposed to believe that they disappeared into thin air?" Heather asked. "There has to be some explanation."

"We brought in some of the best trackers and their dogs in the west. There was no trail with a scent from Tony, Eddie, the Irish priest, or the dog. None."

"I don't care what you didn't find, Randy. My husband, your father-in-law, and that priest stumbled over a massive drug operation. The drug dealers lost tens of millions. They were bound to take revenge. You guys in Arizona know what happened," Gretchen said.

"Gretchen, we don't. Look, it's true that Tony, Eddie, and Father O'Malley got crossways with the Santo Diablo cult. That's why the three of you and your families are all under federal protection. We take that threat seriously. But they didn't get the three missing men and the dog that night. It they had, there would have been a swath of destruction a hundred yards wide," Randy said.

"Randy, I read where the manager of the gift shop at the chapel is also missing. This business gets more and more complicated every day," John added.

"Yeah, that little tidbit is troubling. We're looking into it. There's some disturbing evidence about Mr. Wilson's background. I can't discuss it with you though."

"You know, Mom, they could all be in WITSEC," Heather offered. "The feds might put them in hiding and forbid them from contacting us. It would be for everybody's protection. Randy and Yvette wouldn't be able to discuss that with us."

"Heather," Yvette said. "If my dad were in WITSEC, I'd be overjoyed. I wouldn't be able to give you details, but I'd never mislead you and leave you hanging. Neither would Randy."

"Something bad has happened to your Dad. We'll never see him again," Gretchen said, as she began to cry. "It's worse because that fucker, Don Hansen, has prospered in this crisis. Why hasn't someone investigated him?"

"Gretchen, he is a subject of our investigation. To be honest, he has excellent alibis. He has no known connection to the Santo Diablos. I'll admit that there are half-a-dozen jealous husbands who'd like to do him in. We don't prosecute that kind of scandalous behavior," Randy said.

"Mom, you're going to be pissed. I read in the Drudge Report that they're going to do a reality TV show based on Hansen and his Reiki counseling. He's going to L.A. He's opening up a New Age center in Santa Monica," Tim said.

"For goodness sake. He's such a sleaze. Who'd watch his show?"

"You know what P.T. Barnum said: '…nobody ever lost a dollar underestimating the taste of the American public.' He'll be a big hit." John said.

"There's no justice!" Gretchen said.

"Mom, I want to change the subject. I think this is the time and place. You guys are the people for this discussion," Tim said.

"OK."

"Something strange happened to me a couple of days ago in D.C. I opened the drawer to my desk at work and found a small envelope," Tim said.

Both John and Gretchen stopped cold and looked at Tim in the strangest way. It was like they anticipated his next words. Randy and Yvette looked at each other and nodded.

"Inside the envelope was this item," Tim said as he held up a small golden object that looked like a triangular piece from a round medallion. "It's approximately one third the size of a large St. Michael's Medal."

"Where did it come from?" Gretchen asked in cold tone.

"I don't know. When I looked at it, I saw that it was part of a St. Michael's Medal and had writing in Latin around the edge. I had it translated. It's the beginning of a quote from the Old Testament, Genesis 31:49. On the edge of my coin it says: *Mizpah! May the Good Lord watch.* That's all, though. On the back of the medal, there is an engraved human eye, a heart, the capital letter U, and the Roman numeral II."

"Do you know what that means?" Gretchen asked.

"I think that it means: I love you too," Tim said. "Remember, Dad always would point to his eye, make a heart with his hand, then a U, and then signal two fingers. He called it our gang sign."

"That's wild." Gretchen said. "Someone is playing a cruel joke."

Randy reached over and gave his new bride's hand an affectionate pat.

"I don't think so, Mom," John said. "I got one of those envelopes too, about three days ago. It was in the top drawer of my dresser at home."

"Do you have it?" Tim asked.

"Yep," John admitted. "It's right here."

John held up his gold piece and Tim put his next to it. They fit together perfectly—two pieces of a three-part puzzle.

"What does your part say?" Tim asked.

"Translated from my high school Latin, it says: *out for me and thee, when we are apart,* John said. "I also have the eye, heart, letter U, and Roman numeral on the reverse."

"Two thirds of the translation is "Mizpah: May the Good Lord watch out for me and thee when we are apart," Tim said.

"That's right," John agreed.

"I looked it up. The rest of the words on the missing piece will be *one from the other*, Tim said.

"Mom, do you have the missing piece?" Heather asked, watching Gretchen.

"No. I don't. I have no idea where those things came from or what they mean."

"I think they're from Dad," John said. "He's sending these to us. It's a sign of how much he loves us. Since you don't have the missing piece, he must."

"Mom, are you sure that you don't have anything like this?" Tim asked as he held up the two gold pieces.

"No, nothing like that."

"Yvette had a similar unexplained visitation," Randy said. "Yvette found a golden cameo on the counter in the bathroom."

"What does the Cameo depict?" Tim asked.

"My mother, Mary!" Yvette said, tears in her eyes. On the back is a little code from Poppa. It's a depiction of a fist striking a breast like in a *mea culpa*. Poppa and I would make that sign when we parted. It showed we loved each other. I think it means that Poppa has found my mother."

"This is not possible," Gretchen said, as she covered her face in her hands.

"Mom, what do you have? You have something. I can tell." Tim said.

Without another word, Gretchen got up from the table, walked inside, rummaged through her purse on the kitchen table, picked out an envelope, and returned to the lanai. She removed a thin, flat golden sheet, about six inches long and five inches wide from the envelope. She handed the gold sheet to Tim.

Tim examined the sheet for a few moments and passed it to John. John's eyebrows went up, as he read the words on the sheet.

"What do you make of it? I don't read Latin," Gretchen admitted.

"It's not all in Latin, but the numbers are Roman numerals," John claimed.

"What do you think?" Tim asked.

"It's a boarding pass."

"For whom, what airline, where?" Gretchen asked.

"Tim pull out your laptop and run these numbers; it'll be quicker,"

"Can do," Tim said.

"Who's it for?" Gretchen asked.

"You. Your name is right here. See, *Gretchen* **Giordano**."

"Oh my God!" Heather said. "It looks identical to your name on the box with the stuffed animals."

"What's this about a box?" Randy said.

Gretchen got up again, disappeared into the house, and returned three minutes later. She showed Randy and Yvette the box from her high school days. She explained that she put her name on it next to the Giordano logo ten years before she ever met Tony Giordano.

"Now, I've seen everything," Yvette said.

"That is amazing." Randy agreed. "Is there any other revelation on that boarding pass?"

"Yeah, John. What airline am I supposed to take?" Gretchen asked.

"Can't tell. That's some form of writing I've never seen." John said, as he tried to read the golden sheet.

"Me either," Tim agreed, as he looked over John's shoulder.

"Where's the departure?" Gretchen asked.

"That's in Roman Numerals. Tim, run those through. Let's see what they mean."

"OK, that's 34.83196 and 111.76654," Tim said.

"Hmmm. GPS? Tim, run the numbers through the site that translates digital longitude and latitude," John suggested.

"OK. I put the map in the satellite mode. It's showing a site in north central Arizona. I'll hit the plus sign and see how close I can get. Holy Shit. You're not going to believe this," Tim promised. "The longitude and latitude match up with the Chapel of the Holy Cross in Sedona." Tim said.

"Wow, unbelievable!" Randy said, as he looked at Yvette.

"OK. I'm supposed to believe that I'm going somewhere from that chapel. It won't happen. I'll never go there again. After what happened to your dad, it'll be a cold day in hell. I swear."

"Mom this is an advanced booking. You're not expected there for some time. You may change your mind," Tim said as he examined the gold sheet.

"What are you talking about?" Gretchen demanded.

"Your trip is scheduled for September 2, 2034," Tim said.

"If I find out who's behind this, I'll shoot the son of a bitch. What a sick joke to play on us," Gretchen swore.

"Mom, I don't think this is a joke. Look at the destination," John said as he passed the gold boarding pass back to his mother.

"Where is the destination?" She asked.

"There, in the bottom corner," Tim said.

Gretchen examined the sheet. She wrinkled her pretty nose and shook her head.

"It doesn't mean anything to me. What does the number eight signify?" Gretchen asked.

"You have it sideways, mom. Turn it ninety degrees. See, that's not the number eight, it's the sign for infinity," John explained.

"Oh my. OK, Tony! Play your sick little tricks. I'm still not converting." Gretchen yelled, looking at the sky. "And what's the fucking significance of 2034?" Gretchen shouted.

"Mom," John said. "You're ten years younger than dad now, right?"

"Yes, so what?" Gretchen asked.

"Einstein theory of relativity says that—if you wait until 2034 and use this boarding pass from the chapel to infinity—you'll be ten years older than him, when next you meet," John estimated.

"Tony, you're a bastard!" Gretchen spat, as she looked heavenward, her face morphing into a loving smile.

ABOUT THE AUTHOR

TONY PELUSO is a retired Army Airborne Lieutenant Colonel, who—over 23 years—worked his way up from buck private. During the great adventure that has been his life, he attended a Jesuit Prep in Phoenix, ASU in Tempe, proudly served with the fighting 173rd Airborne in Vietnam, and then earned two separate law degrees. He's practiced law for 40 years, including long stints as a Judge Advocate in the Army, Assistant United States Attorney, and Chief Counsel for the local Sheriff. He retired as an HCSO Major and is currently in private practice.

Archangel of Sedona is Tony's second novel. His friends at WPG published *Waggoners Gap*—historical fiction inspired by the life of a great hero and mentor—in 2012.

Though *Archangel* is also a work of fiction, most of the episodes and vignettes described in the story, including Tony's experiences on September 2, 1966, and the mystery of the missing Christ figure, are absolutely true and accurate in every detail. He's changed names, merged characters, and adjusted small details to protect privacy. There is no serendipity.

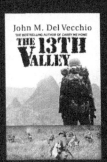

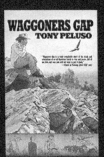

Made in the USA
Monee, IL
12 April 2023

31776776R00154